HER BEST FRIEND'S LOVER

Shiloh Walker

HER BEST FRIEND'S LOVER
An Ellora's Cave Publication, March 2005

Ellora's Cave Publishing, Inc.
1337 Commerce Drive, Suite #13
Stow, Ohio 44224

ISBN #141995041X

Edited by: *Pamela Campbell*
Cover art by: *Syneca*

Warning:

The following material contains graphic sexual content meant for mature readers. *Her Best Friend's Lover* has been rated *E-rotic* by a minimum of three independent reviewers.

Ellora's Cave Publishing offers three levels of Romantica™ reading entertainment: S (S-ensuous), E (E-rotic), and X (X-treme).

S-*ensuous* love scenes are explicit and leave nothing to the imagination.

E-*rotic* love scenes are explicit, leave nothing to the imagination, and are high in volume per the overall word count. In addition, some E-rated titles might contain fantasy material that some readers find objectionable, such as bondage, submission, same sex encounters, forced seductions, etc. E-rated titles are the most graphic titles we carry; it is common, for instance, for an author to use words such as "fucking", "cock", "pussy", etc., within their work of literature.

X-*treme* titles differ from E-rated titles only in plot premise and storyline execution. Unlike E-rated titles, stories designated with the letter X tend to contain controversial subject matter not for the faint of heart.

Also by Shiloh Walker:

Coming in Last
Her Wildest Dreams
Make Me Believe
Mythe & Magick
Once Upon A Midnight Blue
The Dragon's Warrior
The Hunters: Declan and Tori
The Hunters: Eli and Sarel
Touch of Gypsy Fire
Voyeur
Whipped Cream and Handcuffs

HER BEST FRIEND'S LOVER

Chapter One

Lauren glanced up at the sound of a door slamming. Her heart danced wildly for just a moment as she watched the lean hipped, lanky man head her way. At the same time, a weight she carried on her shoulders seemed to grow just a little bit heavier.

He would never love her.

The first time she saw him had been from a hundred feet away and her heart had simply flipped over within her chest. Lauren had been struck by love at first sight, though she had barely been able to make out his face. His face hadn't mattered, because her heart recognized him.

A week later she actually met him, face to face, when Dale strolled up her walk and knocked on her door, flashing that grin at her before holding out his hand and introducing himself. He flirted casually off and on for several months, raising her hopes, only to have those hopes die a slow withering death when it finally dawned on her that Dale flirted with any and every female he met.

The thing was, Dale Stoner loved women, and women seemed to love him right back. He danced around the line that led to seriousness, but any time one woman got too close, he two-stepped back, quick and pretty as you please.

But, lucky her, good ol' Lauren was his buddy. His best friend.

Yippee.

She didn't want to be his best friend. Well, not *just* his best friend. She wanted him. Ached. Hungered. Wanted to eat him down in three big greedy bites.

"Stop it," she ordered under her breath. "This isn't helping you any."

Five years after losing her heart to him, just watching him amble in her direction, her heart still did the same little dance.

More than six feet of mouthwatering, throat drying, smooth talking male made up Dale Stoner. He had the long, lean, muscled build of a runner, broad shoulders, narrow of waist and hip, and the loose-hipped gait of a cowboy. Dimples creased his face each time he flashed his endearingly sweet grin, burnished gold hair fell over his forehead, tempting women to brush it out of that impossibly handsome face.

Sex appeal in spades, there was no doubt he had that. Lauren could feel her body go on alert whenever he was within ten feet of her. Heart racing, mouth dry, nipples erect, her groin tight and wet. Dale was a walking wet dream, one she saw almost every damn day.

But the most mesmerizing feature about Dale was his eyes, the kind of eyes that could put you in a trance. Thickly lashed, heavy lidded eyes, with pale sky blue irises ringed by deep indigo. They could flash hot with need, burn with anger, or freeze with disdain. Every emotion was reflected in those eyes. When he turned them on Lauren, they held nothing but the deepest affection.

Though Lauren had lost count of the different women he had dated, she was well aware that a number of those women spent a night or two wrapped in his arms atop the huge custom-built king-size bed that sprawled underneath a skylight. They'd leave with a slightly dazed smile on their face the next morning, and in a few days, a new face would appear.

He was arrogant, cocky, funny, and at the oddest times, as sweet as any man could possibly be. When Lauren sprained her ankle earlier in the spring, Dale got up early every single Saturday for nearly a month to take care of her precious garden and cut the grass.

When she had the flu over the winter, he hand delivered some of his prize winning chicken soup, a recipe passed on to him from his mother. He had a fear of anything contagious, which stemmed from a serious distrust of doctors. But he braved the flu, just to take care of her.

Lauren sighed, watching him close the distance between them. She had fallen in love with him the moment she first laid eyes on him, maybe even before that. She had known, deep inside, after that one look. *That's him. He's the one I've been waiting for.*

But Dale hadn't been waiting, or even looking, for her.

"G'mornin," Dale drawled, opening the waist-high picket fence that separated their two yards. His eyes were more heavy lidded than normal, his hair still wet from his shower, and a grin of satisfaction curved his mouth.

Lauren Spencer barely glanced up from her precious roses as she asked, "Did you have a good time last night?"

"Ohhh, yeah," Dale murmured. "She's...amazing." The little actress he had spent the night with had picked up some unusual talents. That woman could do things with her mouth...

She rolled her eyes and muttered, "Oh, please." Rising, Lauren dusted her grimy hands off on a towel she had tucked into her back pocket. "I have a feeling you aren't talking about how well she acts with her theater group."

Dale grinned wickedly. "Not exactly. I was referring—"

Cutting him off with a narrowed stare, Lauren said, "Spare me the details."

"And let me guess, you spent the night at home, alone. Again."

"No. I had a roaring orgy with five different men."

"Impossible. You don't know five different men."

"Sure I do. I just don't know any whom I would welcome in my life, or my home. Much less into my bed."

Sighing, Dale followed her through the mudroom into the kitchen. "If you aren't careful, you are going to grow old alone, Lauren. What are you looking for? Why are you so picky?"

Because the man I love doesn't love me. Because the man I love is in love with another woman, a woman he can't have.

Bad enough that he had screwed half the female population between the ages of twenty and thirty-five, Dale was also still in love with a woman from his past, a girl who was happily married to her high school sweetheart.

Several moments passed with no answer from Lauren so he repeated himself. "What is it you want?"

Pausing in the doorway, she looked back at him, one hand resting on the wall. "What do I want?" she repeated. After a moment of silence, a rare look entered her eyes and her mouth curved up in a sad, bittersweet grin. "A fairy tale," she finally replied softly, shaking her head.

"A fairy tale? I didn't think a knight on a white charger was your style, Lauren," Dale responded.

"I want something I can't have, Dale. Just like you do. The difference is that I don't see the point in trying to substitute."

He scowled at her, his brows drawing down over his eyes, his mouth sulky, snarling. Lauren chuckled at the look. "Dale, you're free to see whomever you choose. As many as you choose. And likewise, I'm welcome to see as few men as I want." As she spoke, she headed down the hall, passing the recessed living room, her feet padding silently over the pristine white carpet.

Pausing in the open doorway at the end of the hall, Lauren looked over her shoulder. Calmly meeting his gaze, she told him, "I don't believe in settling, Dale. Surely you know that by now." She then placed her hand square in the middle of his chest and gently shoved him back. "I want a shower, Dale, if you don't mind."

Dale lounged on the deep blue sofa, a can of coke in one hand, the remote in the other. In the bathroom upstairs, the shower was running. He flicked through the channels, frustrated with Lauren, but not sure why.

Her quiet gray eyes always saw too damn much.

It seemed as though she could see right through him, clear down to his soul, yet Dale could never quite fathom what was going on inside that brain of hers. Every emotion she felt was hidden behind cool gray eyes, a serene face, and the smile of a Madonna.

Shit, she had gone and ruined his mellow mood, in less than one minute.

He could spend all night fucking a woman's brains out. He'd wake up feeling pretty damned pleased with himself, and then he would see that appraising, slightly disappointed look in Lauren's eyes.

Tuning off the television, he started mentally trying to work out the kinks in his current work in progress, a tale about a magician who had accidentally turned himself into a mouse and couldn't quite figure out how to turn himself back. A twist of sorts, on the old Beauty and the Beast legend.

Lauren loved it. It wasn't anywhere near finished and he wasn't sure how he was going to end it, but the basics were there.

Absently, his eyes drifted over the familiar room, deep jewel toned furniture on pristine white carpet, the paintings and photographs that adorned the walls, all without really seeing anything.

He glanced over at the canvas by the backdoor, drifting away before being jerked back. A new one.

A landscape of the ocean, but not the way he saw it. The sand, the brush, the seashells, the sea, all glimmered with a pulse of life underneath. On the shore, turned so that the viewer could see only her nude back, stood a woman, hands stretched high and wide overhead, head tipped back, staring up into the sky. A faint glimmer of wings surrounded her.

Her paintings always seemed...otherworldly, almost ethereal, as though she saw it through the eyes of one of the faeries he wrote about. How somebody as down to earth and logical as Lauren Spencer managed to paint like she did was one thing that confounded him.

Lauren had sold her first painting in her first year of college, to an art professor, of all people, who had been astonished at the rough talent of the eighteen year old. By twenty, Lauren had exhibits in Chicago, New York, and San Francisco. By twenty-three, she had refused an offer from a master to come to France for further study. At twenty-five, she was living what most people considered a dream.

One of her pieces hung over his bed, a Christmas gift from her two years ago. The piece of canvas was one of his most cherished possessions. He did the artwork for the stories he wrote, but his drawings were like that of a child's cartoon, rosy-cheeked princes and princesses, witches with hooked noses and warts that somehow managed to be cute and only slightly scary. Cute and clever, not something that could bring a tear to the eye.

Lauren had taken a scene from his first tale, *A Prince's Wish*, and turned it from a child's bedtime story into a painting that seemed too beautiful to have been done by human hands. It was when the prince, Osrel, had stumbled upon the faerie princess in the woods, sitting by a stream. This time, Osrel wasn't a picture perfect, pretty little boy with a playful looking sword and a sweet looking horse. She had painted only the suggestion of a man, standing in shadow, staring at a seductively lovely creature that was reaching out her hand to her reflection in the stream. Tumbled blonde hair fell over a bare shoulder, lowered lashes hid her eyes. The faintest suggestion of wings in the background.

All of her work was stunning. And sad. It was as though she was observing these incredibly lovely things, coveting them, wanting to be part of that beauty, but unsure of how to reach out for it

As she towel dried her hair, scowling at her reflection in the mirror, Lauren decided she should shoot herself. Or maybe just accidentally bust her head wide open. It was bound to be less painful than what she had agreed to do. She was going on a double date with Dale and some golf buddy and the alluring Allison, his latest actress, to see *Joseph and the Amazing Technicolor Dream Coat* in downtown Louisville.

Oh, joy.

Why in the hell couldn't she say no to him? She sure as hell didn't have trouble saying it to anybody else. An hour and a half later, she thought dismally, she was about to get more practice. The golf buddy was going to be another groper. He topped her five-foot-nine by four inches and should have had no trouble meeting her gaze, but he couldn't take his eyes off her chest.

A problem she was familiar with and had been since she had started wearing a 36 DD in eighth grade. Her dress, a sleeveless, long, pale green column that fell to her ankles, slit up both sides to just above the knee, had a high collar that closed at the back of her neck with a single button. It was an elegant and timeless style, modest and classic.

As he introduced himself, his gaze once again fell from her face to land insultingly on her breasts. Later, her back rigid, she told herself if Derek's hand drifted southward from her shoulder one more time, she would shatter every misconception Dale had about her being calm and logical by hunting down a knife and severing Derek Gaines' hand from his wrist and feeding it to him, chunk by chunk.

Dale sat in the seat next to her, where she could feel his body heat, smell the sandalwood scent of his skin, and listen as he murmured in Allison's ear. Where she could watch out of the corner of her eye as he stroked her thigh with long, skilled fingers.

While she sat ramrod stiff and periodically disappeared into the women's room just to avoid the Gaines bastard.

Finally, the play ended and Lauren escaped into the lobby, pretending an interest in the artwork as a ploy to avoid Dale's cheerful banter. Blind fool, she thought morosely.

She caught a glimpse of her reflection in the glass wall that made up the front part of the Kentucky Center for the Arts, her mouth turned down in a grim line. Most people found her attractive enough. Her hair was ebony black and her eyes were a pure clear gray. Her oval face was dominated by those eyes and a wide, mobile mouth. The top lip was a perfect cupid's bow, the bottom lush and full. Lauren had been told, more than once, that her mouth had been designed for sex. The first time, if she recalled correctly, had been by a foster father at the age of eleven.

She stood a curvy five-foot-nine and weighed one-fifty, her body well proportioned, requiring little maintenance to keep its hourglass shape. The three weekly classes of karate were for amusement and enjoyment. She could have easily maintained her weight and size without the classes, thanks to a healthy, quick metabolism.

Even if it was nothing more than a physical attraction, Lauren wished Dale would notice she was alive. On some level other than his 'buddy.' But he was oblivious to the body many women would have cheerfully died for, the body she had given to no man. Until she had met Dale, she hadn't met one worth the trouble.

And Dale just plain didn't want it.

It was really pathetic, she mused sadly. A twenty-five-year-old virgin who would probably live to be a hundred-year-old virgin, all because her neighbor was a blind, deaf, and dumb idiot.

"Maybe you just need to get laid," she muttered to herself. "Maybe if you get rid of the burden of virginity with somebody, losing it with him wouldn't be so damned appealing."

With a sigh, she followed the rest of the group out to the parking garage. Dinner. She still had to get through dinner. Stifling a moan of agony, she dawdled enough that Derek ended up sliding into the back of the car before her, thereby allowing her to avoid his 'helping' hands.

Later, as the Explorer pulled up the driveway to Dale's house, Lauren calculated the amount of time it would take to ditch the bastard who kept running his hand up and down her thigh, no matter how many times she had bumped it off.

When the fingers of that hand grazed her high on the inner thigh, Lauren bared her teeth and smacked the hand away, hard enough to make her fingers sting. She was out of the truck like a rocket and said over her shoulder, "That's it for me, folks. I'm going home."

Dale called after her, but she ignored him, ignored the murmurs that were undoubtedly coming from Derek. She had nothing on her mind but a hot shower to wash the feel of those cold fingers from her body.

She would have been better off to have paid more attention, she realized just a few minutes later, as she was cornered on her porch by a leering advertising executive. He wasn't just plain stupid or too ignorant to recognize a brush-off; he was a disgusting, perverted idiot who wasn't interested in taking 'no' for an answer.

"I know you want the same thing I do." His long blunt fingers wrapped around her arms as he breathed against her neck.

"I seriously doubt you want yourself to disappear off the face of the earth," Lauren snapped, planting her hands against his chest and shoving back with every bit of strength she had in her body.

The ad exec now lay on his back, somewhat stunned. Lauren backed away just slightly, turning so that he couldn't corner her up against the wall, tensing her body.

"Gonna play hard to get?" he laughed from his sprawl on the ground.

Arching a brow at him, she coolly told him, "In your case? Not hard, try impossible. I'd rather bounce on the sheets with a leper."

His eyes widened, then narrowed, as her words sank home. Derek remained on his back as she shifted, his surprise clearly evident in his face. The surprise, though, gave way to anger and Lauren had a moment of fear as he shot to his feet. But when a girl of eleven wakes up to find her foster father leaning over her bed at night, she learns more than caution. She learns self-defense.

At least, this one had.

Dale replayed those words in his head. "She's just embarrassed, I think," Derek had said. "She doesn't want to say anything about it, but she asked me earlier to spend the night." It didn't fit. Lauren going to bed with a man she had known for two hours? Lauren? Embarrassed?

Dignified, cool, collected Lauren Spencer? Dale doubted she even knew what embarrassment was.

Seeing the concern in his eyes, Allison said, "Maybe you should check on her. She was acting rather odd all night, but I don't think it was because she was embarrassed about an illicit slumber party," she said wryly. "I really don't see Derek as her type. From what I saw, she was giving him the brush off most of the night. And even if she was attracted to him, I don't see that woman deciding to fuck a man she just met tonight."

The thought of Lauren fucking anybody didn't settle too well, now that he thought of it. In truth, it settled rather badly, made him feel slightly nauseated. And why was that, after he was always nagging her about living like a nun?

Roughly five minutes after he'd led Allison inside for their own slumber party, he was walking back out, heading toward the gate, jogging. The jogging broke into an all out run when he heard a crash.

He arrived at Lauren's to find Derek on the ground, hands cupping his groin, blood spurting from his nose while Lauren stood sheet white over him, hands up and fisted, ready. Her eyes glinted with rage and fear and challenge while she stood over him, silently daring the man to face her again. A large potted plant had been knocked over, the glazed ceramic shattered.

Her hair had fallen from its neat chignon, tumbling around her shoulders, and the demure neckline of her dress was sagging. Her lower lip gleamed wetly in the porch light's glow, and he realized it was blood. Bruises were forming on the delicate flesh of her upper arms.

She has skin like a baby, Dale remembered inanely.

"Come on, you bloody bastard," she snarled, not even glancing up at Dale as he rushed the porch. Derek was slowly rising to his feet, staring at Lauren with wary eyes while Dale moved a little closer.

Eyes narrowed, Dale saw red as he realized what he had set his best friend up for. Some judgment in character he had, he thought mindlessly as he grabbed Derek Gaines by the lapels of his designer blazer and lifted him to his feet before knocking him clear off them again with a swift uppercut to his chin. His former golf buddy tumbled down the stairs and landed in the middle of one of Lauren's prized flowerbeds.

He started to go down the stairs after him but a soft quiet sound stopped him. He turned and saw Lauren fumbling for her keys, her mouth quivering.

"Damn it, Lauren. I'm sorry," he said quietly, reaching for the keys and unlocking the door before wrapping an arm around her shoulders.

"For what?" she asked, her voice only slightly shaky. "It's not your fault you have somewhat shitty taste in friends." She remained briefly in his embrace before shrugging it off and turning away.

"Has he been hassling you all night?" Dale asked, frowning as she shrugged away his hands, taking deep calming breaths before turning back to face him.

"From the get go," Lauren said, her voice calmer, sedate, almost normal. "You were too busy necking with the future queen of Broadway to notice, but your friend couldn't seem to keep his eyes, or his hands, to himself. I don't think he looked at my face once through out the entire night."

"Why didn't you say something?" he demanded, planting one hand on his hip and the other by the wall beside her head.

"I shouldn't have had to. Any blind man could have seen it," she said quietly. Her gray eyes briefly closed, and when she opened them they were clear and dry. "Please leave, Dale. Go back to your Broadway queen and leave me alone. Don't ask me, ever again, to go along with one of these pathetic ideas of yours."

"Lauren, I was just trying to help. You worry me, how much time you spend alone." He started to reach for her only to be stopped by the look in her cold eyes. "I'm sorry," he repeated. "If I had any idea, I wouldn't have set it up. You're the best friend I've got."

I'm the best friend you've got, she thought brokenly. Didn't he know how much that hurt? She didn't want to be his friend, damn it. She wanted to be his lover, his wife, the mother of his children. She wanted to go to sleep at night with him next to her and she wanted to wake up in the morning curled against him.

And he wanted to set her up on blind dates with his friends because he worried about her.

Defeated, she finally accepted what she had refused to admit to herself.

She was fooling herself.

This beautiful, sexy man with the wicked mouth and heavenly eyes wasn't ever going to notice her. He wouldn't ever love her.

She had to move past him.

Her eyes drifted to the man who sat outside her open door, cursing loudly while trying to stem the flow of blood that gushed from the nose Lauren suspected was broken. Her hand sure as hell felt broken. "If this is all that being your friend gets me, maybe I'm better off not having you as a friend," she said harshly.

Pain, quick and sharp, sliced through Dale as she turned away and left him standing alone in the anteroom. Or so he thought. Allison was standing in the doorway behind him, watching with sympathetic eyes. "Don't take it personally. I doubt she's thinking clearly now."

"Don't bet on it," he muttered, clenching his jaw, closing his eyes for a moment until he had settled. "Lauren doesn't say things she doesn't mean."

"Dale, she is female. That means she is going to say things she doesn't mean from time to time. That's just part of being female. And just because she means it tonight doesn't mean she will mean it in the morning."

Allison only sighed at the implacable look on his face. Surveying the damage on the porch, she decided, "I think I'll call it a night. You give me a call, okay?" Rummaging in her purse, she found her keys and waited for a response.

It was "Uh-huh, sure." With a roll of her eyes, she headed for the car she had parked in Dale's drive hours earlier, certain she wouldn't need it until very, very late, the next morning.

Dale was busy studying Derek who was limping away from the house, muttering things about crazy bitches and lunatic artists.

With cold blue eyes and a mean smile, Dale decided he'd do something constructive with the anger that had built.

Later that night, after hours of tossing and turning, brief periods of sleep interrupted by old nightmares, Lauren faced her pale reflection over the sink. The brightly lit makeup mirror highlighted every flaw, her pale skin, grim mouth, solemn eyes. A tiny nick on her lip remained, just slightly swollen. She'd had worse, she knew. Her right hand throbbed like the devil and her knuckles were swollen. The exec had a face of stone.

Why did she do this to herself?

It was pretty damn sad when a woman got more depressed over a friend sleeping with some bimbo actress than an attempted rape.

Tears burned her bloodshot eyes and she closed them, but not before two tears broke free, sliding hotly down her face. Why'd she have to fall for the one guy who saw her as a buddy, not a woman?

With the back of her unhurt hand, she dashed away the damp tear tracks from her cheeks. "What are you going to do about this?" Lauren asked the sad-faced woman in the mirror.

"This cannot continue."

* * * * *

The following morning he eyed his torn knuckles and smiled, quite pleased with himself. Of course, smiling didn't feel too good. For an ad exec, Derek had packed a pretty decent punch. Now, if only they could meet up on the green somewhere and have round number two, Dale would be even happier.

But thoughts of Lauren ruined his good mood. He had to make sure she was okay. He realized that she had been shaken up the past night, very much so. No doubt it reminded her of the rough times she had gone through as a foster child. Twice a foster father had tried to molest her and only Lauren's speed and quick thinking had kept it from happening. That, and the grace of God.

He didn't want to think about what kind of bad memories last night had probably brought on. But Lauren had no choice but think about them. So Dale did as well. Had she had nightmares? Had she slept?

Had she forgiven him?

But one look at Lauren's icy gray eyes quickly told him the night hadn't done much for her temper. "You could have at least taken the brawl off my property, Dale," she said over her shoulder as she knelt in the dirt of the flowerbed, repairing the damage done by two men rolling through them. "You completely ruined my marigolds."

Taken aback, Dale paused in the act of reaching for the pile of refuse at her side. Slowly, he straightened and tucked his hands in his pockets. "I beg your pardon?"

She glanced at him and said, "You heard me well enough, big shot. You tore the hell out of my flowerbeds."

With an absent frown, Dale studied the grounds. Sure enough, several small bushes had been flattened and almost every single flower in this particular area was trampled. But he still couldn't quite believe what he was seeing in her face. "You're ticked at me because I tore up some flowers?"

"A little bit upset, yes. Did you enjoy yourself?"

"Excuse me, but that guy tried to rape you. Should I have just calmly escorted him off your property?"

"You calmly escorted him onto it without any trouble." She shrugged, a negligent move of her shoulders, as she continued pulling up destroyed plants. "If you hadn't nagged me into going out with him, there wouldn't have been a problem, now would there?"

Guilt flushed his cheeks red but was chased away as self-righteous anger settled in. "I had no idea he was like that. He always seemed like a pretty decent guy," Dale said, taking a deep breath and trying to calm down. He was on edge anyway, too little sleep, sore to boot, and madder than hell over what had almost happened last night. What would have happened if Lauren hadn't known how to take care of herself? He might have calmed himself down. If Lauren hadn't deliberately been goading him.

"I'm sorry."

"Mmm," she said softly. "Maybe now you'll keep your nose out of my life. Then again, you probably won't be happy until my social calendar is as full as yours."

"I'll keep my opinions about your social life, or lack of one, to myself," he said through gritted teeth. "And don't go laying last night at my feet. In the first place, you could have told me you weren't interested. And, second of all, if you were worried about him, which you obviously were, you should have said something to me."

"I might have, if you hadn't been so...busy with Miss Broadway," Lauren replied, digging her hands deep in the dirt. "Every time I tried to talk to you, you'd mumble something under your breath and go back to nuzzling Allison."

I'm such an idiot, she thought sadly. Setting myself up for heartache like this. After all, how many women had there been? She knew of at least seven in the past six months, one or two lasting a few weeks before another lovely thing took her place. Allison had been around now over a month, showing no signs of leaving. "I hated to interrupt you with my complaints about your choice in friends."

"Pretty shitty taste, I guess," he agreed, narrowing his eyes at her. "After all, my best friend is a selfish bitch who can't accept an apology when it's offered."

The insult rolled like water off her shoulders. Or seemed to. He wouldn't know how deeply it cut into her heart to see that anger on his face, the hurt in his eyes, and worse, the knowledge that she had put it there. With seeming calm, she rose, dusted her filthy hands on her shorts. If his mind hadn't been so cluttered, and he hadn't been reeling inside from shock, he might have seen the minute signs of a sleepless night that showed on Lauren's face.

As it was, he had little time to do more than absently notice the smudges of dirt on denim before he started seeing red. One slim thigh, bared by the rather brief shorts, had the angry imprint of a hand, turning the deep blue of a fresh bruise. More bruises ringed her arms.

Gently, he traced the tips of his fingers over one of those bruises. He opened his mouth to speak but Lauren forced herself to step away from his hands, forced herself to say, "Selfish? Is that what I am? Remember, Dale, I went out on the date as a favor to you. I spent the whole night trying to keep my distance from a man who was more interested in my bust size than my tailor would be."

"You don't use a tailor."

She smiled sweetly. "Good thing, too. Otherwise that would have been one hell of an expensive dress that was ruined last night when that bastard tried to rip it off of me. I'm rather surprised you even showed up. I figured you were too interested in ripping that little vamp suit off of your actress."

"What the fuck is wrong with you, Lauren?" Dale demanded, his eyes huge and bewildered.

"I have no idea what you mean," she said, turning away from the hurt in those dreamy blue eyes.

"The hell you don't. You're going out of your way to pick a fight, but I can't figure out why. Care to explain that?" He followed her up the three steps that led to the porch, followed her to the front door and through it before he finally reached out and caught her elbow, gently turning her around.

"I suppose it's because I'm tired of this, Dale. Almost every other week, you've hooked up with a new lady, the flavor of the month, if you will. A couple of dates, a couple of romps in the sack and then you're off to the next one. I don't approve, but that lifestyle obviously makes you happy."

"I prefer a quiet life, the life I have, and yet you insist on shoving your friends at me. Hell, you've even introduced me to total strangers you meet at the gym just because they look like my 'type.' Every time I listen to you, it ends up a disaster. And you aren't satisfied. But if I dated all the guys you've tried to get me to date, and led the type of social life you lead, I'd be branded a tramp."

"I was almost raped last night," she finished coldly, backing away from him, even though all she wanted to do was reach for him. All she had ever wanted from him was for him to love her. Even a little. "By a man you called your friend. Maybe this will wake you up. I don't need your interference in my life. I have enough problems of my own."

Dale studied her, his jaw clenched tight. Where in the hell had all that anger in her eyes, on her face, come from?

Had it been there a while and he just hadn't noticed? "Fine," he said, hollowly, the skin across his taut cheekbones a dull red. "Fine. I'll just stay the hell out of your life, Lauren. Take care of yourself."

And quietly he left, his head tucked down, hands shoved deep in his pockets, leaving the door open behind him.

If he had paused to look back, he would have seen the tears that welled up in her eyes. Might have heard her whisper, "I'm sorry, Dale. But I can't afford your friendship."

It hurt too much.

The back of her hand pressed to her mouth to muffle the sob, she fell to her knees and cried, again, over a man who could never love her back.

Dale stood at the window an hour later, watching as Lauren climbed into her fire-engine red convertible. Her shoulders were slumped, her head low. But he couldn't see her face. And, too clearly, he remembered the words she had uttered earlier.

He really didn't see what was so terrible about trying to find her a guy. Lauren was the type who should have a family, kids running around, a husband to coddle her, love her out of her moods when she got too melancholy.

Yet, she was alone, always alone.

But maybe he was wrong about her, maybe she didn't want a family. Maybe that was why she stayed alone. Hell, maybe she didn't even like men. He hadn't thought of that, but he obviously didn't know her as well as he'd thought.

With a heavy sigh, he turned his eyes back to the damaged flowerbeds in front of her house. Her pride and joy. She had only cleaned up roughly half of the mess.

Resolutely, he hunted up a pair of work gloves and a bucket before heading over to her house. Setting his jaw, he planted his hands on his hips and surveyed the damage. With a muttered curse, he dropped to his knees in the dirt, donned his heavy gloves and reached for the trampled remains of a flowering bush. She may have had reason to be upset over last night, but he'd be damned if she'd come yelling at him over the mess she had in her front yard.

Lauren didn't return home until late that night. Dale's car was gone, all the lights out. Too tired to drive around to the garage, she left her car out front. She paused, halfway up the steps, unsure of what had caught her attention.

Slowly, she backtracked and studied the yard. The bare, but ruthlessly clean, flowerbeds. The bushes had been tended to, broken branches cleared away. And sitting in a cardboard box by her front door were various potted seedlings. Summer and fall flowers to replace the ones she'd had to remove earlier today.

Reaching out to trace a bright yellow marigold, she blinked away tears.

How could a man sweet and sensitive enough to know how much she loved those flowerbeds be so damn blind?

Bad tempered, Dale slammed the door on his way into his house. This damn week has sucked, he thought furiously. First, the fight with Lauren. They still hadn't spoken and Dale was slowly realizing he had lost his best friend. She wasn't just in a little snit that she would eventually work herself out of. He should have known better. He had never known Lauren to have snits. God forbid, that was too human for her.

He had tried after two days to talk to her again, but the temperature had dropped thirty degrees before he had even opened his mouth.

She was blaming him for what had happened. Which was just as well, he was blaming himself too. Then three days ago, Allison had announced that she was ready to settle down and get married. If Dale wasn't interested, then there was no reason to call her any more.

His editor had called and was nagging him about some kind of deal with a cable network, after he'd told her for the millionth time, absolutely no. He'd sliced his hand when he'd changed his oil the other day. How he'd managed that would forever remain a mystery. He had been working on cars for more than twenty years, and ten of it had been as a fucking mechanic. So how in the hell how he managed to slice his hand open while doing an oil change?

This morning, out of the blue, his computer had crashed, taking God only knew how much information and work with it, since he sometimes forgot to back up his work on disc.

His gut churned queasily and he dropped to the couch, throwing his arm over his eyes. To top it all off, in his back pocket was a letter from Abigail Lightfoot, Nikki's daughter. Stepdaughter, technically. A feeling of foreboding had filled him when he had seen the letter, setting all alone, in his mailbox.

After putting it off a few more minutes, he went and snagged a bottle of beer from the fridge, opened the letter and settled down to read the childish scrawl.

Thirty minutes later, the letter lay saturated in a puddle of beer. A leather-bound journal lay open on the floor, sketches done over the past years spilling out of it.

Three empty beer bottles lay on the floor. He had realized that this was not an occasion for Miller, so he dug out the Irish. A pint of whiskey sat on the table. With an unsteady hand, Dale took another swig from the bottle, his eyes tearing up as it burned its way down his throat. While he could usually handle a couple of beers without a problem, he had passed drunk several swigs earlier.

The only real problem being that he generally lost the time between getting tipsy and waking up.

Another baby. Their fourth.

Damn it, it hurt to think of Nikki cuddling a baby to her chest, to think of the love that would be shining out of her eyes, directed at some bastard who didn't deserve her. Wishing himself into that mental picture, knowing it was just his imagination, hurt even more, so he washed that thought away with another swig of whiskey.

And so on, and so on.

Lauren stood in front of the canvas, paintbrush poised over it, ready to work her magic. She closed her eyes, trying to summon up an image to put on canvas, immortalized through strokes of her brush.

But the magic wasn't there. It hadn't been there since she had tossed Dale's apology in his face and thrown him out of her life. Heaving a sigh, she set the brush and her palette down, thrusting her hands through her hair.

Clasping them behind her neck, she turned to stare out over the backyard.

It wasn't his fault that he didn't love her. He had given his heart long before he had ever met her. But that hadn't kept him from caring for her, or from being one of the best friends she'd ever had.

The past week had been empty; the days had lost their color and the magic had slipped from her hands. Two canvases had been ruined, relegated to "file thirteen."

Even her plants were suffering. She killed the mums she had been transplanting. The dogwood she planted the previous fall had suddenly died and none of her efforts to save it had brought forth any results.

And Lauren couldn't get his expression out of her head, the way he had looked at her that last time before he had walked silently out of her house. Like she had walked up to him out of the blue and plunged a knife in his heart. Those mournful, deeply hurt blue eyes haunted her at night.

Walking into the living room, she threw herself face down on the couch. She couldn't do it. Even if he was only a friend and never anything more, she couldn't live without Dale Stoner in her life.

Damn it all to hell and back, she thought viciously. She felt like she was compulsively beating her head against a wall of cinderblock. It was painful, she hated it and wanted desperately to stop, but couldn't.

But the fact remained unchanged, regardless of how much she might wish otherwise.

This past week had felt as though half of her entire soul was missing.

Chapter Two

Two hours later, she had a tin of fresh chocolate chip cookies in her hands and a penitent look on her pretty face as she headed out the front door. Lauren had dressed carefully, hiding the fading bruises on her arms with a ruffled poet-styled shirt tucked into a pair of her favorite jeans.

Around her neck she wore a silver chain, an amethyst wand hanging from it to rest in the hollow of her throat. Dale had given it to her the past Christmas.

She had a little apology speech already prepared and was fully ready to eat crow, if necessary. But she would do it her way.

Her first knock brought nothing but silence from the house. Starting to deflate, she knocked again. What if he wasn't home? And after she went to all the trouble to prepare herself for this, a humiliating experience to be sure. But then she heard crashing from within the house and muted cursing. When the door opened, the stench of whiskey washed over her and she stood there, staring in bemusement at one very drunk man.

His tousled golden hair fell in a tumble over his forehead, and a sexy little scowl darkened his face. His shirt was hanging loose and unbuttoned over a lean tanned belly. A light scattering of golden hair trailed down to disappear in the vee of his unsnapped jeans.

Oh, hell. Can't I just have one taste? she thought frantically, much like a child denied an ice cream cone.

Lauren hesitated a moment, unsure of her ability to speak. She was afraid that if she tried, all she would utter was incoherent babbling. Her heart danced wildly around in her chest, and unconsciously her tongue darted out to lick her lips.

Oh, please. Just one bite?

Glaring at her, Dale slurred, "What? Are you here to beat me over the head again? Helluva thing to do, kick a man when he's down." He started to slam the door, but she caught it easily, coming out of her daze and slipping inside. She followed him as he stalked out of the anteroom, veering left into the living room.

Inside the arched entranceway, she paused, shocked.

"Ah, I came over to apologize," she started, cautiously setting the tin down as she looked all around. The oak coffee table had been upended. The normally neat living room was a disaster, empty beer bottles all over the place, scattered pieces of paper and pictures lying on the floor. She knelt over one that caught her eye. A hand drawn sketch of a woman nursing a baby. The love that had been poured into the picture told her who it was, even if 'Nikki' hadn't been printed below the picture.

Every line had been carefully, lovingly done from the dimple that winked in the left corner of the woman's mouth to the little curls of hair that graced the infant's head. She closed her eyes against the dagger in her heart and carefully scooped up the papers—more drawings and letters—then she righted the coffee table and gathered them together in a pile, setting them on the surface before raising her head and looking into Dale's bleak eyes.

A humorless smile pulled up one corner of his mouth as he repeated, "Apologize, huh? Yeah, fine. You make your pretty little apology and get the hell out, 'kay, Lauren?"

"Dale, what's happened?"

"Whaddya mean, what's happened?" he asked, lifting a half empty bottle of whiskey to his lips. Lauren's belly tightened as she watched that tanned throat work, imagined him drinking from her lips the way he drank from that bottle. She forced her attention back to his words.

"Lemme see." Ticking his statements off on his fingers, he started, "First, my best friend damn near gets raped, and blames it on me. Guess she got a good 'nough reason. Then the girl I've been dating decides she's ready for marriage and unless I want to be the one, I ain't to call no more. My damn editor won't leave me alone." As he counted, he spilled whiskey from the nearly empty pint. "I slice my damn hand wide open during a freaking oil change. What in the hell am I changing the oil in my car for anyway?" He studied the ugly red gash on the back of his hand with a dark scowl.

His deep southern accent thickened as his face grew darker. "And—"

He cut himself off, reaching for one of the drawings on the table. The first one Lauren had picked up, of Nikki nursing a baby. "And what?" Lauren asked softly, going to sit beside him, taking his hand in hers.

It tightened on hers as he whispered, "And she's pregnant."

"Nikki." Lauren said.

"Yeah. Nikki." he replied, his voice gone flat.

"Dale, why are you doing this to yourself?" she asked, knowing he'd never be able to answer.

He gazed up at her with dazed eyes, clearly befuddled.

"She loves him, Dale. She can't help that," Lauren said, taking the picture from him and turning it face down before catching his cheek and forcing him to look at her. Holding his face in her hands, she stared in to his eyes, her own heart breaking. "She loves him," she repeated slowly. "Love doesn't follow logical rules. We don't always love who we want to, or who we ought to. You have to let her go. She's beyond your reach now."

"What in the hell do you know about love?" he snapped, jerking free from her gentle touch.

She smiled sadly. "A lot more than you would think, Dale. I know what it's like to love somebody you can't have. And I know how hard it is to let it go, to carry on life as normal while that person lives a life that doesn't, and never will, include you."

Shoulders slumped, Dale stared dejectedly at his hands, trying to tune out the sound of her voice.

"I know what it's like to love somebody who doesn't love you back, Dale," she repeated. With a delicate shrug of her shoulders, she quietly finished, "You won't be able to replace her with somebody else, Dale. The women you date deserve better than to be treated as a substitute for the one you really want."

"Who the hell are you to give me advice on my love life?" he demanded, slamming down the whiskey. The potent amber liquid splashed out of the bottle, spraying Lauren with droplets as Dale surged to his feet.

With a steady hand, Lauren wiped a trickle of liquor from her face before rising and meeting Dale's turbulent gaze with her own. "You don't have a love life, Dale. You have a sex life, in which you pretend every woman you sleep with is Nicole Kline. And you have a dream life, where you imagine yourself in his place, the father of her children, the love of her life."

His eyes closed and he turned his head away. "I can't put her out of my mind, Lauren. I try, but I can't," he said, his voice tight and shaky. "Do you know how he treated her? What he did? They were going to be married, for pity's sake, and just a few months before the wedding, he knocks another woman up. So he married that bitch and left Nikki alone. He broke her fucking heart, but when his wife died, he figured he could get Nikki back."

"He didn't deserve her!"

"If she had been mine, I would have cherished her every day of my life, she never would have been hurt the way she was. I would have treated her like a queen and I never would have hurt her."

Very calmly, very succinctly, she said, "Bullshit."

His head snapped up and his startled gaze flew up to meet hers. "Excuse me?" he said, his voice going cold once more. Glacial ice had already formed in those blue eyes.

"You can't love somebody without hurting them from time to time. You'd be a fool to think otherwise. Pain is a part of loving. Without it, we'd probably take all the good things for granted."

"I would treasure her. I love her, damn it!"

"You worship her," Lauren countered. "You've put her on a damn pedestal and would kneel at her feet if you could. She is the cursed princess from one of your kid's tales, Dale. You've told me this story before, buddy. I know all about the betrayal, all about her rough childhood, and all about how you fell in love with her only to lose her to him. You don't love her."

"You want to rescue her, help her put her life together and coddle her. But she's a real woman, with real needs. She doesn't need worshipping and she doesn't need to be treasured. That makes her sound like some kind of possession. She needs a man to love her as a woman, not as an ideal."

"What in the hell do you know about it?" he demanded, stumbling to the side and nearly tripping over the coffee table. With a growl, he shoved it, sending the whiskey sailing through the air and the heavy oak table upended on the floor. "What in hell do you know about love? You don't even let a guy within ten feet of you."

"That's because I don't have anything to offer one. My heart belongs to somebody and I don't believe in casual sex." Lauren turned her gaze away so that Dale wouldn't be able to read that he was the one who owned her—heart, mind, body and soul.

Her elegant shoulders lifted and fell in a casual shrug before she loosely linked her hands in front of her. "Dale, I'd rather be alone, just me and my wishes, than to fall into bed with every other guy who comes along. I might forget for a little while, but then it's over. I'd be even more lonely than I was to begin with."

Dale sat silently staring at the puddle of spilled whiskey that was seeping into his deep, plush carpet. *How could she so accurately describe it?* he wondered. How did she know about the ache that lived within him?

He scowled as the answer came into his drunken mind. Because, as she had told him, she was in love with somebody who didn't have the sense to love her back. "Better off without him," he announced, wishing for another swig from the bottle.

"Pardon?"

He grinned foolishly at her and mimicked her formal, regal tone, "Pardon?" before laughing. "That's what I love 'bout you, Lauren. You're such a damn lady, even with a drunk ass idiot." He glanced around the room, wondered if he'd actually drunk enough to make it spin or if the fault buried below Kentuckiana had finally started shifting. "Better off without him," he repeated. "Probably ain't good 'nough for ya, anyway."

Arching a slim black brow at him, she agreeably said, "Probably not."

"This place is a damn sty," Dale said, his foul mood gone in the blink of an eye. "What kind of pig lives here?"

"Hmmm, I wonder," Lauren murmured, tucking her hands into her pockets to keep from reaching for him. He was so damned adorable. So damned sexy and rumpled.

He chuckled under his breath and dropped back down on the dark gray couch, staring up at her. Her face was turned sideways, studying the unholy mess, treating Dale to a clear view of her perfect profile. Clear ivory skin, deep smoky eyes, wide lush mouth. "You sure are pretty, Lauren," he said, grinning up at her. "If you don't mind my saying so."

"Thank you," she said politely, a smile tugging the corners of her mouth as she turned her head to look at him. "Of course, I realize your judgment is a tad bit impaired right now."

"Tad bit, my ass," he muttered, enjoying the sensation of the room spinning around. The only thing in focus was Lauren, with her watchful gray eyes and amused smile. Dale lowered his gaze to her mouth—that wide, lush mouth, curved up in amusement. Carefully, concentrating on each separate movement, he rose to his feet.

"Why don't I fix you something to eat and then clean up this mess?" she asked, sidestepping neatly when he reached for her, then positioning herself at his side as he tried to steady himself.

"Not hungry," he told her, a sweet smile on his face. He reached out, stroked his hand down the satiny skin of her cheek. "Soft," he murmured, turning his hand around and stroking his knuckles down her jaw to her neck.

"So are we friends again?" His gaze, bleary and bloodshot, wandered over her face. "You here to make me feel all better?"

"Yes. That's why I'm going to fix you something to eat so you don't wake up with a hangover the size of Kansas," she said steadily, even though her heart started tripping when his eyes started to linger, none too subtly, on her mouth.

"Don't wanna eat," he sulked, reaching up to touch his index finger to her bottom lip. "Not unless you're on the menu."

Drunk or not, he knew heat in a woman's eyes. And what he saw flare in her gaze was a damn forest fire. He moved up, aligning his body next to hers. With a slow, wicked grin, he asked, "So whaddya say? Can I eat you?" Lowering his head, he lapped at her neck, one long slow stroke of his tongue that set his mouth ablaze, craving another taste.

"Back off, Dale," she said, taking a quick step back.

"Hmm," he murmured, following each retreating step. "Why don't you kiss me and make me all better, beautiful?" he asked, knowing exactly where he wanted her to kiss.

A reluctant, amused grin tugged at her mouth but she shook her head. "Fuck off," she ordered, dodging him yet again.

"I'd rather fuck you," he replied, reaching out and catching hold of her hand.

"You need to eat, take some aspirin and go to bed," she told him. "Otherwise you are going to wish you were dead in the morning. You'll feel better about all this tomorrow."

"Not hungry," he repeated. "And I can feel better now, if you'll just let me." Curving his hand around the back of her neck, he drew her to him, leaned down and pressed his mouth to the corner of hers, nibbling. "Hmm, that's better, baby." Dale was pretty certain he was doing something he shouldn't. But he was drunk enough, needy enough. Damn it, lonely enough. And here was Lauren. He thought he had lost her; sweet, gentle, logical Lauren who could put his chaotic mind to ease just by being there.

"Dale," Lauren said, her voice shaky now, as well. "Dale, stop it."

"Why?" he asked absently as he moved from the corner of her mouth to her stubborn chin, then down to her slender neck. Lauren fit against him perfectly, he noted. Curve to curve, she fit against his body as if she had been made specifically for him. Why in hell had he been focusing on delicate little women that he had to bend over to kiss?

"You're lonely. I'm lonely. Maybe together, we won't be so lonely." A little warning light went off in some distant corner of his clouded mind, but he easily ignored it, intently feasting on the taste of soft smooth flesh.

"Didn't we just get done discussing this, Dale?" she asked, forcing a light-hearted tone into her voice even as her knees went weak and her throat went tight.

"I dunno. Did we?" he asked, nuzzling her ear.

"Sex isn't the answer to everything," Lauren said, trying to step back, only to have him bring her firmly up against him once more.

"Doesn't have to be. Just needs to be the answer for this," he whispered, nibbling along the line of her collar bone while one hand roamed to her waist, freeing the tail of her shirt from her jeans. She tasted good. His mouth meandered back up and locked onto hers while he pressed the flat of his hand to her waist and slid it upward, bringing her body in full contact with his, locking her against him.

This. Lauren had been dreaming of just this for an eternity. And her dreams were nowhere near the reality, she decided, as he crushed his mouth to hers as though he meant to devour her whole. Lauren quivered under that clever mouth, quivered as he ran those long-fingered, callused hands over her bare back.

This is wrong, she thought, this has to stop. Right here and now. She would. End it. Right now. As she swore that, he pulled back just slightly to lower his mouth to her neck. The end result was a shudder that wracked her from head to toe and back again as he left her neck to cruise back up to her mouth.

Then her arm snaked up and curled over his shoulders. This was every dream she had ever had, that he would one day turn to her. The feel of his skin, hot and smooth, under her hands, the press of that beautiful, clever mouth against hers, the feel of his heart pounding against her own, that long lean body tight against hers, his arms holding her against him.

Lauren told herself that she didn't care that he was turning to her for comfort, not for love. That he was drunk out of his mind. She ignored the little voice that signaled that her common sense was not quite dead—almost, but not quite. She ignored it, the soft little voice that kept whispering, *"This will change everything."*

After five years of loving him in silence, of needing him, knowing she would never have him, didn't she deserve something? This would be the only chance she would ever have to be with him. With a murmur of assent, her eyes drifted closed and her body went pliant.

And she just felt. Let him tip her head back and continue to rain kisses over the exposed flesh of her throat. Let him slip her shirt over her head and loosen the clasp of her bra.

It fell to the floor unnoticed as Dale cupped her breasts in his hands, leaning back to study the sight of his tanned hands on her pale flesh. Damn it, but she was built, filling his hands to overflowing. The rounded globes of her breasts were satin soft, her nipples puckering and drawing tight as he rolled each one between finger and thumb. Lowering his head to take one reddened tip into his mouth as his hands trailed lower, over her narrow ribcage, over the indent of her waist before settling his fingers on the softly rounded curve of her hips. Grasping one firmly curved ass cheek in his hand, he dragged her lower body against his as he feasted on her sweet, hot nipples.

He kissed his way back up to her throat before leaning back to stare at her with hot, hungry eyes. His fingers left her throbbing nipples to stroke the underside and outer curve of her breasts while he whispered, "You've got the prettiest damn tits I've ever seen. And you taste so fucking good."

God, did she taste good. Soft and warm and female. Damnation, he needed more, needed another taste. Needed to taste her skin, to feast on those lovely white tits while he buried his aching cock in that lush body.

This was what mattered. Now.

He shifted, rubbing his hips against hers but couldn't find the angle he needed. Taking her mouth in another drugging, mind-blowing kiss, he walked her backward until she came up against the wall. Pinning her there, he lifted her hips until she locked her legs around his flanks. Groaning, he buried his face in her neck.

Her scent rose to haunt him, sweet and erotic, innocent and tempting. He lowered his head and gently bit the underside of one breast as he ground himself against the heat between her legs. He snarled in frustration at the heavy cloth that separated them and reached for the zipper of her jeans, jerking them open and down in two quick movements. Lauren fell back against the wall, her head spinning dizzily, as Dale knelt in front of her and pulled her jeans completely off and away, before he leaned forward, nuzzling the front panel of her panties briefly before he rose and grabbed her hips again, fitting his cock into the notch between her thighs and rocking against her.

Through the heavy denim, Lauren could feel his shaft, hard and long, as he thrust against her silk covered flesh. Her nerve endings sizzled, and she swore some exploded with little pops when he gripped her ass with one hand while the other slid further down and under, sliding inside her panties until he could circle her wet opening with one fingertip while he rocked her against that hard cock. She shuddered and gasped, her hands flying up to clutch at his shoulders, then fist in his hair. A weak whimper rose in the air before dying away into the silence. A choking gasp. Shuddering with heavy breaths, and a weak, moaning whimper as Dale thrust his hand past the silky barrier of her panties, arrowing in on the delights they hid. Her cleft was covered by a small triangle of damp, soft, ebony curls that felt like silk when he brushed them with his hand as his fingers slid slickly across her wet flesh, plunging deeply into her hungering body.

She closed around him, tight and wet, unbelievably sweet. The tight walls of her sex gloved his fingers like a second skin, satin slick and clinging as he worked first one finger, and then a second inside, working her body and circling the pad of his thumb around her pulsing clit. Her sheath clung to him, gripping his fingers so tightly that his head started to pound as he imagined what it was going to feel like when he got his cock inside her. Son of a fucking bitch, he'd explode.

Her head was thrown back, her cheeks flushed, her mouth swollen. A chain of silver hung at her neck, a wand resting in the hollow of her throat. His heavy lidded eyes took the sight in, even as dim recognition started to flutter in his mind. No. Damn it, he didn't want to think, didn't want to do anything other than taste this woman, to bury himself inside her.

Dropping to his knees, he drew her panties down her long, sleekly muscled thighs, stroking one long narrow foot as he spread her legs. Leaning forward, he used his tongue, drawing it up her wet slit in one long stroke. She shrieked, tried to pull him away. "Let me," he murmured, pulling away long enough to take her hands and pin them down to her sides. "God, you're sweet."

She was reluctant. It had been a while since he'd had to coax a woman into spreading her thighs for him, but he hadn't forgotten how. Gentle, nuzzling kisses against her belly while one hand lazily stroked her clit. As she moved closer to climax, she lost her resolve and didn't notice as he worked his way down with his mouth and eventually replaced his fingers with his tongue. He stabbed at her clit with his tongue before taking it between his teeth and sucking as he started to fuck her with his fingers, groaning as her cream flooded his hand. He lapped it up greedily, taking one of her thighs and draping it over his shoulder, opening her folds. Spreading them with his fingers, he thrust his tongue inside her, lapping at her slick walls, gently biting at soft plump lips that guarded her passage, before returning to suckle on her clit again.

He pulled away briefly to stare at her sex before glancing up at her. "God, you're good. I could eat you for hours," he muttered before diving for her again.

She was wet. Hot. Tasty. Cupping the firm cheeks of her ass in his hands, he ate at her, sucking, licking, drinking her down while her hands clutched at his head. He could hear her panting, moaning, finally crying out as she climaxed in his mouth.

He rose, planting hot, biting kisses against her flushed torso as he stood. His mouth gleamed wetly with her cream as he covered her mouth with his, groaning as her eager hands clutched him against her.

"Now," he muttered, and he once again lifted her hips and positioned himself between her legs.

Lauren froze as he ended the kiss to work his way to her ear. She could taste herself on him, and it set her to blushing all over again. Which was foolish, since he had just had his face buried in her crotch, his tongue gliding in and out of her pussy.

But there was also the taste of whiskey strong in her mouth and the odor of it hung in the air. The hot thick cloud of pleasure that fogged her brain tried to clear up, allowing her a moment of sanity.

"Dale," she said, with half a mind to put a stop to this. Then he brushed against the damp triangle between her legs, hot, smooth and hard. She gasped, arching back as he slid once, twice, three times against her. On the fourth pass over the knotted bundle of nerves, she cried out as waves of pleasure washed over her, radiating outward from the center of her body.

He chuckled, and lowered his head to purr in her ear, "Like that?" He repeated it, stroking the fat head of his cock against her, as if checking her response, and he hummed a soft little praise against her throat. "Yeah. You like that. You're gonna like it even more when I'm inside you. You're so hot, so wet. Tight."

She gasped and cried out a second time as he slid inside, thrusting deep, forcing himself through her tight channel as it strained to accommodate him, hurting despite her arousal. She instinctively arched again, squirmed, whimpered. *Oh, shit,* she thought in a panic.

This isn't going to work. He was too big and it was stretching her, burning and filling her.

But then he started to circle her clit with his thumb again, pressing, plucking it gently, and she forgot her panic, focusing just on that hand, whimpering and crying, silently begging for him to continue.

As Dale slid his thick cock further inside her she moaned, half in fear, half in mindless pleasure. "Shh," he murmured in her ear, recognizing the distress, if not the cause of it. "Relax, honey. Just relax," he crooned softly, withdrawing just a little before sliding in again. "Shh, baby. You're fine. Damn more than fine."

Bracing her against the wall, Dale shifted his grip until one arm was wrapped beneath her buttocks. He nudged himself in a little further, groaning as she clamped around him tighter, hot wet silk. He raised his head, found her mouth without opening his eyes. She was so tight, her body trying to resist, and he couldn't for the life of him figure out why. Didn't care. She was hot and wet and ready and she wanted him every bit as much as he wanted her.

He nipped sharply at her lip and her eyes flew open, yelping a little, before catching her breath, arching up as he withdrew and plunged back into the wet, silken depths of her, burying his cock to the hilt. Her flesh writhed convulsively around him, forcing Dale to grit his teeth against his body's impulses.

She was so tight, gloving his cock like he was a size or two too big, her muscles squeezing around him.

The tide ebbed a little, enough for him to be able to move without fear of immediate explosion. Eyes closed, face buried against her neck, Dale rocked against her as he held her pinned to the wall, gently rotating his hips, adjusting his thrusts so that he brushed against sensitized flesh every time he moved. She was quivering against him, around him. Each breath she took tightened her muscles in a slow, maddening caress around his cock. He pulled out a little further, thrust in, groaning helplessly when it set her muscles to writhing, and her inner walls to clinging around his length.

She moaned softly, straining to move, to do something before she flew apart. He was so big, so full inside her, stretching her sheath as he worked his shaft back and forth in tiny strokes that spread licking flames through her belly.

It was more than she could handle; she shifted and squirmed against him. Tried to pull away from him as the tension started to grow inside her belly. Her eyes flew open, desperately wanting to see his face, see those glorious, sexy eyes, the eyes of the man she loved, but they were closed. Closed, and she knew, seeing another woman's face.

She tried, then, to turn away, to twist out of his grip, even though the damage, so to speak, had already been done. His eyes opened slightly at the withdrawal and he whispered, "No," as he tightened his grip.

Blindly, he caught her chin in his hand, forced her face back to his as he lowered his mouth to hers, brushing her damp mouth with his. All the while, he crooned to her, pressing kisses against her cheek, her ear, the tip of her nose. "Easy, sweetheart. Don't fight it." With a shift of his body, he forced her further down, opening her more.

"It's gonna be good," he murmured against her ear. "Just relax, angel. Just let me…Yeah," he said roughly as she whimpered when he moved against her again. "Yeah, that's it." She could feel him inside her, long, hard and thick. The thick head of his cock kept rubbing against a rather extraordinary little button deep inside her slick, wet vagina and it was robbing her of the ability to think. Each thrust set off magical little explosions inside her belly, heat spreading outward from her center, until she thought she would go up in flames.

And even though she hated herself for being so weak, she stopped caring if he wasn't seeing her. He slid one hand up to cup her breast, pushing it upward until he could suckle the nipple. Gasping, she threw her head back, rapping it into the wall and never noticing as he pulled further out this time, thrusting back inside with more force.

It hurt. No. It wasn't pain...oh, damn it, what was it? That hot little ball of need grew stronger as he trailed a line of kisses back up to her face. He tugged her lower lip into his mouth as she strained against him, silently begging. "It's okay, baby," he whispered, adjusting his grip, sliding his hands down and grasping her behind each knee, lifting her weight. Then he hooked his arms under her knees, leaving her open and vulnerable. Lowering his head, he bit her shoulder as his hips jack-hammered against hers. The tight silken walls of her sex started to tighten and cling as she neared orgasm.

Dale swallowed her gasping scream with his mouth, felt the woman convulse around him. His eyes were open now, but they were not seeing the woman he held against him, the woman who loved him with every breath in her body.

He came inside her, in hot, wet jets, startled when he felt her body clamp around his a second time. Those milking little caresses sent shivers up his spine and he felt his balls drawing tight, his cock still full and hard and eager. Again.

Taking her to the floor, he draped her thighs over his, holding her ass in his hands while he fucked her slowly, smiling when she whimpered and strained against him. "Such pretty tits," he murmured, releasing her butt long enough to guide one of her hands to the tits in questions. "Play with them for me."

Her hands were hesitant but willing and her mind was too far gone to care as he whispered what he wanted her to do. When he whispered, "Pinch your nipple," she did it, rolling and plucking until each movement tightened the muscles lower in her body. The other hand he guided to her clit, where her opening stretched tight around his penis. When he gruffly said, "Show me how you like to have it touched," she showed him, her torso twisting and straining while her fingers circled repeatedly against her clit, harder and faster until she was whimpering in time with her own touch.

Dale's breath shuddered out of his lungs as he watched the play of those long graceful fingers stroking over naked flesh. A swollen pink nipple pinched and rolled, the other hand working at her clit. A picture straight out of his dreams, hot, wet dreams, centered around a hot, wet woman willing to touch and be touched. He stayed upright on his knees, staring down as her long, slim fingers rolled and rubbed the hard swollen bead of flesh. Moisture from their bodies soon had her fingers gleaming. Taking her hand yet again he guided it to her mouth, forced two of her wet fingers inside, until she licked it off, her eyes smoky and hot as she stared at him

"Gimme a taste," he ordered, leaning forward over her body. She reached up to touch his lips but he shook his head. "Uh-uh, darling. Get me more."

So she played with her throbbing clit again as he stroked in and out, lazy and slow. The fingers he took into his mouth were wet with her cream and his come and Dale was certain he had never tasted anything so good before. Her hips started to rock feverishly under the play of her fingers and he pinned her in place with his hands. "Not so fast," he rasped as he drove his cock home inside her.

Her puckered little nipples stood upright, begging for his attention. Shifting, he lowered his body across her, forcing her breast up until he could feast on her nipple while he rode her body in hard, sure strokes.

Her hand slid up to clutch at his shoulders when he took her legs and put them high in the air, opening her body so he could take her hard and deep. Lauren flinched when he pounded into her, forcing his cock deep inside her already swollen, sensitive passage. He bit delicately on her nipple while he pumped into her, pulling a muffled scream from her.

"That's it, baby. Scream for me, come for me," he murmured, lifting his head and transferring his attention to her other breast until both nipples were hard, red and wet from his mouth.

She screamed, all right. When he rose up and shoved her legs to her chest, fucking her hard, she screamed as she climaxed around him, feeling his come spurt inside her, hot and deep. The climax tore through her belly, tearing open a dam deep inside that gushed forth beneath the pounding of his body.

In his mind, Dale had pictured a face, one he saw with every woman. Her image wasn't quite as clear, but he hardly noticed as the silky flesh around him sent him into an explosive climax, the likes of which he'd never before experienced.

Without even realizing he had spoken, he roared out her name while he shot his semen into Lauren Spencer's tight little sheath, her climax milking and squeezing around his cock like a greedy fist.

Moments later, exhaustion crowding his already dazed mind, he collapsed on top of her. The unreal pleasure, combined with the unholy amount of liquor he had consumed, dulled his mind enough that he didn't see anything wrong with curling up around the warm, naked female he held against his sweating body.

Dimly, he tried to remember who she was, but couldn't. And he didn't have the energy needed to open his eyes and look. She'd be there when he woke up, and then he'd find out. After he buried himself in that body again.

Turning his head, eyes still closed, he breathed in the incredible scent of her soft skin before burying his face in her hair and falling into oblivion.

Lauren was pretty certain she was going to be sick. Just puke her guts up right there. And since Dale's long, heavy body still pinned her to the floor, she was pretty certain she would also choke on her own vomit, and asphyxiate right there. It couldn't possibly be any more humiliating than hearing Dale cry another woman's name while he was coming inside her.

What had she done?

Her body aching, her mouth swollen from the rough kisses, Lauren lay staring at the ceiling in Dale's living room.

What had she done?

She forced herself to breathe evenly, deeply, slowly, until the nausea started to pass. The anger still lurked but she restrained it. God knows, she had certainly set herself up for this.

Carefully, after deciding he had definitely passed out, Lauren, shifted, twisted and shimmied her way out from under him. She pulled her knees to her chest, flinching as muscles never before used went on protest. A dull throb between her legs lingered, but the minor pain was worth the pleasure.

So that was a climax. That was why people sought out the opposite sex. With a shaky smile, she decided she could understand the appeal it held. But even though her body was so sated, so relaxed she could curl up and happily sleep for a week, her heart was breaking.

Baby. Sweetheart. Never once had he said her name. Not once had his eyes looked into hers.

And in the end, he had cried out, "Nikki," as he emptied his body into hers.

Another substitute, that's what she had become.

And she only had herself to blame. She knew Dale well enough to know if she hadn't been willing, hadn't shown any interest in what he was offering, this wouldn't have happened. It never would have gone past that first glorious kiss. If he hadn't been drunk, that kiss, oh, that wonderful kiss wouldn't have happened either.

Quickly, Lauren shoved the thought from her mind. This was so pathetic, she thought miserably. She had come over here to apologize and had ended up giving her virginity to a man who had been making love to another woman in his mind. It had meant everything to her, and meant less than nothing to him. Any woman would have done.

Humiliation stained her cheeks red and she couldn't even begin to think of how she would explain this.

Maybe he won't remember.

Lauren shrugged away that persistent little voice, shaking her head and the unlikely possibility.

Then, again, he had been awfully drunk. Otherwise, he wouldn't have touched her. The thought never would have crossed his mind. Maybe he really wouldn't remember.

Frowning, Lauren thought back. Dale had mentioned he didn't like to do any heavy drinking because he lost too much time, too easily. Three beers and quite a bit of whiskey from the stink of it. Running her tongue over her teeth, she started to wonder.

She had gotten more from him than she had ever hoped to have, regardless of the circumstances. His face was relaxed now, free from the pain she had seen etched there when he had opened the door. He had gotten some comfort from it. Nobody had been hurt. If he didn't remember, would it matter not to enlighten him?

Pregnancy was unlikely. Completely wrong time of the month. Her period was due in three or four days. And though Dale was casual about sex, he wasn't casual about health. She knew he always wore a rubber, no matter what a woman said.

The sticky dampness between her thighs reminded her that perhaps always wasn't a good word to use. But he was healthy.

Lauren couldn't be any healthier, not in that area.

Would it hurt anything?

Slowly, gingerly, she got to her feet, gathered her clothes. She only donned her jeans and shirt, gathering her shoes, panties and bra and setting them in a bundle by the door.

Gnawing on her lip, she studied him lying at her feet. He still wore his shirt. His jeans were shoved, uncomfortably she imagined, just past his hips. His penis lay against his belly, soft, wet and shiny from their combined climaxes, from her body. Her eyes lingered briefly before she made up her mind. First, she retrieved a paper towel, wet with warm water and cleaned him, his cock twitching in her hands, lengthening and hardening. Carefully, she tried to tug his jeans back into place. He woke slightly, smiled a tipsy smile at her, and she doubted he even really saw her. "Sorry, sugar. Can't just yet," was all he said before falling back to sleep. Finally, she had his jeans up and he was decently covered.

Of course, she wasn't quite certain 'can't' had been particularly accurate. He was already hard again, even though he was sound asleep.

Nervously, fingers fumbling, she got the buttons on his fly secured. Then she spied the whiskey bottle and snatched it up, setting it close, but not too close to his outstretched hand. Tossing the paper towel in the garbage, she wondered if she had done enough to erase any evidence.

Feeling slightly guilty, she took her underwear and the tin of chocolate chip cookies and quietly sneaked out the front door, using her own copy of his key to lock it. Taking a deep breath, she headed down the stairs.

* * * * *

A smile lingered on her lips sometime later as she lay in a tub of water, soaking away the faint discomfort. No wonder so many of those women left the house with smiles on their faces. No wonder Allison had lingered so long, despite Dale's obvious avoidance of any type of commitment.

The man had magic in his hands, she mused, scooping up a handful of bubbles and stroking them down her arms. And sin in his blood. Those hands, that mouth, she gave a low hum of appreciation as she slid a little lower in the scented water.

Granted, she felt somewhat cheated. She doubted that any of those women left his house after a few minutes upright against the wall in the living room, or even after a harder fuck on the floor. But she also doubted that any of those women had felt the way she did, had loved him the way she did. The smile was now tinged with sadness. She could have made him so happy.

Then she sighed, reality settling in. Until Dale was ready to let go of a woman he had never really had, nobody could make him happy. Not even the one woman who loved him with everything she had in her.

Morose now, she gazed at the reflection the mirrored wall at her right sent back at her. Sure, she was pretty enough. But she'd been a pretty child, and that hadn't made her family want her. Nobody had ever wanted her. Why should Dale be any different?

With a sigh of disgust, she arose, dripping wet from the bath. Jerking a warmed towel off the rod, she wrapped it around her and left the room.

"Feeling sorry for yourself changes nothing, Lauren," she told herself.

* * * * *

Cautiously, Dale opened his eyes. He had been lying awake for a good five minutes now, taking stock. He remembered the letter, the first and second beer clearly enough, but after that, things started getting a little fuzzy. He hadn't eaten since breakfast so the alcohol had hit him harder and faster than it normally would have. The whiskey bottle, uh, yeah, he was thinking he remembered the whiskey bottle as well.

Pushing himself onto his elbows, he surveyed the mess around him with squinted eyes. The pint lay just a few feet away from his right hand. Empty. But from the smell of things, it was likely there was more whiskey on the floor than inside him.

A faint headache throbbed behind his eyes and his mouth was incredibly dry, but other than that, there were no aftereffects from his attempt to drown his sorrows in booze.

Unless he counted the lost time.

What had happened?

Hell, he hated getting drunk, hated the loss of control that inevitably happened, even if it was just the inability to remember what he had done, where he had been. Who he had been with. Scowling, he wondered where that thought had come from.

A woman. Had there been a woman here? Vaguely, he remembered soft arms, soft skin. A scent that lingered in his mind, and faintly, he thought, on his skin.

Though he couldn't taste anything beyond the stale taste of whiskey in his mouth, he thought he remembered tasting, no, devouring a woman. Thrusting, rocking, fucking a woman.

Loving. *Loving?*

But his mind was a blank. There was no face to go with the body. Had he been dreaming?

Even if his mind was foggy, his body remembered, tightening in remembered pleasure.

It had to have been a dream. If there had been a woman here, she would likely still be here and they would be in bed. Naked, their bodies wet with sweat and come. Instead, Dale was sitting on the floor of his living room, completely dressed, alone. And clean.

Sex hadn't ever been clean in Dale's experience.

"I've really got to stop doing this," he muttered, slowly getting to his feet, thankful there was no nausea. Just a little shaky and a lot curious. A lot horny. What had he dreamed about? The distant echo of a gasping cry lingered in his ears. A blinding sense of pleasure, a sense of homecoming.

Maybe a better question would be whom had he dreamed about, he decided. It hadn't been Nikki. He was absolutely certain of that.

That faint, subtle scent clung to him, tightening his flesh, making his mouth water. He glanced downward in wry amusement and muttered, "Down, boy," as his already interested cock stood up at full attention. There was nobody here, and from the look of things, there hadn't been anybody here all day.

The stink of the place was nearly enough to make him blanche, and he doubted his body was in much better condition. Rubbing a hand down his stubbled jaw, he grimaced. He'd have peeled all the flesh from a woman in the shape he was in.

Thirty minutes later, revitalized by a hot shower and hot coffee, a smile lingering on his face, Dale straightened the living room. Clean shaven, clear-headed, and inexplicably cheerful for some reason, he whistled a jazzy tune as he gathered up sketches and replaced pillows on the couch. He was cleaning the carpet where the whiskey had spilled, when the doorbell rang. Settling back on his heels, he wondered. Hoped.

It was past ten o'clock. And he could think of only one person who could be on the other side of that door. When he opened it moments later, he decided the only way he could have been more pleased was if it had been Nikki. Or the dream woman.

Lauren stood there, her eyes hesitant, clad in a baggy sweatshirt and rumpled jeans, clutching a colorful tin. He could count the number of times he had seen Lauren look so . . .touchable. She was always so reserved, so elegant and cool.

"Hi," she said, her voice soft, uncertain. "Are you, um, alone?"

"Yeah," he said, unsure whether he wanted to open the door and make it easy for her or stay there while she shifted from foot to foot, nervous and uncomfortable. But her downcast eyes and the unhappy set of her mouth decided the matter for him. He stepped back and said,

"Come on in." As she started to move past him, an image fluttered in his mind. A soft pale gray shirt, a ruffled neckline, a slim pale neck surrounded by a length of silver. The way she smelled…vanilla, musk, baby lotion.

Oh, shit.

And Dale started to worry a little. "Uh, you didn't come by earlier, did you?"

She smiled sheepishly and said, "No. I've just now worked up the nerve." Then she shoved the tin at him. "These are for you."

He took the tin, deciding to make it just a little hard. "Worked up the nerve for what?" he asked, inclining his head, tucking the tin against his side without looking in it. He already knew what it held. Homemade chocolate-chip cookies with pecans. Her specialty. His mouth was already watering.

"Apologizing."

"For what?"

Her cheeks were slightly flushed and she turned her head away. "For what I said last week, how I acted. It wasn't your fault and wasn't anything you did. I was just feeling a little nasty and took it out on you." Then she turned her head, met his eyes straight on and said, "You're the best friend I have. You've been there for me whenever I needed you, helped me out more times than I can count. I shouldn't have jumped on you and I'm sorry."

"You have no idea how glad I am to see you," he whispered, tugging her into a friendly embrace. She held herself slightly rigid for just a moment then relaxed, squeezing him tight around the middle before backing away.

"Does that mean I'm forgiven?" she asked solemnly. "If not, I'll just take those cookies home and drown my sorrow in them."

He snatched the tin up and carried it into the kitchen. "I don't think so," he said, opening it and popping half a cookie into his mouth. She started toward him, a grin curving her mouth upward and he almost choked as an image of him covering that wide mouth with his loomed in his mind. Quickly, he grabbed his coffee and swallowed, burning the roof of his mouth. Where in the hell had that come from?

She eyed him oddly, her face paling a little. Or did he imagine that? Then she popped a cookie into her mouth before looking around. Her nostrils twitched and she pronounced, "It smells like a distillery in here." Her tongue darted out to catch a crumb at the corner of her mouth. "And you're looking a little rough there."

He dragged his gaze and attention away from her mouth. "I, ah, decided to do a little drowning myself. It's been a hell of a rough week." She hitched herself onto the counter across from him and the relief settled even deeper into his bones. Normal. Things were back to normal again. And, helping himself to another cookie, he told her about it.

Something flickered in her eyes as he told her about the letter. Hurt? Pity? She sighed, pulling her legs up against her chest, quietly saying, "How much longer are you going to do this to yourself?"

He turned away from her, busying himself with getting out a couple of glasses of milk to enjoy with the cookies. Out of the blue, he said, "I'm wondering if maybe I'm in love with her, or just the idea of it." Since his back was turned, he didn't see Lauren stiffen, missed seeing her eyes widen. By the time he turned around, she was just watching, waiting for him to continue.

He frowned, wondering where that thought had come from. Of course he loved Nikki. He had for years. "Anyway, after the way the week has been, I decided to cap it off with a gallon or so of alcohol."

Lauren grinned at him and said, "That would explain that smell." Her eyes narrowed and her smile turned mischievous. "Lose any time?"

"Guess so. I woke up a little after nine. The last time I saw the clock it was about four thirty." He watched her from the corner of his eye, nonchalantly asking, "Did you see Allison here, crawling back to me?" He had to force the teasing note into his voice. "Declaring she would take anything I wanted to give her?"

"No. I can't say I did. But I just got back a couple of hours ago," she replied, shrugging before popping another cookie into her mouth. "Keep the rest of those things away from me. I already ate five before I left the house."

He bit his lip to keep from asking, "Did you see anybody?"

A dream, he told himself. Just a dream.

But that didn't keep him from trying desperately to piece together the fragments of his memory.

* * * * *

The Dream Woman plagued his thoughts. While the sun was out and he was busy, he was able to shove her to the back of his mind. But at night, she slipped out of the shadows, always hiding her face, taunting him. Soft sleek female flesh, the heady scent of musk and something innocent—baby lotion? A firm body pressed against his, taking, demanding everything he could give. He would wake up in the middle of the night, aroused beyond bearing, unable to remember a damn thing, his cock unbelievably hard and aching.

At his desk, he sat, a fine sweat breaking out all over his body, as he replayed the dream in his mind. So vivid, he had thought he would turn over and she'd be there next to him in bed. Shit, he couldn't work like this. He tore his jeans open, wrapping his hand around his shaft, falling into a quick rhythm while he imagined it was her, riding him, or better yet, sucking him off, on her knees.

Cupping his balls with his other hand, he groaned, grunting as thick white jets of semen spilled onto his belly and hands.

"Am I losing my mind?" he muttered out loud, wondering. Why else would a woman who didn't exist haunt him so?

He glanced out his window to see Lauren trudging down her driveway, lugging a large trashcan. He pulled his shirt off and used it to wipe the come away before he stood and fastened his jeans. Absently, he saved his work on the computer and straightened up his sketches before heading outside, pausing to wash up a little better and grab a clean shirt. He caught up with her as she was setting the can down beside a very sorry looking, very dead bush.

"That's your third dead plant this summer, pal," he commented, taking the string from her and binding up the branches. "Losing your touch?"

She scowled at him and loftily informed him, "It's been a dry summer."

"Oh, yeah. I forgot," he said, sarcastically, glancing around at the verdant green grass, the blooming flowers. The small garden he had in the back of his house was nearly over run by thriving tomato plants.

"How did your date go last night?"

He shrugged and replied, "We called it quits early. That girl could talk of nothing other than herself and the plastic surgeon she works for. Filled me in on how well he had helped her fill out, and at a discount, too." He'd retreated to his bed alone, something rare for him after a date.

"You like them filled out," Lauren reminded dryly.

"I prefer to think that Mother Nature is responsible for it, though. Kind of loses its impact when the woman's bragging about how flat-chested she used to be," he said with disgust. Eyeing Lauren with a playful leer, he added, "Definitely not a problem you'd be familiar with."

She flushed, dropping to her knees beside the small flowering bush, now brittle and dry. "Not since about seventh or eighth grade, no." Donning her thick rubber gloves, she started digging in the earth to get to the root. "Maybe she should be dating her plastic surgeon. He's certain to appreciate his own work."

"Mm," he muttered. The woman in question (Sissy, or was it Stacey?) had tucked her phone number into his pocket, whispering coyly for him to call her when he was feeling better. Fat chance. Apparently the woman was too stupid to recognize a brush off when she received one.

"I've got to fly to New York next month," he said suddenly, remembering why he had headed out here. "I'll be gone a few days. Would you mind dropping me off and picking me up?"

"As long you don't plan on catching any red eye flights," she responded, hissing under her breath when the root ball proved to be rather persistent. "Help me out here," she ordered, nodding at the other side of the plant.

"Jeez, Lauren," he muttered, getting to his knees. "I don't have this fascination for digging around in the dirt the way you do. I can't do it and stay clean, like you can." Nonetheless, he dug his hands into the soil and helped her work the root ball toward the surface.

"Buddy, you use to be a *mechanic*. You made your living getting filth," she reminded, giving a satisfied grunt when the root ball broke free. Several wayward roots had remained in the earth, so she left Dale to dispose of the plant and root while she settled down to dig out those little pieces.

"You could just leave those be," he said after he had tossed the plant.

"No, I couldn't. I'm planning on putting a weeping willow here and I don't want little baby bushes springing up next year to choke it."

Later, he followed her into her house to scrub up his hands while she washed up and changed. Thursday night. They had developed a tradition for Thursday nights over the years. Pizza, beer for him, wine for her, and a movie or two. He had already ordered when she padded back into the living room half an hour later wearing baggy cotton pants and a cotton top that didn't quite reach the waistband of those pants. Every time she moved, he found himself enjoying the sight of her pale torso. He shifted uncomfortably, finally tearing his eyes away and watching the screen.

A faint cramp tightened her belly momentarily and Lauren shifted, drawing her knees to her chest. Over the next hour, throughout the movie, the cramps worsened. She slowly straightened her legs, scooting towards the edge of the couch. "I'm sorry, but I think I need to go on to bed," she said, trying to keep her voice level. No wonder she'd been feeling so damn moody all day.

"You okay?" Dale asked, a faint frown marring his forehead. He'd spent the past forty- five minutes day dreaming, not paying Lauren any attention at all. Now he saw her pale face, the faint line between her eyebrows, the hand she had over her stomach.

"Yeah. Just need to get to bed," Lauren replied, trying to keep the crossness from her voice. "Lock up for me, will you?"

She started to push herself to her feet, but Dale had already risen and taken her hand, helping her up. "You don't look okay," he said, worried. "You getting sick?"

"No," she said shortly, trying to shrug his hands off her shoulders.

"Then what in the hell's wrong?" he demanded, the worry increasing.

She narrowed her eyes at him and said, very slowly, as though speaking to a small child, "Think about it, Dale. What makes a woman very tired, very cranky, and makes her belly cramp?"

Understanding dawned in his eyes and he quickly yanked his hands away, a dull flush darkening his cheeks. He jammed his hands in his pockets and moved back a few feet. "Ah, hmm, okay," he mumbled. "You . . .you need anything?"

Amused at his obvious discomfort, she smiled a little, despite the twisting pain in her belly. "Yes. I need some Advil, a heating pad and my bed. I think I can handle it myself. Go on home," she said, heading for the stairs. "Lock the door, if you don't mind."

She didn't glance back at the noise behind her, intent only on getting that Advil, the heating pad, and most definitely, her bed.

After picking up and locking up over at Lauren's, Dale opened the door to his house and went into the living room. He put on some music and turned it up loud before heading upstairs. But he barely got inside the arched open doorway before he froze in his tracks, stumbled and fell back, banging his shoulder against the wall.

An image, so strong and so damn clear, of him pressing Lauren up against the wall, right where he was resting, her long body naked, her midnight hair falling around those strong slim shoulders. His hands tangling in that hair, pulling her mouth to his.

Of him going down on her, sliding his tongue inside her wet little cunt while she gripped his hair and moaned. So vivid, he could almost taste her cream on his tongue.

Of him shoving her to the floor and shoving his cock inside her body while she still trembled from her last climax. Pumping in and out of her body until she climaxed around him again, feeling like heaven, as he emptied his come into her receptive body.

Nearly blind, his chest tight, Dale slid down the wall until he sat on the floor, propped up against the wall. The blood in his veins pounded heavily, slowly, and his hands closed into tightly clenched fists as he struggled to hold onto that image. But it faded, so quickly, so suddenly, he wondered briefly if he had gotten a hold of a bad mushroom.

His breathing slowed as he convinced himself she was only on his mind because he was worried about her. He had only pictured what he had pictured because he was so damn horny. Perfectly logical, perfectly sound.

But it didn't explain away why he had this sudden urge to find out what she really looked like without her clothes.

Early the next morning, Lauren climbed out of bed, her mind sluggish, her body aching. Jeez, her period had never bothered her like this before. She had started to worry a little the past week. Her period hadn't started when it was supposed to and she had a couple of bad moments trying to figure out what in the hell she would do if . . .

Hell, it hadn't happened.

Now she stood staring at her reflection, so pale and drawn, and felt like crying. For a while there, she hadn't allowed herself to acknowledge the faint hope she had harbored when her period hadn't started.

A baby. Her eyes drifted closed as she tried to imagine it. She had never really thought about having children. After her own pretty rotten childhood, she had never quite seen herself raising kids. She wouldn't have the faintest clue as to how to do it. She always felt so...clumsy and useless around kids.

But having Dale's baby. She cut that train of thought off, disgusted with herself. And how would she go about explaining that? And how would she deal with it? How would he deal with it?

She knew Dale. He'd feel obligated. She didn't want his obligation. She wanted his love.

And she'd never have that. And that thought was enough to make the tears welling in her eyes come trickling out.

Chapter Three

Nearly three weeks had passed, but Lauren wasn't feeling much better. The light period had passed, but the fatigue and general depression hadn't. While she was sitting in the doctor's office in Jeffersonville, Indiana, Dale was slow dancing a delicate little red haired woman who bore a remarkable resemblance to Nicole Kline Lightfoot around a New York penthouse. Had she known that, her strained nerves would have snapped. As she was being weighed, he was dancing Beth Greer into her bedroom, his hands busily unzipping her snazzy little two-piece green business suit.

Insurance information from Lauren was given to the receptionist while he guided Beth's mouth to his shaft, and Beth was sliding a rubber on him while Lauren was led to the bathroom.

While she was peeing in a cup, he laid the owner of a ritzy little art gallery down across a bed made up with silk sheets. He was lifting her body over his, up and down on his cock while Lauren was having her blood pressure checked.

The moment the doctor confirmed her pregnancy, he was climaxing, his face buried in Beth's hair.

It might have made her somewhat happy to know that this time it wasn't Nikki's face he saw, Nikki's body he pictured under him. Rather, it was a long tall woman whose face slipped away from him, as ephemerally as the dreams that haunted him at night.

"I can't be pregnant," Lauren repeated, her voice shaking. "I had my period two weeks ago. And I was with him just that once, over a month ago."

The OB, a small- framed woman with long brown hair she wore caught in a ponytail, smiled, held Lauren's hand. "You are pregnant. Four to six weeks pregnant, by my estimation. The test is without a doubt positive. And you probably just had some very light spotting. Some women have that the first few months of pregnancy."

"Will . . ." she licked her dry lips. "Will that hurt the...the baby?"

"I seriously doubt it. Of course, I do want to do some tests, an ultrasound, make sure everything's okay. But I'm sure everything is just fine. You're young, you're strong, and you're healthy." She paused, her light brown eyes sympathetic. "You weren't expecting this."

"No. No."

Dark eyes serious, Dr. Flynn offered, "There are options-"

"No!" Lauren hissed, her hand flying to her still flat stomach. "Expecting it or not, it's my baby."

"And the father?" Dr. Flynn asked.

"It...it doesn't concern him. It was a fluke. He doesn't want kids, doesn't want a family."

"Being a single mother is a tough job, Lauren," the woman said softly. "Being a mother is a tough job, period. I know. I have four kids of my own."

Lauren smiled slightly. "There's not much choice. I won't force him into something he doesn't want. We'd both regret it, but the baby would pay for it. And I'm financially able to provide for the baby." It was getting easier, she realized, to actually say it. To actually think it.

"You're not having morning sickness?"

"Not yet. When does that start?"

"If you're going to have it, it will start soon. It if does, the best thing you can do is keep crackers at the bedside, eat one before you get out of bed and take it real easy until your body adjusts to this." The doctor was actually beaming now, looking so happy.

Lauren started to smile, that happiness contagious. "You love your job," she said, out of the blue.

Dr. Flynn cocked her head and smiled even brighter. "Yes. I do." Catching hold of Lauren's hand once more, she squeezed it gently. "You're about to become a mom. That is the number one job. And I think you're going to love that."

Hand resting on her belly, Lauren smiled, shakily this time. She was starting to worry now. What in the world was she going to tell Dale? God, please, she thought in a very rare prayer, please. I don't want to lose him.

* * * * *

Morning sickness hit four days later, with a vengeance. Crackers, crackers, and more crackers. From the time she woke up, which lately was around nine, until after ten or ten thirty, she was sicker than a dog. She popped those crackers like an addict and sometimes, they actually helped. During the oddest times of the day, certain smells, certain sights would just set her off all over again. So, it was more crackers. And more.

She catnapped three or four times a day and fell into bed, exhausted, before ten o'clock at night. Before she realized it the day to pick Dale up from the airport had come and gone. She slept through the phone calls that started at two in the afternoon and continued until nearly four.

* * * * *

Both mind and body relaxed, Dale smiled at the pretty dark haired flight attendant. She was a Louisville native and had offered him a ride home early in the flight. With just a tiny bit of regret, he refused. He wanted to settle down and relax a bit now, maybe catch a movie with Lauren in a day or two.

He was hungry, though. Maybe he could talk Lauren into stopping off someplace to eat.

Passing quickly through the terminal, his long legs ate up the distance between him and the baggage claim area. Lauren had told him she would meet him there and keep an eye out for his bags. The airport was fairly quiet and only a few people lingered in the baggage area.

Lauren wasn't one of them.

His steps slowed and halted as he frowned. Lauren was never late. Hell, the woman left nearly an hour early for a doctor's appointment in Jeffersonville. He scanned the area one more time for a sleek, elegant woman, but she wasn't there. A leather clad teenaged girl with a nose ring, a harassed looking mother of three, two bored looking businessman.

No Lauren.

Flagging down a young uniformed security guard, he asked, "Have you seen a tall, dark haired woman here recently?"

Tossing him a glance, the guard replied, "Hundreds of times a day."

Rolling his eyes, he dug his wallet out of his hip pocket and flipped it open to a little snapshot he and Lauren had done at Six Flags the previous summer. Her normally serene eyes were sparkling with laughter and her wide mouth curved in a captivating smile. He flashed it at the guard and waited.

The guard, hardly more than a kid, let out a low appreciative whistle before saying positively, "Nope. Haven't seen her."

"You're sure?"

Smirking, the guard said, "I wouldn't forget a woman that looks like that." And then he was walking away, telling himself if he had a babe that looked like that, he sure as hell wouldn't be flying away from her.

Dale tucked the wallet away, absently rubbing his growling belly. Maybe she was just caught up in traffic. The Louisville highways had been under construction for the larger part of the past decade. His face blanched when his vivid imagination suddenly formed a picture of Lauren trapped in her beloved Mustang, something he had pictured a time or two before. If anything about Lauren was less than ladylike, it was her driving. She drove that car around like a bullet and had been pulled over more than once.

Of course, Dale reflected with a scowl, he had more tickets than she did, even though she was pulled over on a fairly regular basis. Having had the pleasure of being in the car with her a time or two, he was aware that she didn't really flirt, not exactly, but she sure as hell did something. She'd lower her lashes, smile demurely, and promise, insincerely, to be more careful. Promise, my ass, he thought in remembrance. Lied through her teeth was more like it.

Dale had to restrain himself from going to the nearest pay phone. His cell phone was stowed somewhere in his bags, and most likely, in need of recharging. After retrieving his bags, he settled down in a hard uncomfortable chair to wait, hunger eating a hole in his belly and a tension headache brewing.

Thirty minutes after he and Lauren had agreed to meet, he gave up and went for the pay phone. After counting some fifteen rings, he assured himself she was on the way.

At two twenty, she still wasn't there, so he called again, worry forming a heavy knot in his gut.

It was a little after three when he called a friend on the Jefferson County PD who assured him there was no wrecks involving a classic fire engine red Mustang in Louisville or the surrounding area. Somewhat relieved, he started to get irritated.

By four, he was downright pissed. "I'm gonna wring her damn neck," he snapped, slamming down the phone before stalking over to his luggage and swearing under his breath, passing a white haired little old lady who shot him a disapproving glare that melted into a reminiscing smile as she remembered similar words coming from her dear departed husband any number of times throughout their fifty years together. He had the look of John, she thought, tall and rangy, his lean face dark with a sexy scowl.

It was just before five and she had been up, moving somewhat sluggishly, the past thirty minutes when the front door flew open. Somewhat befuddled, she raised her head, a book on pregnancy in her lap, to stare at Dale who stood in the doorway glaring at her.

"I hope to God you've got a good reason for forgetting me," he stated, his eyes narrowed. "I waited at that damn airport nearly two hours, worrying myself to death about you."

Her color was somewhat revived since she had just wakened from a good nap. She had been reading about the baby's development, which had put a tiny little smile on her face, and a dreamy look in her eyes.

Dale stood there, glaring at her, thinking she looked like she had just tumbled out of bed with a man. She had forgotten him, her best damn friend, in favor of a lay. That was the first thought in his mind. But the only car in the driveway was hers, she was fully dressed, and alone. "Well?"

She looked somewhat puzzled, raising her hand to shove her tumbled hair back and then her eyes widened. "Damn it," she whispered, snapping the book closed and rising. "Damn it, Dale. I'm sorry. I was sleeping. I've been so tired." Her voice trailed off as he moved closer, peering at her closely.

"Are you still sick?" he demanded suddenly. She looked exhausted, actually, the color fading from her cheeks with each passing second. The sly little female smile was gone and her eyes just looked weary.

"Ah, no," she said, shaking her head. "I'm not sick." She turned away, clutching the book to her chest.

"How do you know? Have you been to the doctor?"

"Yes," she replied, truthfully. "And there's nothing wrong with me."

"There has to be, if you're taking naps in the middle of the afternoon. And you don't look like you're eating very well." Hell, she didn't like she was eating at all.

"How much weight have you lost? I swear, if you're trying to do one of those starvation diets-"

With a familiar bit of her normal fire, she shot him a withering look and said, "Please." Then Lauren moved away, pacing the living room. "I'm not sick, Dale," she said, distractedly. Now is the time, she thought. To tell or not to tell?

"Then what in the hell is wrong?" he asked, gritting his teeth. And worrying. Have mercy, but she was starting to scare him. Her face was pale, almost gray, and her smooth cheeks were hollowed. Large purple half moons were under her eyes and her hair was as disheveled as he had ever seen it, loose and tumbled around her slumped shoulders.

Voices echoed in Lauren's mind as she gripped the book tightly to her chest, so tightly her knuckles were white.

Being a single mother is a tough job, Lauren.

If I can't have a family with her, then I don't want one, period.

You weren't expecting this.

I love her, Lauren. Even if she doesn't ever love me, that doesn't change the fact that I lost my heart to her the first time I saw her.

Do or don't. Will or won't. Lauren stopped her pacing and turned to face the father of her child. And decided fiercely, that she wouldn't. She couldn't. She would not bind him to her, wouldn't destroy their friendship. And she wouldn't destroy herself. He would come to her now, if she told him, but it would be for the baby. Not for her, never for her.

She knew, from experience, what it was like to be an unwanted child, a burden. By God, she swore fiercely, this child will never know that feeling. She had been given a gift, the most precious gift she could have imagined. Her child would never be an obligation.

Dale took a few steps forward until he was just a few feet away from Lauren. Her face was pale and fierce, her eyes glittering brightly. Something inside his gut twisted and he decided he didn't want to know what was going on.

But he reached out anyway, carefully taking the book that she held clutched to her chest.

What to Expect When You're Expecting.

"This isn't just some recreational reading," he said, raising his eyes to hers.

"No."

"You have been sick. Morning sickness?"

"Yes."

Taking a deep breath and letting it out slowly, Dale studied her pale face. "You're pregnant."

"Yes."

"You just had your period the week before I left. I was only gone three weeks. Are you certain?"

"It wasn't my period, turns out. It was just some cramping. A little light bleeding. Some women have that early in pregnancy." She almost smiled as he flushed a dull red. "I'm a little over a month pregnant. It should stop within another month or two." She breezed nonchalantly through that sentence, hoping he wouldn't start to remember anything about that little-over-a-month ago time period. Hoping he would.

"Who's the father?" he asked calmly, although inside he was jumping with nerves. Had it been her? he wondered. Had it really happened, or was he going crazy? Had it been her? That night that he couldn't quite remember, and wasn't able to forget. And why didn't the thought scare him to death?

Looking at him out of those clear gray eyes, Lauren lied through her teeth. "Nobody you know."

"That's going to have to be remedied soon, don't you think? After all, we're best friends and you're carrying his baby."

"No. I'm carrying my baby," she corrected. "He doesn't want a family."

"Maybe he should have thought of that before he took you to bed without protecting you," Dale snapped, tossing the book to the coffee table. "I don't want a family either, which is why I damn well wear a rubber every time I sleep with a woman. And what if he has something?" Before she could speak, he turned around, looked at her and demanded, "Who is he? I'll go talk to him."

"No, you will not, Dale," she said, reaching out, catching his arm. There had been hope for a second that he remembered, and changed his mind about wanting a family. But the cold, flat look in his eyes totally destroyed that faint hope. "Dale, listen to me. It's my responsibility as much as it his. More. I knew how he felt about a family and I didn't care."

"Lauren, he's got a responsibility."

"No. If I couldn't provide for the baby, it would be different. But I can. Birth control is just as much the woman's responsibility." Granted, Lauren had never needed it before, and certainly hadn't planned on needing it the night in question.

"You can be both father and mother?" he asked sarcastically. "I'm talking about more than money here, sweetheart."

"And so am I," Lauren replied calmly. "I grew up in a house where I wasn't wanted. My dad didn't want me, and my mother really didn't either. You don't know what that's like, Dale. Your parents adored you. Mine tolerated me until I was ten years old and then my father up and left. A few weeks later, my mother left me in a hotel room and took off." Her voice trembled slightly and she paused taking a deep breath. With her eyes hot, her voice intense, she said, "I know what it's like not to be wanted. First hand, I know what it's like. Being passed around from one home to the next, sometimes just for the money you bring the family. And just as you find one family you like, who likes you, they take you away again. I know, Dale, how it feels to not be wanted. You can't hide that sort of thing, especially not from a child."

He opened to his mouth, once again, to argue. But he closed it on a sigh, recognizing the steely determination in her eyes. And he couldn't fight her logic, nor could he blame her. "He knows you're pregnant?"

With a guileless smile, she honestly answered, "Yes."

"And he won't live up to his responsibility?"

"If I asked, he most certainly would." Her hands came up and closed over her still flat belly and her voice shook with urgency. "But this isn't a responsibility. It's a child, my child, Dale. If he wanted me, wanted a family, it would be different. But he doesn't. And I won't subject myself, or my baby, to that, not in this lifetime."

Dale smiled slightly, his admiration for her, already high, climbing yet another notch. She was so damn regal, so proud. "This isn't an easy road you're walking, Lauren."

"Since when have I ever wanted easy?" she asked, smiling. "That's your road, not mine." Hell, Lauren thought, I probably wouldn't know easy if it bit me on the butt.

Cupping her face in his hands, he smiled down at her. "You'll be a great mom," he told her, placing a chaste kiss on her forehead. "Congratulations."

She gave a weak laugh and said, "Thank you."

And then she promptly passed out in his arms.

* * * * *

Dale decided, later, thinking back, that he had handled it quite well. After all, it's not every day your best friend passes out on you. If he hadn't gone to hug her, she'd have slid to the floor in a boneless heap. He had carried her to the couch, panicking, calling 911. Her eyes flew open and she yelped when a cold washcloth was swiped across her face. Dale was cussing and swearing a blue streak, hands shaking, his heart jumping around inside his chest. Worry and fear knotted in his stomach and he figured it would be sometime before they faded.

The worry and fear was shortly joined by embarrassment when Lauren stared at him as though he had grown two heads after he told her he had called an ambulance. But, bless her heart, she said nothing, simply picked up the phone, called dispatch and informed them the ambulance wasn't needed.

"How do you know you don't need to go to the hospital? You passed out!"

"I am pregnant, Dale," she said slowly. "Pregnant women do that sort of thing. I get dizzy. I get morning sickness. I spend more time in the bathroom than I ever did before. I spend more than half of the day sleeping."

"How do you know something isn't wrong?" he demanded, staring at her pale face and worrying. "Damn it, you shouldn't be here alone."

Lauren rolled her eyes and started to stand up only to have him grab her shoulders. "Stay off your feet, for crying out loud. You ought be to be resting."

"Dale, I'm pregnant, not sick, not dying. I feel fine," she insisted. She stared at him, bemused and wondering if he was this bad now, how would he have acted if she had told him he was the father?

Knowing him, he'd worry himself sick and drive her insane. He'd end up resenting her, because she wasn't the one he wanted. And suddenly, her eyes filled with tears. Staring at her, seeing those clear eyes suddenly full of distress, watching as her lower lip started to tremble, Dale decided it was time to panic again. "What's wrong? I'm sorry. Whatever I did, I'm sorry."

Disgusted with herself, she firmed her lower lip and blinked the tears away. "Nothing. I also start crying for no reason. I hate that," she whined. Hating hearing the petulance in her voice, but unable to do anything about it.

Compassion filled him and he wrapped his arms around her, tucking her head against his shoulder. "Honey, you have every reason to cry, if that's what you want to do." Those words, so gently spoken, broke through her decision to be strong and not cry. The tears welled up again and started leaking out. And she couldn't think of any reason why she shouldn't stay there, her face pressed against his shoulder, crying silently.

Lauren rose earlier the next morning than she had in the past few weeks. It was just a little before eight when she stood in the kitchen, drinking decaffeinated coffee. Didn't seem the same, kind of like drinking nonalcoholic beer, but she was hoping to fool her body.

She had hardly slept. She knew she was doing what was best for all of them, but that didn't make the guilt any easier to bear. She had lied to her best friend, the man she loved. She was depriving her child of its father. But she didn't see how she had any other choice.

Lauren couldn't live with Dale, let him be the father he would insist on being, knowing that he loved another woman, knowing that he resented that his child wasn't hers. She wouldn't lie under him in bed at night while he made love to her with his eyes closed so he could pretend she was Nikki.

Lauren had dealt with a lot in her life, had put up with a lot, made sacrifices. But that wasn't something she was willing to do. She downright refused.

If only he could love her.

If only, she scoffed silently. 'If only,' she thought wearily.

Movement outside caught her eye. She turned her head, cocking it as she watched Dale drop to his knees in her vegetable garden, weeding. A smile spread across her face as she realized what he was doing.

Dale was of the mindset that pregnant meant fragile. He had been adamant last night that she lift nothing heavier than a glass of water, do nothing more than rest on the couch. Scowling, she raised her false coffee to her mouth. She was tired of resting already. And she'd be damned if she'd give up her gardening.

She flinched when Dale nearly trampled a fledgling rhododendron bush. She tossed the rest of the coffee and stormed outside. Nope. She wasn't giving up her garden.

* * * * *

Lauren was barely three months pregnant. She was still so tired, but the morning sickness had passed. Once she was up and about, her energy built up and she was moving around almost normally. Standing naked in front of the mirror in the bathroom, she studied her body. So far, she couldn't tell. At least, not by looking. But her breasts were becoming more sensitive. She had already made the decision to nurse the baby, at least for a while.

Were they getting bigger already? she wondered, turning sideways to look. She couldn't tell. She generally paid her breast size as much attention as her shoe size. But her bras were getting tighter, or seemed to be. Of course, if they got much bigger, she'd need a damn crane to help lift them, she decided with a scowl. The full white globes were still firm, though.

All in all, Lauren thought smugly, she looked better than most women ever did.

A knock at the door interrupted her somewhat involved study of her chest. Flushing, she yanked the robe from the back of the door and headed out of the bathroom. She swiped a hand through her tangled damp hair as she peered through the window. Dale.

Biting back a sigh, she wondered what in the hell he wanted now.

Dale felt like an idiot. He didn't even know how to act around her any more. She seemed so damned fragile, sometimes. Tearing up for no reason, laughing and smiling at nothing at other times. She wasn't sick much any more, but she still slept so much. And talk about moody. She had been acting more or less like the Lauren he knew the other day, then for no reason that he could discern, she went into a sulk that lasted the rest of the afternoon.

She didn't have anybody here to watch out for her. No family, no boyfriend or husband, no close friends other than him and a girlfriend from high school, Jenny Something or Other. She was so alone.

Which explained why he was standing at her door at ten thirty in the morning, a stuffed bunny behind his back. Dale felt like a moron, but he had seen the little thing and hadn't been able to resist buying it.

He was so damn curious. He kept waiting for her to start showing, but from what he could tell, she wasn't showing at all. She was more than three months pregnant now, but Dale had absolutely no experience with pregnant women and had no idea what to expect. Of course, he still kept several books handy. Some women didn't start showing until half way through their pregnancy. Some gained very little weight at all.

Lauren wouldn't gain much, he figured. She was so damn graceful-

The door swung open and he turned his head, a smile on his face. That smile froze.

She was wearing a terry cloth robe that hung somewhere between knee and butt, leaving an awful lot of leg bare. Wet legs. Wet hair, pushed back from her face.

Tiny little beads of water clung to her neck, ran down into the vee of the robe between her breasts. Dale had never felt so thirsty in his life.

She was wet and naked under that robe.

Wet and naked…

Pregnant! His brain shouted. *Pregnant, remember that?*

Damn it. He really had to get over this damn fascination he was developing for her. Feeling even more like an idiot with each passing second, he thrust the little bunny at her. She stared at the bunny for just a second and then raised her eyes to his as she reached out and took it, a foolish little smile on her face as she held it clutched against her chest. A mighty fine looking chest, Dale decided, then felt like kicking himself in the butt.

Lauren stroked the soft brown fur as she moved out of the way, holding the door open. Dale moved in, passing close enough to her that he could smell the scent of the soap she used on her skin. The scent rushed straight to his already befuddled mind and made him want to grab her and bury his face against her neck.

What in the hell was wrong with him?

"Thank you," Lauren said, coming up close to him, kissing his cheek. Dale's eyes closed and he fisted his hands in his pockets to keep from grabbing her. His eyes slid down, catching sight of those big, beautiful tits as she kissed first one cheek, then the other before sliding back down to stand flat on her feet in front of him and smile at him.

As she moved away, he had a vague flash of something, the scent of her tickling some memory buried in his mind.

"I'm going to get dressed," she told him, still holding the silly little lop eared bunny against her chest.

Dale decided then and there that he envied the little rabbit. As he turned away, he raised his hands and rubbed his face. What in the hell was wrong with him? Why couldn't he stop thinking about her? She was his best damn friend and he wasn't supposed to think of her like that. So why did he keep seeing her face as he drifted off to sleep at night?

His gaze drifted up as Lauren came back into the room, locked on her face, unable to stop staring. She still held onto the little rabbit, still had that silly little smile on her face, wearing neatly cuffed khaki shorts and a sleeveless white button down top. Her hair had been pulled up into a simple twist. He wondered how she always managed to look so neat, so collected. Hell, his life was in turmoil and he wasn't the one pregnant.

She didn't look the way he would have thought a pregnant woman should look. She looked so...serene. At peace.

She shot him a smile as she gracefully sat down in the papasan chair, drawing her knees to her chest. "How is your story going?"

He shrugged, flopping down on the couch. "I haven't been working much lately."

She arched a black brow, her eyes concerned. "Something wrong?"

"Nope. I just don't feel like working on anything," he replied, studying the ceiling intently. "Lauren, how come you and I have never gone out?"

"We go out all the time, Dale. We went to the mall just last weekend."

Keeping his eyes fastened on the ceiling, he said, "That isn't what I meant. I mean like on a date."

If he had been looking at her, Dale would have had the rare pleasure of seeing Lauren totally shocked. Her eyes widened, her mouth fell open and she just stared at him. Finally, she managed to close her mouth. "Ex...excuse me?" she stammered out, sitting up straighter, her feet settling on the floor.

He swung his legs over, now looking her in the face. She looked perfectly normal to his eyes, that creamy complexion the same, those clear gray eyes the same.

That mouth...Nope. Better off not thinking about the mouth, he decided. "I meant like on a date. I buy you dinner, take you to a movie, a play, a concert. How come we've never done that?"

Calmly, she smoothed her hands over her legs, a faint, mocking smile on her mouth. His eyes dropped to those lean legs as she crossed them elegantly at the knee, then his gaze slowly rose until he was staring at that amused little smile as she said, "Dale, I'm not exactly your type. I'm only a few inches shorter than you, I don't have red hair, and I'm not about to let you pretend I'm a substitute for a woman you can't have."

He narrowed his eyes at her, started to open his mouth to say something pithy, only to snap it shut. How many of the women he had dated fit exactly that description? The vast majority. Granted, Lauren was tall for a woman, but he rarely dated anybody taller than five foot six. And so he was attracted to red heads. Lately, that midnight black hair of hers looked mighty tempting. He was tempted to tug it down from its knot and bury his face in it.

But he was mildly insulted at the last part of her statement. Whether it was because it was the truth or because it wasn't, he didn't know.

So he took a deep breath and said, somewhat cautiously, "Maybe I've decided it's time I changed my type."

"I don't want to be your guinea pig, Dale. If you're ready to start looking for a real relationship, fine. I'm happy for you. But you're not going to use me as a test drive," she stated, flatly, her eyes expressionless.

Now he was more than mildly insulted. "Is that what you think of me? That I'd use my best friend just to find out if I'm ready to get back in the swing of things?"

"Isn't that what you're doing?"

"No," he snapped, shooting to his feet. "I was trying to work up enough nerve to ask you on a date, but now that I realize what your opinion of me is, I think I'll just forget that idea. I'm going home." He barely made it three feet before she was standing next to him, her hand reaching out to him.

"Dale, I didn't mean to hurt your feelings. Or imply anything." She sighed and closed her eyes briefly before continuing. "Dale, you've lived next door to me for five years now. Why in the world are you asking me out now?"

"I wasn't aware I was required to explain myself," Dale said coldly, looking over her shoulder to the door.

"Under the circumstances, Dale, I think maybe I'm entitled to a little explaining. I'm three months pregnant. This isn't exactly the time for me to start dating," Lauren said drolly, continuing to block his way. "Is that what this is about? Is it because I'm safe? Because you don't have to worry about me getting serious?"

"It's because I've been wondering, Lauren. But, don't worry. I'll keep the wondering to myself." He started to push past her.

"Don't you think it's a little late to be wondering?" she asked quietly as he reached for the door. "Why didn't you wonder before now? Why not a few months ago? A few years ago? Why now?"

"Beats the hell out of me," he muttered, dragging his hand through his already rumpled golden hair.

Why couldn't he have asked her before she met this guy and fell in love with him? Why couldn't he have been the one to...Damn it, what in the hell was he thinking? Was he actually jealous of the father?

He looked over at her, met those beautiful dove gray eyes, and knew the answer. Yes. Without a doubt, he was jealous. He studied her intently, watched as a minute shudder raced through her long body. She turned away from him, staring at the wall. "Why, Dale?"

"I don't know. But, lately, you're all I think about."

"Isn't that kind of awkward?"

"Why would it be?" he asked wearily. He laid one hand on her shoulder, gently tugging her around. "You already said this guy's not interested in you or the baby." He forced a grin and pointed out, "That right there proves he's a dumb ass."

Lauren didn't smile and Dale studied her. She was hiding something. Not telling him something. "He does know, doesn't he?" he asked, suspicious.

"I already told you, he knows I'm pregnant. He was the first person I told," Lauren said, sighing, running a hand over her French twist. "Dale, you're still not making any sense. I'm pregnant. If I were to start dating, it would only be because I expected something to come from it."

"I wouldn't have asked if I didn't expect something to come from it," Dale said evenly, meeting her sober gray eyes with his.

"What..." Lauren huffed out a breath, closed her eyes. Inside, her heart was starting to jump around. "What do you mean?"

"I mean, that I'm an idiot for not noticing sooner. You're my best friend. You know me better than anybody. We care about each other." He reached out a hand to stroke her cheek. Her skin was every bit as smooth, as silky as it seemed. "And you're so damn beautiful."

Her pale skin flushed a soft pink. He was doing a damn good job of controlling himself until her tongue darted out to wet her lips. He groaned as his control slipped out the window. "Come on, Lauren. Give it a chance," he whispered, hooking a hand over the back of her neck and drawing her closer. He brushed his lips over hers, dying for just a small taste of her.

She gasped, then a tiny little whimper rose and died in her throat as she tilted her head back. "Dale." But as he lowered his head to kiss her again, her eyes flew open and she shook her head slightly, as if to clear it. She backed up a step, her eyes dark as storm clouds. "What exactly did you mean? What in the world are you thinking may come of this?" Even as she asked, she was ready to kick herself. He was asking her out, for crying out loud. A chance. And she was questioning it.

"Why do women always want things explained?" Dale muttered to himself, shoving his hands in his pockets. The small taste of her rested on his tongue, making him ravenous for the whole feast. "I don't know what could come of this. But I do know I want to find out. There's only one woman out there who's ever mattered to me, Lauren. Until you. For the longest time, you mattered as a friend. But, lately…Lately, I've been starting to think you matter as more."

"Does this mean you're not in love with Nikki anymore?"

Dale froze in the act of shoving his hair out of his eyes. Slowly, his hand lowered and he stared into space as he asked himself the same question. "I don't know how I feel about her any more. I do know that you've been on my mind more in the past few months than she has. Does that count for anything?"

"I don't want to be second best, Dale. Not to anybody."

A slight grin lifted the corner of his mouth. "Lauren Spencer wouldn't know how to settle for anything less than first," he said softly. "I want you to go to a movie with me this weekend, Lauren. I want to see if this could lead to something." He turned back to her as he spoke, meeting her eyes with his.

"Dale…" Lauren's voice trailed off as he moved closer to her, using his index finger under her chin to lift her face to his.

She stared into his eyes, her heart breaking at the depth of the sincerity she saw there. If this led nowhere, it would break her heart. She started to say no, but a tiny little voice in her mind asked, *and what if it does lead somewhere?*

No. She repeated it firmly to herself. She was a practical woman, not a dreamer.

"Yes." The word left her mouth before she even finished reminding herself of how sensible she was. She opened her mouth to change her mind, but a brilliant smile came and went on his face, momentarily leaving her senseless. By the time she remembered what she was saying no to, he had already left.

* * * * *

"Pregnant women do not go out on dates," she muttered to herself three days later as she slipped into a loosely fitting pair of linen pants. They were one of the few pairs in her closet that weren't getting uncomfortable to wear.

She topped the pale gray trousers with a short sleeveless fitted camisole style top. She wouldn't be able to wear it much longer either, she mused, eyeing her reflection. The pale ivory shirt fit fine through her breasts and waist for now, but not for much longer. She was starting to gain weight. The first two months, she had lost nearly six pounds, but she had gained back three just in the past five weeks. Her OB wasn't concerned about it. The female vanity in Lauren had her cringing at the thought of gaining any weight at all, something she had never had to worry about.

Slipping her feet into a pair of soft gray sandals, she scolded herself a little more. And she wondered over it. Maybe Dale had just been suffering a little mental breakdown the other day. He hadn't ever shown any interest in her before.

Standing in front of the mirror, she absently reached for the long amethyst wand that Dale had given her, only to drop her hand before she could pick it up. She hadn't worn it in three months. The last time she had worn it, it had been the only thing she had been wearing. Instead, she sifted through the tangle of chains, selecting a pearl necklace she'd bought on a whim after selling her first painting. Without thinking about her reluctance to wear the amethyst, she fastened the pearls around her neck, turned out the lights and left the bedroom.

* * * * *

Dale was nervous. He couldn't ever remember being this nervous, not even the few times he had taken Nikki out that summer years before. He had loved Nikki so much it hurt, but he was nervous as a teenager about Lauren, his best friend. It was because of how fragile she seemed lately. He insisted it was that and only that. But that didn't make him feel any better about it. He knocked quickly, tucking his hands into the back pockets of his Dockers. Rocking back on the balls of his feet, he stared into the distance as he waited for her to answer.

What if this didn't work out? What if he messed up their friendship? Damn it, she meant too much to him for anything to mess this up. What in the hell was he doing? A guy didn't date his best friend, for crying out loud. Even if his best friend was female. A fine looking female.

The door swung open and he amended that to a damn fine looking female. Only Lauren could make something as simple as an ivory shirt and a pair of gray pants look so elegant, and so sexy, at the same time. Her long hair was pulled back, woven into an intricate braid. A simple strand of pearls adorned her long white neck.

Automatically, Dale's eyes coasted the length of her figure, looking for obvious signs of pregnancy. The only one was the delicate glow to her face.

"They're right, you know," he said conversationally. "Pregnant women do glow."

Her eyes rolled and dryly, she said, "It's not a glow, Dale. It's oil. Pregnant women look like they glow because their skin gets so damn oily."

"Lauren, you really need to do something about that romantic soul of yours. It gets so damn soppy, you know?"

"You try having the complexion of a teenager all over again and see how you like it," she muttered, grabbing her purse from the table by the door before digging her keys out. Dale took the keys from her before she could lock the door, locking it himself before lifting her face to his.

Smooth ivory skin, a lush rose mouth, a glow to her face that hadn't always been there. He announced, "Your complexion looks fine to me," taking her arm as they walked to the car.

She remained silent, her eyes sober and serious, making Dale wonder what she was thinking, then she turned her face away from him. "You asked me if I was still in love with Nikki. I told you I didn't know." He waited until she turned her eyes to him before he asked, "Do you still love the baby's father? Is this a waste of my time?"

The question had been plaguing him ever since she had agreed to go out with him.

Calmly, so very calmly, Lauren smiled. "I never said that I loved him."

He eyed her suspiciously.

She returned his look levelly. "Dale, you didn't love every woman you slept with, now did you?" she asked, an amused smile playing at her lips. "You should know better than anybody, love isn't a requirement for sex."

He opened his mouth only to snap it shut as she continued to stand there watching him with that sly little female smile, her eyes all but dancing with amusement. Irritated, but unsure why, he jerked the car door open for her without speaking.

It never occurred to him that she hadn't answered his question.

* * * * *

Lauren's stomach was dancing wildly and it had nothing to do with morning, or evening, sickness. She sat across a dimly lit table from Dale, her hand resting in his as he played with her fingers. Her short, neatly trimmed nails, painted a soft, pale pink, her long slender artists' hand, the narrow palm, all received equal attention as he studied and stroked her hand as they waited for their dinner.

She was on her third glass of ice water, no lemon, when Dale raised his eyes to hers as she lowered the half empty glass. Her throat was drier than the Sahara, thanks to the dubious pleasure of her hand in his. Those wicked blue eyes were now studying her face, so full of concern, so gentle, it made her chest ache.

"How are you feeling? Not sick any more?"

"What?" she asked, still looking at her hand in his. She jerked her eyes up and replied, "Ah, no. I haven't been sick for a few weeks now. Almost a month."

"When do you go to the doctor again?"

"Monday," she answered, casually drawing both hands into her lap, fisting them there. Her heart was racing madly, just from holding hands. "I'm still only going once a month right now."

"Everything's fine, right? Your doctor doesn't think you'll have any trouble?"

"No. I'm young and healthy. I've always taken care of myself. There is no reason for there to be any trouble."

He dropped his eyes, idly rubbing his index finger across the smooth linen tablecloth. "I've been wondering. About the classes you're supposed to go to. You're going to need a coach."

Her eyes flew up to his, only to find him studying the tablecloth with intensity. "I'll find somebody."

"Why settle for somebody? I live right next door. I can be there in no time flat if you need me. I don't have to worry about leaving work or anything like that. My time is my own."

Swallowing the knot in her throat, Lauren asked, "Why would you want to?"

"Because it's your baby. You're going to need somebody with you, at least for a while. I want to be the one."

"Do you have any idea what it is you're asking?" Lauren asked. "Childbirth is messy. It's painful. I'm not going to be in a good mood."

"I've seen you upset before," Dale said mildly. He leaned closer, watching her. "Lauren, you matter to me. I care about you, and your baby. I want to help. I've been thinking about this for a while now and I know I want to do this."

Staring into those slumberous eyes, Lauren felt her heart begin to swell, felt herself begin to hope. Something was changing here, she realized. Something very important. "If you're certain, Dale," she said, keeping her voice level through sheer will alone.

* * * * *

Lauren didn't realize when he had offered to be her coach that he wanted more than just that. Until she was sitting in the car next to him, directing him to her OB's office, she didn't realize how much he wanted to be a part of her entire pregnancy. She was signing herself in at the window when she caught his eyes on a couple across the room. The obviously happy father-to-be had his hand resting on the swollen belly of the woman. Both looked blissfully happy.

And the look in Dale's eyes was wistful and envious.

He wanted a family. No matter what he said, or what he thought he wanted, he wanted a family of his own.

Lauren's hand crept up to rest on her still flat belly as he led her to a seat. She was going to have to tell him.

She took a deep bracing breath, telling herself she had to do it, while she had the nerve. He was idly tracing a design over the back of her hand with a roughened index finger, sending goose bumps dancing across her skin.

Oh, he was going to be so angry. *What if I lose him?* she wondered. Could she handle it if he turned away from her? Oh, he'd never abandon the baby, but what if it killed whatever feelings he had for her?

Now, Lauren, she told herself. Whatever it cost her, it was the right thing to do.

But when he turned those sexy eyes her way, smiled so gently at her, she decided to wait. Who knew what could happen in the next few months?

The nurse called her back and Lauren rose, started to walk to the door, and paused. Looking back over her shoulder, she held her hand out and said, "Why don't you come back with me?"

Dale tried to act casual about it but his eyes lit up and his hand folded over hers so tightly, Lauren wondered if he was going to turn loose. As the nurse directed her to stand on the scale, she shot a warning glare at him. "Say absolutely nothing," she told him. "Forget this part."

The nurse chuckled and jotted down her weight. "One fifty six," she announced cheerfully. "You've gained back what you lost. Not getting sick any more?"

"No," Lauren answered, stepping off the scale. As they followed the nurse back to the exam room, she slid Dale a look out of the corner of her eye. He was staring straight ahead, mouth set in somber lines. But the twinkle in his eyes gave his amusement away.

After having her blood pressure checked and peeing in the little cup, Lauren was instructed to sit on the table. "Dr. Flynn will try to hear the heart beat today," the nurse said on her way out the door.

"They can do that?" Dale asked, awed.

"Yes. I think it's something like an ultrasound." She plucked at a loose thread on her lightweight sweater. "Dale, she's probably going to think you're the father." She kept her eyes on her legs as she spoke, so he wouldn't see the truth in her eyes.

He shrugged, his movement casual, a complete opposite of how he felt inside. *The father*, he thought to himself. He should be running scared right now. So why did he want to go over to her, fall to his knees and wrap his arms around her, bury his face against her still flat belly? "I don't mind," was all he said out loud, while inside his mind shouted *I want to be the father.*

Did he really?

Was he that serious about this?

Lauren raised her head, her cheeks pink. "I mean, I'll tell her you're going to be my coach, but she-"

He got up then, walked over to her, laid his finger across her lips. Her soft gray eyes stared into his as he laid one hand on her belly. "I don't mind," he repeated softly, and he stroked her belly through her clothes. Lowering his head, he covered her mouth with his.

Why did she taste so familiar? he wondered. As a moan rose up in her throat and shimmered out into him, he wondered how he knew she would do that. She fit against him as though she had been made just for him. Was it because this was what he had been looking for, that she was the one meant for him? A gentle knock sounded at the door as he pulled away from her. Right as the door opened, he repeated in her ear, "I don't mind."

That was as close as he could come to saying what he really wanted.

As Lauren had expected, Dr. Flynn treated Dale as though he were the father. When she tried to correct the doctor, Dale squeezed her hand before neatly cutting her off with a series of questions.

And the look on his face as the OB moved a little instrument over her belly, and together, they listened to the rapid heartbeat for the first time was worth the guilt she was silently bearing.

A fast paced steady thumping filled the room and Dale's hand tightened convulsively on Lauren's. He swallowed, his mouth suddenly dry. "Sweet God," he whispered, closing his eyes against the flood of emotion that filled him. "Sweet Jesus, isn't that amazing?" he asked, his voice reverent.

He opened his dreamy blue eyes, met Lauren's, bright with tears. He raised their linked hands and pressed his lips to the back of hers, closing his eyes once more, listening to that steady little heart.

If she had known how he was going to be, she would have told him. She had been so afraid he would be there with her, but only out of a sense of responsibility. Now he was there because he wanted to be.

With tears leaking out of her eyes, she lay on the table, her hand in his, while Dr. Flynn probed this way and that. "Now this noise," she said, pausing to let them hear a whooshing sound, "is the uterine blood flow. You've been taking good care of yourself, Lauren. Eating what you should and exercising. You are as healthy as you can be and it sounds like you have a healthy little baby in the there." She once again found the heartbeat for them, knowing that was what they wanted to hear. She allowed them to listen in silence for another moment before stepping back, a beaming smile on her face as she handed Lauren a tissue to clean the gel from her belly.

Lauren lay there, unable to think, as the sound of that racing heart echoed in her mind. Dr. Flynn watched as Dale took the tissue and wiped Lauren's skin clean. On her way out the door, she wondered how her patient could have thought that the father didn't want a baby. It was written all over his face that there was nothing he wanted more.

Dale was thoroughly shaken as he escorted Lauren from the doctor's office. He had never, never, in his life wanted anything the way he wanted the baby Lauren was carrying. When he heard the heartbeat, he thought his own heart was going to explode. It was pure instinct, but everything in him shouted, *Mine!*

As he opened the car door for Lauren, a different type of instinct was shouting the same thing. He crouched down beside her and spoke her name. She turned her head to look at him, her shiny black hair swinging with the movement before settling around her shoulders. He reached up with one hand, threading it through that dense thick hair, pulling her face to his.

Dale kissed her gently, sucking at her lower lip before seeking entrance to her mouth. The taste of her, something innocent and sweet, touched lightly with the dark heady taste of sex. It was the same as her scent, a complete contradiction in every way. He craved more of it.

He wanted her.

And he was realizing that it wasn't just some temporary need. He wanted her always. He wanted the baby that was growing inside her. He wanted to see her face in the morning when he woke up and wanted to lay down next to her at night. He wanted to make love to her, with her. He wanted to have a family with her and grow old with her.

Gradually, he ended the kiss, pulling back to study her face. She looked at him out of confused eyes, her mouth wet, her cheeks flushed. He decided it was best that the baby's father wasn't interested. Dale Stoner had every intention of taking his place, in both Lauren's life, and in her baby's.

Chapter Four

Lauren's hands shook slightly as she prepared decaffeinated coffee early the next morning. She hoped he couldn't tell. "How long are you going to be gone?" she asked, hoping her voice sounded nonchalant.

"Just a few days. I haven't seen my family in a while. I was planning to go home at Christmas, but I've changed my mind," he replied, his back to her. Hopefully she wouldn't notice the bags under his eyes.

Dale Stoner was going back home to Somerset. To face the woman he had been dreaming of for the better part of a decade. He had thought, right up until the past few weeks, that he had fallen in love with Nikki the moment he had first seen her. But how could he love her and feel the way he felt about Lauren?

He hated leaving, especially right now, but there was no other time to do it. If he waited much longer, Lauren would be too far along. She was already past her third month. And he wanted to be here for the fourth month; that was when they'd do another ultrasound. His hands started sweating at the thought of that, of putting a picture to the rapid heartbeat he had heard only the day before.

Lauren pretended not to notice his preoccupation. Pretended not to notice the way his eyes lit up as he spoke of going back home. He did it every so often, as though just the sight of Nikki soothed his broken heart. She wouldn't have believed him if he had told her he hadn't seen her in years.

Of course, he hadn't. He had started avoiding Nikki after seeing her pregnant some years earlier. It had broken his heart, at the time, but now he wondered if it had hurt as much as it should have. He turned his eyes to Lauren, watching her move slowly, gracefully around the kitchen. Her long body was encased in a men's oxford, knotted at her still flat waist and a pair of cuffed blue jean shorts. The thick, sturdy hiking boots on her feet would have looked clumsy on some women. On her, they just looked right.

The thought of that baby made his heart swell. The attempt to bring up a picture in his mind of the baby's father made his hands clench into fists. He was far better off in pretending that Lauren had gotten pregnant all by herself. Or better yet, that he had put that baby inside her.

The thought of another man touching her made him see red.

And that was why he was going to Somerset. He had to look Nikki in the face, find out once and for all if it was love he felt. And once he knew if his heart was his own, and he was pretty sure it was, he planned on giving it to Lauren.

If she would have him.

On the drive down, he pondered that worrisome thought. If she would have him. She told him that she didn't love the baby's father, but Dale was wondering about that. Lauren so rarely dated, he certainly couldn't see her just up and making it with somebody she didn't care about. She would have cared. A lot. What if she was too in love with the baby's father to care about him?

He stopped in Danville to fill up the gas tank and refuel on caffeine. He had been running on pure adrenaline the past hour or so and it was wearing thin. He hadn't been home in almost a year. He hadn't seen Nikki since that summer three years earlier, when she had been outside the movie theater, her belly swollen with Wade Lightfoot's child.

Abigail Lightfoot, Nikki's stepdaughter, always wrote him and thanked him for the books he had sent. He always sent the first copy to them, Abby and Nikki. Nikki was the one who had encouraged him to try to get his stories published. So, always, the first copy to them. The last letter, the one he had been reading that night he got shit-faced, had been another thank you letter, and Abby mentioned how she was going to have a new baby brother or sister.

In addition to Abby's sweet little thank-you's, he also had the parental grapevine, and knew that Nikki still lived in her castle on the hill, sharing it with her quiet solemn husband. Dale scowled automatically at the thought of Wade, but it faded long before it usually did. The jealous urge to pummel his fists into Wade's face didn't even appear.

It was nearing dusk when he pulled up in front of the house made of wooden beams and sheets of glass. It hadn't changed much. A few small flowerbeds full of pitiful looking buds and blooms. He thought of Lauren, kneeling in her flowers, plants blooming all around her. A child's bike lay on its side by the steps, next to an expensive mountain bike. He climbed the few steps to the porch, his boot heels ringing hollowly on the wood.

He raised his hand and knocked on the beveled glass door, his heart thudding slowly in his chest. The door swung open to reveal a pintsized mirror of Nikki, only with dark curling hair and dark eyes. A small dimple winked from under the corner of her mouth, which was streaked liberally with chocolate. "Who are you?" she demanded, her rosebud mouth pursed in a scowl.

Before he could answer, Nikki was behind her, her face lighting with pleasure. "Dale!" she whispered, throwing open the screen door and hurling herself at him, wrapping her arms around his neck. Dale's eyebrows rose. She hadn't been this demonstrative before. At one time, he would have started to hope.

And as she pulled back to smile up into his eyes, Dale had the answer to his question. His feelings for Nikki had changed.

"Hey, Nik. How are you?"

"Who's at the d- You. What in the hell are you doing here?"

Dale raised his eyes and met the threatening gaze of Wade Lightfoot. Though shorter than Dale by a good six inches, he exuded menace. His proprietary gaze settled on the hand Dale had wrapped around Nikki's waist to return her embrace. "Nice to see you, too, Lightfoot. Yes, it has been a long time."

Wade was remembering a night when he had seen the two of them in a lip-lock just a few feet outside this very door. With a dark scowl, he replied, "Not long enough."

"Wade, watch it," Nikki warned, grabbing Dale's hands and squeezing. "It's so good to see you. I've been meaning to write you, to thank you for the books you sent."

Dale smiled at her. "It was your doing, Nikki. You're the reason I sent them off to begin with. Thank you for that."

"All I did was tell you to give it a shot. You did all the hard work. Come in, Dale," she invited, holding out her small hand. Dale accepted it, throwing Wade a smirk.

"Don't mind if I do."

"She's pregnant?"

Dale nodded, taking a swig of beer before meeting Nikki's puzzled eyes. "She won't tell me who the father is. But it doesn't matter. He had his chance."

"What's she like?"

"Beautiful," Dale whispered, his voice almost reverent. "Serene. Soothing. She's got this way about her; whenever I'm near her, I feel so settled." A wicked grin lit his face and he tipped back his beer. "And she's sexy as all get out."

Nikki smiled, relieved, at that. "She was sounding like Mother Teresa for a minute there."

Dale laughed. "I never said she was a saint. She's stubborn, got a mean streak from time to time. Damn it, the truth is, at times, she's a downright ice queen. And I can never tell what she's thinking. But she's . . . she's . . ." He fumbled for words only to have Nikki find them for him.

"She's perfect for you," she said quietly. "In a way I never could have been."

He met her eyes levelly and agreed. "Exactly."

Nikki smiled a little. "I can't say that doesn't hurt my pride a bit for you to agree so easily." She sipped at her glass of milk and grimaced. "He nags me to drink three glasses a day." Then she set the glass down and curled her legs up next to her. "So how do you feel about her?"

"I don't know just yet. That's why I had to come here to see you. I had to get that straightened out so I could figure this out."

Nikki shook her head. "I don't think you've got to worry about that." She smiled, studying him with knowing eyes. "You're in love with her. I'm happy for you, and her."

He grimaced and said, "Don't be happy yet. I have no clue how she feels about me."

"Unless she's an idiot, she's going to love you just as much as you love her."

He cocked an eyebrow at her and asked, "Did you love me?"

Softly, she said, "No." Her eyes dropped to her lap and she studied her wedding band. "But you never looked the way you look right now, not with me. Not about me." She took a deep breath and said, "I wanted to love you, Dale." Her voice was quiet, soft, mindful of her husband who no doubt lurked outside the door. "I really did. If I could have chosen, I would have chosen you. But it doesn't work that way. And that's a good thing. I wouldn't have made you happy."

"Lauren makes me happy."

"Good for you."

* * * * *

Lauren wasn't happy.

She was huddled on the couch, miserable. An untouched box of bonbons sat next to her, along with a nearly empty milkshake from McDonald's. How stupid she was. She had started to think that maybe Dale did care about her. He'd sat with her in the doctor's office, listening to that strong little heart, holding her hand. His eyes had been almost as wet as hers.

And then, before she could so much as blink, he was on the road to Somerset.

To her.

"Idiot," she mumbled, dashing away a tear with the back of her hand.

Her hair was pulled up into a messy ponytail and her shirt hadn't been ironed. As another tear rolled down her cheek, her head fell back and she stared up at the ceiling. "Moron," she muttered. A leopard can't very well change his spots, now can he? How could she expect Dale to stop loving a woman he had been in love with for years? She couldn't expect it. He would no more fall out of love with Nikki than . . .than she would fall out of love with Dale.

Why should he love her anyway? Nobody else ever had. What was it about her that kept people from loving her? Was she missing something?

"Fool." She dashed away another tear. Everything inside her felt broken. Dale had been gone only two days, yet it felt like an eternity. No doubt, he would come back all morose and depressed, the way he had the time he had seen Nikki eight months pregnant. I hope she was the size of a horse, Lauren thought spitefully. I hope she got so fat, nobody recognized her.

Smoothing a hand down her still flat stomach, she smugly thought, I bet she wasn't able to still get into her normal clothes at four months.

And I hope she's blindly in love with her husband. I hope she doesn't even remember Dale.

But who could forget him?

Lauren had certainly tried, and failed more times than she could count. Morosely, she picked up the shake and emptied it with one last slurp. "You ought to be ashamed of yourself," she muttered. "Sitting here feeling sorry for yourself. Why can't you just accept it? You're not his type." Resentfully, she thought of the delicate little women he squired around town. Skinny, petite little things, all of them.

And that brought another scowl to her face. Why in the hell was she doing this? How did a calm, sensible woman let herself get so damned depressed? "Quit swearing," she muttered out loud. "Don't even swear while you're thinking."

It's the baby, she told herself. Your hormones are all out of whack. That's why you're feeling this way. Taking a deep breath, she counted to ten and closed her eyes, summoning up all the composure she had in her. And with a monstrous effort, she forced herself off the couch. Stowing the bonbons for a later time, she tossed the empty milkshake container out.

"We're going shopping," she said to the baby, patting it absently. "I'm going to buy you a big stuffed animal. And I'm buying me whatever catches my eye."

Several things caught her eye. An oversized silk camp shirt in sapphire blue, which she could wear throughout her pregnancy and after. A pair of tennis shoes. A diamond tennis bracelet. Then she treated herself to a box of Godiva's and a new book. A small stuffed bear sat on a chair, a small board book in his paws, watching her with kind, friendly eyes.

Eyeing her purchases the next morning, she decided it was a good thing she had a lot of money in the bank. And it was good that she rarely got depressed enough that she used a shopping trip to cheer up. Otherwise, that nicely filled out bank account would become anorexic.

She stroked a hand down the nubby stuffed animal. Winnie the Pooh. When she had been little, she guessed about five, she remembered seeing a Winnie the Pooh stuffed animal, and asking for Santa to bring it to her. What she had gotten had been a backhand across the face for interrupting her mother's television shows for such a dumb ass question. She raised one hand to her cheek in memory. She had never asked for another thing.

In recent memory, she hadn't asked for anything.

She had wanted, she had hoped, but she had never expected to receive anything. And she had learned long ago, to pretend not to want something. That way, it hurt less when you didn't get it.

"You can ask for whatever you want," she whispered softly. "You won't get everything you ask for, but you don't ever have to be afraid of asking."

She closed her eyes against the memory of a loud, screeching voice, the crash of a glass hitting the wall, the stench of alcohol. With a grim effort, she tore herself away from the past. She was past that, beyond it, and her child would never know it.

She decided to decorate the nursery in a Winnie the Pooh theme. The stuffed animal would sit in a rocker until the baby was old enough to play with it. Lauren bought a second, larger storybook of the cartoon character to look at. She'd paint a mural on one wall and put up a border, or maybe paint the border herself. The walls were already painted a soft ivory with hints of beige. That would go perfectly with what she had in mind.

Cuddling the bear to her chest, she settled herself onto the couch, smiling absently. A mobile over the crib. One of those nice cribs, with drawers built under it. Oak. Natural color, not painted. A dresser and an armoire with bookshelves. Lots of books. Dale had already helped her move things out of a spare bedroom that was never used. It was just down the hall from her room, with a huge window that faced west. They could watch the sun set at night.

She settled Pooh in the corner of the couch and got up. She hunted out some pencils and took the storybook.

No time like the present to get started.

Winnie ended up on the southern wall, roughly sketched in pencil. His pot of 'hunny' was on its side, while the chubby bear licked one sticky paw. She'd add in background, just a little, and maybe Tigger and the little pig—what was his name? She was stretching her hands high over her head when she heard the door being unlocked. Freezing, she looked out the window, uselessly. She couldn't see the driveway or the house next door from this room.

"Lauren?"

She lowered her hands slowly. A quick trip. He had only been gone two days. Nastily, she wished he had stayed gone a little longer. She wasn't in the mood to try to cheer him out of the depression that always followed a trip home. "I'm upstairs," she called out, blowing out a deep breath and counting to ten to steady herself. If he were too morose, she would just tell him to leave. After all, she was pregnant, wasn't she? If she didn't want to deal with mooning, she didn't have to.

But when she turned her head and met his eyes, she saw that he wasn't upset. Wasn't morose or sad. She could read those eyes as well, if not better, than she could read her own. She knew every detail of his face, down to the smallest line, how to judge the looks on his face, how to judge his emotions.

He looked . . . happy. His impossibly blue eyes were smiling and a pleased grin curved his mouth. Cold chills ran up and down her spine. Had Nicole remembered him after all?

"How did your trip go?" she asked levelly as he walked over and studied the faint drawing on the wall.

"Great," he answered, absently, stroking one finger along Pooh's cheek. "Where's Piglet?"

Piglet. "I haven't decided whether or not to use Piglet. I just decided on Pooh today," she answered. "You weren't gone very long this time."

Rising, he turned to meet her eyes, tucking his hands into his pockets. "No reason to be gone long. I took care of what I needed to. No reason left to stay."

"Oh?" she asked, arching one eyebrow, pleased that her voice was even. "Didn't mooning over Nikki take long this time?" Just the lightest touch of sarcasm in her voice, just to let him know what she thought of it.

"No mooning, Lauren. I saw her yesterday for the first time in three years," he said, rolling his eyes at her disbelieving look. "I went out of my way not to see her ever since I saw her that summer, pregnant. But that's beside the point."

"And what is the point?" she asked, turning away to gather up her supplies. The job was simply busywork, to avoid looking into his eyes. Three years? she thought.

His hands came up to rest on her shoulders. Gently, he turned her to face him. "I don't love her, Lauren. We only dated off and on a few times, right after Wade moved to Somerset. And it was Nikki's idea, to try to get him to leave her alone. The few times I tried to get her to go out with me, when she first moved to town, she very politely brushed me off. I don't love her now. Maybe I did at first, a little, but not the way I thought I did. I care about her, yes. But I don't love her. And I don't think I ever did."

Her lashes dropped to shield her eyes and she sidestepped out from under his hands. "Took an awful long time to figure that one out, did you?" she asked, quivering inside and unwilling to let him see.

"You knew." It was a puzzled statement. She knew he was thinking, *how could you know how I felt when I didn't know?*

There was no way to tell him that she knew him the way no other could, knew him inside and out. She knew that what he wanted wasn't always what he needed, and what he needed wasn't necessarily something he wanted.

After all, he didn't want her, she thought sadly. And she was the best thing to ever happen to him.

With a sigh, she said, "I knew she wasn't the type of woman you needed. Maybe the type you wanted, but not what you need. You wanted to rescue her, like some cursed princess from a fairy tale. You were blind to the fact that you were all wrong for her, and she was wrong for you."

"You don't even know her," Dale said, slightly irritated. How did she know him so well?

"I know you," she said softly. "That's all it took. She sounds too much like you, too volatile, too hot tempered.

Do you have any idea how terrible you two would be as a couple? You'd kill each other in a matter of days."

"We got along pretty damn good for a while," he said, edgily.

Smiling, Lauren turned to face him. "That's because you were friends. Just friends, no matter how much you wanted it to be otherwise." She started past him, certain she had done the best she could at hiding the emotions running rampant within her. "I'm happy for you, Dale. You're free now." She patted his shoulder absently as she moved past him.

"No," he said, reaching out and snagging her arm. "No, I'm not."

She went still, turning her head, meeting his eyes. The look in those eyes made her knees weak, but Lauren locked them and remained upright, kept her eyes clear and focused on his. She knew what kind of crazy things hoping could do to her head. "Realize that you love your little actress, Dale?" she asked calmly, while his hand braceleted her wrist. "She steal your heart along with the show?"

He smiled, shook his head. "No." Her pulse was rabbiting under his fingers and the thought of what might be causing that made his smile grow wider. She looked completely indifferent, one brow arched arrogantly, a half amused smile on her face. But her hand was shaking, he could feel it, and her heart was pounding.

"If you know me so well, Lauren, why don't you tell me what I need? Why don't you tell me why I'm not free?"

Through the lowered fringe of her lashes, she watched him. "Knowing you well doesn't make me a mind reader,

Dale," she said calmly, tugging against his hold. "I don't know what goes on in that thick head of yours."

"Don't you?"

Hot little flip-flops were turning in her belly, and her chest felt unbelievably tight. Keeping her voice level became an act of sheer will. "No, Dale. I don't." She tugged again, trying to free her wrist.

"Why don't I give you a clue?" he murmured as he drew her closer, up against his chest. She was simply staring at him, those wide gray eyes locked on his face. Her hands came up to press against his chest, her fingers curling into the soft material of his T-shirt. With one arm wrapped around her waist, his free hand buried in her hair, he lowered his mouth to hers, his eyes on hers as he brushed her lips with his.

She gasped, eyes fluttering closed as he nipped at her lip. He angled his head and covered her mouth with his just as her hands crept up to lock behind his head, tugging him closer. *Oh. Oh, my,* Lauren thought, right before her mental capacity went out the window.

His tongue slyly darted across her tongue, danced within her mouth before withdrawing once again so he could nibble at her lower lip, her chin, her jaw. His hands, oh, his clever artistic hands cupped her breasts, gently, thumbs brushing over her sensitive nipples. Against her belly, she could feel the hot length of him. A slow, molten heat grew in her belly and spread throughout her body. She wanted that inside, that long, hard magical cock of his buried inside her. Whimpering deep in her throat, she searched for his mouth again.

So familiar, Dale wondered, dipping into her mouth again and again. *How do I know how she tastes? How do I know that she whimpers like that when she's excited?* That whimper sounded again as his hands slipped under her loose shirt to find her flesh. Those lush breasts strained against her bra as he massaged the heated flesh with greedy hands.

He jerked her shirt up, dipped his head and caught the tip of her nipple in his teeth, tugging at it delicately before swirling his tongue around the crest. One hand streaked down her middle, and he knew the firm bulge hadn't been there long. It was subtle, so subtle he shouldn't have been able to even notice. He straightened, one hand resting protectively on her belly as he took her mouth again.

A hot thrill speared from her mouth down to her belly. Her hips arched up, seeking. Desperately, her hands unlocked from behind his neck as he lowered his head to nip at her shoulder. Her hands locked on his butt, tugging him closer, needing to feel his heat against her.

His eyes nearly crossed with pleasure as he tore his mouth from her. Her strong agile hands had already tugged his shirt free and one was currently trying to undo the buttons of his fly. "Lauren," he said, his voice catching as her fingers brushed against him. *How had one kiss led to this?* he wondered frantically, pulling away from her questing fingers. He caught her hands in his, and in the name of self-protection, locked them both behind her back.

"Jeez, Lauren," he gasped, moving back a step. "I was trying to give you a clue, not a quickie against the wall." Even as he said it, that image loomed large in his mind, of him pressing her up against the wall, burying himself into that long elegant body. A fantasy, he knew. So why did it seem like a memory?

Knowing he had to either take her or move away, he released her hands and stepped back.

Scrubbing his hands over his face, he missed seeing her pale.Whirling away, Lauren cupped one hand over her belly, forcing down the panic. *Tell him,* something inside her whispered. *Tell him now.*

I can't. He'll be so angry. And what if he's wrong about how he thinks he feels?

Lauren had played second fiddle for so long, had been his buddy instead of his lover, his confidant instead of soul mate. "I beg your pardon," she said, embarrassment and fear making her voice icy.

"Don't," he said quietly, forcing her to turn around. "Don't. That meant something, Lauren. You know it. I know it. That's why I went back home. I had to see how I would feel if I saw her again."

Lauren only continued to stare at him, wanting desperately to ask. Unable to find the courage to do so.

"You won't even ask, will you?" he said softly. "Not because it doesn't matter. Because it does." He pulled her close again, willing his unruly body to calm. "I think I know you pretty well, too." Pressing his lips to her temple, he breathed in the scent of vanilla, musk and the innocence that was Lauren. Holding her against his chest, simply holding her, felt more right than anything in his whole life had ever felt. "I looked at her and felt no more than I would have felt looking at my high school sweetheart, Bobbi Jo Myers, who is happily married to the minister of my parents' church. Just a little…smile, you know? The kind you feel on the inside when remembering something sweet."

"And that was nothing compared to what I felt when I walked in here and looked at you," he finished, drawing back, looking down into her eyes.

Her mouth fell open, and her eyes closed. He watched as she drew in a deep breath and opened her eyes, the sheen of tears that glistened there making his throat tighten in panic. "I love you," he said rapidly. "I don't know why it took me so long to see you. It's real, though. I love you so much it makes my head spin to even think about you. I want this. I want to help you raise this baby. But I can wait until you're ready to see me, too. To love me."

Her heart pounded in her chest, swelling until she thought she'd faint from lack of air. Looking deeply into his eyes she searched for confirmation. He loved her.

A laugh bubbled out of her throat and she threw her arms around his neck.

She felt lightheaded and dizzy, and she wanted to laugh and cry at the same time. "You fool," she whispered, twin tears spilling over to trickle down her ivory cheeks. "I already do."

His hands, in the act of reaching up to hold her against him, went limp. "Lauren?" he asked, almost afraid to ask if she had said what he thought she had said. What if she hadn't? Pulling back, he stared down into her tear bright eyes.

In response to that unasked question, she raised her hands until she could cup his face. Staring into those bottomless blue eyes that had haunted her dreams for years, she pressed her lips to his. A quiet groan sounded deep in his chest as he wrapped his arms around her waist, dragging her against him. The kiss was gentle, soothing, an answer all on its own. When she pulled her mouth from his, he rested his forehead against hers, his eyes closed. "Lauren." Her name left him on a quiet sigh.

"I've loved you for so long," she whispered, her breath coming in shuddering gasps. "All I ever wanted was to be with you. And every time you left to go home, you took a part of me with you. I thought I'd die when you went back this last time."

Pulling back, he stared at her with bewildered eyes. "How long?" he asked, his voice rough. "Why didn't you ever say anything?"

She smiled sadly, shaking her head. "You wouldn't have wanted to hear it, Dale. I never thought you'd love me."

"You never showed it."

"I couldn't. Friendship was all you wanted, so that's all I gave," she whispered, her voice breaking.

He pulled her back against him, holding her there, feeling her heart pound against his. "I want everything you have to give me, Lauren," he told her, rubbing his cheek against her silky midnight hair. "More."

"All you ever had to do was ask." She rose on her toes, kissing his cheek, grazing his mouth with hers.

He captured her face when she would have pulled back after that butterfly touch. "I'm asking now," he said, his voice rough and unsteady. "Lauren, lie with me tonight. Let me love you."

A tingle of lust shot through her body, followed by the rush of love that nearly swamped her. "Tonight, and every night. For as long as you want me."

"Always. I can't even think of a life without you in it."

She wrapped her arms around his neck and he lifted her, boosting her hips up until she could wrap her legs around his hips. Silently, he carried her down the hall to her room, eye to eye. She pressed a kiss to that smiling mouth, as she had so often dreamed of doing.

It never dawned on him until later that he had never been inside her room before. He had glimpsed it from time to time, but the door, most often, was closed and he had responded to the unspoken need for privacy. He laid her on the pretty fancy of a bed, never realizing how little it seemed to suit Lauren, or suit the Lauren he had not seen until recently. Wrought iron black poles rose from the corners of the king sized mattress, each connected at the top by another pole. Swatches of gauzy white fabric draped over the bed, creating a canopy effect.

The comforter beneath her was deep rose, shades darker than the walls she had painted herself. Throw pillows of hunter green were grouped at the head of the bed. With one sweep of his arm, they all tumbled to the floor. Straddling her hips, careful to keep his weight off of her, he settled back on his heels, his eyes on hers as he unbuttoned the practical white cotton shirt.

Beneath it was totally impractical white lace and satin. The white lace cupped the milky white skin of her breasts, the darker pink of her nipples pressing firmly against the lace, straining and swelling in invitation. Parting the shirt, he merely stared at her for a long moment before tracing one finger along the edge of the ivory satin, whispering, "You're so damn pretty, Lauren." Her slim torso narrowed slightly at her waist before flaring into rounded hips and long, sleek legs he hadn't been able to keep from fantasizing about.

A quick smile lit her face, her cheeks flushing. "You're not so bad yourself," she replied, reaching up to run a hand through his gold streaked hair.

Rolling off of her, he pulled her up, until they were facing each other, kneeling on the bed. Slowly, he slid the open shirt from her shoulders. Her breasts filled that sexy bra to overflowing and he chuckled as he cupped her in his hands. "And these...how did I miss these for so long?" he asked, only half teasing. Pale blue veins streaked under the fine marble of her skin and he wondered why he was so certain those were new. Her rose colored nipples pressed hard against the lace, tempting him.

"Beats me," she murmured wryly. "They're kind of hard to miss."

"Do you always wear things like this?" he asked, flicking the lace with one finger.

She nodded, ducking her chin. "I like pretty things. But I won't be wearing them for much longer. Pretty bras in my size are easy enough to find, but I doubt they'll be comfortable for much longer."

"Do they hurt?" he asked, lowering his head to nuzzle the valley between her breasts. He locked one arm at the small of her back, pulling her up against him as he grazed her skin with his mouth.

"N-no," she whispered, her head falling back as he worked his way up to her neck. "Just...sensitive," she finished on a sigh as one warm hand closed over her, gently massaging the soft flesh.

He pulled back and released the front catch on her bra, watching in lazy satisfaction as her breasts tumbled free. Cupping her again, he gently urged her onto her back, bending over her. "I'll be gentle," he promised. True to his word, he caressed her lightly, lovingly, as Lauren sank into a deep pool of pleasure.

His mouth closed over one nipple, started a gentle suction that had her hips arching up in response. "Dale," she whimpered. So gentle, so tender, but the remembered fury of passion was sneaking up on her, turning her own hands greedy and demanding. "Dale." She tugged at his shoulders, rubbed her hips against his when he lay down fully against her.

"Easy, Lauren. We've got all the time in the world," he said, brushing his thumb over the stiff peak of her nipple.

"Maybe you do," she muttered, eyes glazing over when one clever hand cupped her between her thighs. Opening them wider, she urged him on with a rocking motion. Her damn jeans were in the way, she thought disgustedly. She reached for the button only to have him brush her hands away.

"Let me," he murmured against her ear. He eased the jeans down her legs slowly, pulling the swatch of ivory lace down as well before he settled back on his heels, staring down at her long pale body. Studying, memorizing. For this wasn't familiar. Flashes and glimpses, the taste of her, the scent of her, they all seemed so damned familiar. But he knew, as certain as he was sitting there, he had never seen the glory of Lauren Spencer, naked as the day she was born. Her eyes, half closed, stared at him from a face flushed with need, that wide, sexy mouth curved up in a small smile. Long, strong limbs, lightly muscled and ivory pale. Those heavy, beautiful breasts tipped with rose nipples, long torso, belly just slightly curved, and the small patch of black down at the juncture of her thighs, gleaming wetly. He caressed her flesh lightly, just the tips of his fingers lightly grazing her skin as he studied her. Brushing against her nipples in a butterfly stroke, smiling when she gasped, before roaming down to circle her navel, then trailing one lone finger down her wet, hot cleft.

"Beautiful," he muttered thickly, before lowering his head, nuzzling that downy patch.

"Dale!" she half screamed, her hips arching up.

He slid his hands beneath them, holding her hips open as he drank from her. Sweet, spicy woman. The taste of her was more arousing than the scent, as arousing as the sight of her. He stabbed at her clit, worrying it with his teeth before soothing it with his tongue, lapping at the plump lips of her sex as cream started to pulse from her. Her hands gripped his head, at first, trying to hold him back and then, gripping him closer as he thoroughly loved her with his mouth.

He stroked one hand down her leg before catching her behind the knee, forcing her leg upward, forcing her body to open even more. "Dale, stop," she pleaded, gasping. His tongue swirled and dipped into her. A slick sheen of sweat rose on her body, her nipples beaded and flushed. "Dale-"

"No," he whispered, pulling back just a little, licking the taste of her from his mouth, shuddering with pleasure before lowering his mouth to her again, drinking from her once more. He shifted, changed his angle until he could nibble at the bundle of nerves at the top of her wet slit. As his tongue circled and massaged her clit, she flew apart.

With a gasping cry, she fell straight into a deep downward spiral, the breath knocked from her as a storm of white-hot pleasure pummeled her from all sides. Her hips bucked up once more as Dale slid one finger inside her and pressed. The unexpected touch of his finger brushing against her sensitized flesh drew the orgasm out until she could hardly see, could barely breathe as it flooded her through her. A long moan was ripped from her as her body trembled and shattered. Something seemed to open low inside her belly and a dam burst, drenching them both. The heat engulfed her and she knew she would die from it.

No one could feel this kind of heat, this kind of pleasure and live.

But, untold moments later, her eyes drifted open and Dale was crouched above her, watching and waiting. Moisture gleamed along his mouth and when he kissed her, she tasted herself on him. "Roll over," he murmured, guiding her onto her belly. "I'm dying to see you, all of you." Her body quaked with nerves from the recent climax as she lay on her belly while his hands stroked down her sides, over her butt, down her legs.

"You've got the prettiest ass," he told her, lowering his head to press a kiss to the soft, firm mounds of flesh. Then he ranged his body behind hers, rocking his cock against her butt and groaning when she shuddered and bucked against him.

"I need you," he whispered, brushing her hair aside and biting her neck. "I need to be inside you, feel that hot little pussy of yours around me, feel you come."

She whimpered and squirmed under his hands. "Dale," she whispered, arching her hips instinctively. The cheeks of her ass closed around him, cuddling the length of his cock and Dale froze, before he rocked gently there, a bead of moisture escaping from the tip to dampen the flesh there, easing the slow, maddening strokes. He thrust against her, with his cock cuddled between the cheeks of her ass, and the feel of it, of her soft hot body, nearly drove him insane. "Not like this," he panted, rolling her back onto her back. I want to see you, this first time, see you while I fill you."

"You're mine," he whispered as he settled between her thighs. Gripping one leg behind her knee, he opened her wide and plunged into her, deep, until he was settled inside her. "And I'll never let you go."

"I sure as hell hope not," Lauren whispered, clenching around him as the heat started to build inside her once more. Rocking her hips to meet his, she stared up into his eyes, hardly able to believe this was happening, that this was real. She could feel him deep inside, the head of his cock rubbing against that nifty little G-spot a woman was lucky enough to be born with. Each time he nudged it, it pushed her just a little closer to mind shattering ecstasy.

He slowed his thrusts until he was barely rocking inside her, until she was writhing beneath him and pulling at him, her fingers biting into his ass while she tried to pull him further inside.

"Want more?" he asked, pulling out a little farther before easing back inside her. She was tight and hot and wet, her sex gloving his shaft, her muscles caressing him until he was nearly blind with the pleasure of it.

"Please, yes," she groaned, thrusting her hips high to take him deeper.

"Tell me," he purred, grasping her hands and pinning them beside her head. "Tell me what you want." Lowering his head to her ear, he whispered, "Tell me you want me to fuck you, Lauren. I feel like I've been waiting my whole life to hear it."

Her cheeks flushed as he lifted his head, staring down at her, waiting. But her lips parted and the words left her on a sigh, "Fuck me, Dale. Fuck me hard. I *have* been waiting my whole life."

Keeping her hands pinned beside her head, he rose up, shifted until he was riding high on her body and started to fuck her, hard. Just like she had asked.

He felt the muscles low in his spine starting to tighten and tingle as his balls drew tight against his body. "Shit," he muttered against the side of her neck, "I can't wait, Lauren. I need you too much." His head swooped down and he set his teeth against the curve of her neck and bit down just as he lost control, semen pulsing out of his body in heavy, hot spurts of fire.

She started to seize around him, her pulsating vaginal walls stroking and gripping his cock, drawing his orgasm out slowly. Her shuddering, convulsing sheath closed around him tightly, until each time those silken muscles tightened around his cock, it seemed to pull a little more come from him until he felt like she had drained him completely.

And when she came around him, those same muscles vicing around him, Dale felt like he had found his way into heaven.

"Are you okay?" he asked later, his voice drowsy. One hand lay protectively over her belly as he cuddled her up against him.

"Never been better," she said honestly, cupping her hand over her mouth and yawning delicately. "Sorry."

He grinned against the back of her neck. "Me, too. I thought I had you so worn out you'd forget your manners."

"Manners? What are they?" she asked, sighing in pleasure as she stared out the window. The sun had already set, leaving the room bathed in pale twilight.

As they drifted towards sleep, only one thought bothered Dale.

Had the baby's father made her feel this way?

When her eyes drifted open hours later, silvery moonlight was coming through the window, gilding everything with its gentle glow. Against her back, Dale slept on. She was certain she was dreaming. Could this really be happening?

But she could smell him. Pressing her lips together, she could still taste him there. Against her back she felt the solid steady beating of his heart. A dull ache between her thighs remained, a reminder of how they had spent the night.

And what had happened earlier. Her legs went weak just thinking of it, and her insides were turning to hot molten lava. Oh, it was happening all right. Her imagination worked just fine, but nobody's imagination worked fine enough to conjure up something like that, certainly not without experiencing it in the flesh.

Slowly, she moved out from under his arm, turning around to stare at him. Pale white moonlight lit half his face, casting the other half into shadow. The smile lines at the corners of his mouth and eyes were relaxed. A small smile, a remnant from a dream or what had happened only hours earlier, had the corner of his mouth turned up just slightly.

He said he loved her. Said he wanted to raise this baby with her. Her eyes closed. Oh, how was she going to explain this?

She turned her head away, tears stinging her eyes.

A gentle hand cupped her elbow. "What's wrong?" Dale asked sleepily, watching her through his lashes. "Regrets already?"

Dashing away tears, she forced out a smile she really didn't feel. And without even realizing it, took the coward's way out. "Not one bit. I'm just a little too emotional. Hormones, I guess." She tucked her chin against her chest, letting him pull her back up against him.

"I think your hormones are working just fine," he murmured in her ear, one hand gliding up and down her side. "You've certainly got mine stirred up and hopping, though."

His erection pressed against the small of her back. With a quiet moan, she arched back against him, squirming to get closer. "You're not sore?" he asked, resting one hand on her belly.

"No," she whispered, tilting her head to allow him better access to her neck. His teeth nipped at the curve where neck joined shoulder gently before urging her onto her knees. But when she started to turn, he held her still, stroking his hands over her buttocks and hips before one hand slipped between her thighs, long fingers parting her flesh, testing her.

On hands and knees, she tensed when he pressed against her. "Easy, Lauren," he whispered, rocking gently against her, entering her gently. With each subtle thrust of his hips, he moved deeper inside her. Face buried against the mattress, Lauren whimpered under his touch. Filled almost to bursting, she shuddered as he nudged forward, easing the rest of his length inside her. When he was buried inside her, he smoothed his hands over her hips, before changing his grip, nudging her just slightly forward before pulling her back to meet him. "Tight," he muttered. "So tight and wet."

Slowly, he stroked her, caressing her bottom with his hands, murmuring softly to her until the tension left her body. And then, he pushed a little deeper, a little harder.

Hands closing tightly over the linens, she clenched her inner muscles around him. He felt so deep. Tight, yes, damn it. Almost too tight. She moaned now, as he pulled her back a little harder. She thought it hurt, but then she shuddered, moving back this time to meet his hips eagerly, faster and faster, until he was slamming into her, hands clamped on her hips tightly enough to bruise.

She convulsed around him with a scream only moments before he emptied himself into her. Her upper body collapsed, air sawing in and out of her lungs. Behind her, Dale groaned deep in his chest, pulling back before seating himself inside her once more. And then, locking one arm around her waist, he rolled to his side, without breaking their connection. "No regrets, Lauren," he whispered in her ear before falling back into sleep.

Chapter Five

The morning after. Awkward?

You don't know the half of it, buddy, Dale said silently to whomever had coined the phrase. Awkward didn't quite describe how he felt at six thirty two in the morning, crouched around Lauren's heaving body as she wretched over the toilet. He kept his forearm locked around her waist, the other hand holding her hair back from her face. Her hands were wrapped around his arm, clutching it to her chest, short neat nails biting into his skin with every spasm.

He had been awakened violently when she had shoved out of the bed some twenty minutes earlier. The dry heaves had been wracking her ever since. Tears and sweat soaked her face, and beneath his hands, her body trembled violently.

Five more minutes, he swore. If she doesn't stop in five minutes, I'm calling that damn doctor.

Four months pregnant, for crying out loud. The morning sickness had stopped weeks ago, hadn't it? Smoothing a gentle hand over her sweaty hair, he closed his eyes in sympathy, and a little pain, as her nails bit into his forearm when another spasm hit her, this one was longer in duration, stronger.

And final.

The five minutes was up and Dale was wiping a damp cold cloth over her flushed face. Her eyes closed, cheeks pale under the flush, soft wide mouth still trembling. "Are you okay now?" he asked quietly, using the cloth on her neck.

"I- I think so," she whispered, letting her head fall back to rest against his shoulder. "Sorry." Her voice, slightly stronger now, was prim and polite and quite lady like.

"Not a problem," he replied, amused at both of them. They had spent more time engaged in bedtime sports than in sleep. Instead of sleeping late and waking to a leisurely bout of morning sex and breakfast, they were up at the crack of dawn while she lost what little was left in her belly after a rather busy night.

Resting his cheek on her head, he rocked her back and forth, perched rather precariously on the edge of the deep bathtub. Once the tremors had passed, he raised his head and brushed her tangled hair back from her face. Studying her, he realized this was the first time he had seen her this defenseless. Even when she'd caught the flu a winter or so back, she had looked better than most women could look on their best days. Granted, he hadn't seen her the first two days when she had practically camped on the bathroom floor.

"Is there anything I can get you to help?"

"Crackers," she said, eyes closing again as weariness settled in.

Five minutes later, he had her back in bed, seated behind her, propping her weary body against his while she munched on a saltine. "I thought you were past this stage," he said, finger combing the tangles from her ebony hair.

With a wry grimace, Lauren responded, "So did I. That doctor is fired."

A smile tugging at his mouth, Dale told her, "I don't think she's to blame for this." He rested the flat of his hand on her forehead, testing. "You don't feel warm, but maybe you're coming down with something."

She shook her head. "No. I'm feeling better already, just really tired." She rested her head against his shoulder and rolled her eyes over to meet his. "For some reason, I didn't sleep well."

He frowned, face folded in somber lines. "Lauren, a woman in your condition should take better care of herself. Early to bed, a stout breakfast in the morning. No wild sex." His eyes narrowed thoughtfully. "No, scratch that last part. The wild sex isn't hurting anything."

She smiled, closing her eyes and rolling her head until it rested in the curve of his neck and shoulder. "No. Not a thing," she murmured. The bout of nausea was gone, as though it hadn't happened. She sighed in pleasure as his hand rested on the curve of her belly.

Dale was no longer able to keep from asking, "Who was he, Lauren?"

But she had already fallen asleep, a peaceful smile on her face. Her head rested on his shoulder and as he watched, she shifted, raising one hand to rest on his chest, right above his heart.

Dale closed his eyes, breathed out slowly. Was it better this way? Dale had the weird idea that as long as she didn't speak his name out loud, the father of the baby wouldn't be real. He wouldn't have to face it.

He desperately needed to know.

He desperately didn't want to.

* * * * *

Lauren was certain she had never been so happy in her life. The man she had dreamed about for years, had loved endlessly, finally loved her back. She didn't doubt it; she recognized the look in his eyes when he smiled at her. She ought to, after seeing that same gleam in her eyes for so long.

Only one thing managed to put a pall on her pleasure.

She hadn't told him.

Several times, she had tried. But she was so scared of what might happen. And Dale didn't seem to care about it. Since that first time he'd asked, no, demanded to know, he hadn't spoken of it again.

If her guilt cast a slight pall on her joy, it was a small price to pay. She told herself he didn't want to know, so she didn't need to tell him.

She knew she was being a fool, and a coward.

There were no more bouts of morning sickness. She eased into her fifth month, and then her sixth, before she finally had to start wearing maternity clothes. Even then, few people who knew her realized she was pregnant. Resting his hand on her belly as they waited for her turn to have the ultrasound, Dale asked the question for the millionth time, "Let's find out what the baby is. We can be more prepared that way."

"No," she replied, pleasantly, flipping the pages of a glossy magazine. She shifted on the hard chair before glancing at her watch. These things always took forever. Sometime in the fourth month the obstetrician had decided she wanted monthly ultrasounds to monitor the baby's growth. She hadn't been very pleased with Lauren's birth canal; it was too narrow. Lauren had snorted at that, well aware of her more than adequate hip width.

"It's not the hips that concern me, Lauren. It's the rest of it," Dr. Flynn had remarked dryly. "If that baby weighs more than eight pounds, you'll be having a cesarean."

Dale had paled and panicked at that, his hand closing tightly over Lauren's, questions shooting from his mouth like bullets, one after the other, hardly giving the doctor a chance to answer.

So far, so good, Lauren mused. She got the munchies often enough, but she was carrying the baby so high, she was forced to eat much smaller meals any way. She rarely indulged her sweet tooth. It wasn't that the baby's size worried her. she was a mature woman, capable of handling a crisis should it come her way.

No. She wasn't worried at all about the baby's size.

It was the word *cesarean* that worried her. The idea of surgery is what had her pale and panicky. Not that she would let Dale know. The man was a basket case already, quoting advice from pregnancy books from dawn till dusk. He was being so damn sweet, coddling her, cuddling her, comforting her. If he knew how worried she was about the thought of having to undergo a cesarean, he would be doubly worried about it.

She sat there, fretting about the possibility of having her flesh sliced into by some knife welding M.D., pretending she was interested in how to better her self esteem and boost her sexuality. Doctors were screened for psychopathic tendencies before they got their medical degrees, weren't they?

She sat waiting for the word game to begin.

A monotonous tapping drew her eyes from the magazine. Dale was rocking back in his chair, tapping his feet, causing a shortened chair leg to rattle on the bare floor. "Must you?" she asked mildly, eyeing his feet.

"Nope," he replied, continuing his little drum roll with his size elevens serving as the drumsticks.

"Will you please stop?" she politely requested, rustling the magazine in front of her.

"Sure. Once you agree to find out what the baby is," he responded, tapping a little more enthusiastically.

"No."

"Why not?"

"Because I enjoy making you suffer," she said pleasantly, laying the magazine down on her lap and folding her hands over her belly.

With a grin, he lowered his chair back to the ground. "I'll make you a deal. Let me find out what it is and I won't tell you," he suggested, hope gleaming in his eyes. "I'll even pretend to still want to know, so you can pretend to make me suffer."

She slid him a look from the corner of her eye and repeated, "No."

Groaning, he slumped in the seat. "Can't you say anything else?"

"Certainly. Can't you ask a different question?"

This was a repeat of the past two trips to have the ultrasound. Now Dale would reply, *Sure. If you give me the answer I want to the first one.* The bantering would continue until she was called back.

But Dale had risen out of his chair and knelt in front of her, a little different from the normal script. As he caught her hand in his, she arched a brow at him. "Going to beg me? This ought to be interesting. Might have been more fun at home though."

He didn't smile. "I have a different question now," was all he said, before raising her hand to his lips and kissing it. Her left hand.

She met his eyes, going still. The magazine slid, forgotten, from her lap as he whispered, "I love you more than my own life. There's nothing I wouldn't do for you, nothing I wouldn't give. I want to be a husband to you."

Lauren's heart stopped beating.

"I want to be a father to your child," he added. "I want that more than life."

Her breath stopped within her throat.

"I want to wake up to you in the morning, fall asleep next to you at night. I want to raise this baby with you and grow old with you."

A single tear fell, rolled down her cheek.

He slid a gold band, set with a pearl flanked by sparkling diamonds, onto her finger. "Lauren, will you marry me?"

Her eyes closed and another tear fell. Turning her hand over, she clutched his, feeling the weight, the fit of the band on her finger as she slid off the chair into his lap, in front of the small audience that sat in the waiting room. A little girl giggled, a couple of watery sniffs came from behind her as she wrapped her arms around his neck. Across the room, one woman sighed in envy before elbowing her husband and asking, "Why couldn't you ask me like that?"

"Yes," she whispered, as another onlooker shook his head, smiling a bit himself.

"Heck of a place to propose," the onlooker muttered, enjoying the show. Much better than the talk trash on the TV, in his opinion. The woman was a looker, tall, willowy, black, black hair and smoky gray eyes. Stacked. And he had to admit, all those sweet words the man had spoken had done the trick. Bound to get something special for that.

"Yes," she repeated as Dale held her tightly against him. A sigh of relief escaped him as she leaned her head back, staring into his blue eyes.

Just then, the door swung open and a tiny gray haired woman boomed out in a voice like a cannon, "Lauren Spencer?"

Dale smiled sweetly and bussed her mouth. "Not for long."

* * * * *

You have to tell him, Lauren told herself.

She stared at herself in the mirror, brush held limply in her hand as she held her free hand over the hard mound of her belly, feeling the tiny little fluttering kicks within. Her eyes burned with tears, her teeth closed over her lower lip. She had put it off, knowing full well she hadn't expected him to stay with her, like this, for long.

But he wanted to marry her.

Oh, he was going to be furious.

Dale was on his way back from the store, chasing down lime sherbet for her.

For her, a selfish, self-centered coward of a woman.

She sat down on the toilet, face buried in her hands. "That's it, Lauren. When he gets home, you're telling him."

Dale's house had just sold to a young doctor and his bride. He'd volunteered to sell his house and make hers their home, a gesture that made her cry. He knew how much she loved this place, this home she had made, the only real home she'd ever known. He knew how she loved her garden, every flower, every bush and tree. And they had worked side by side to finish the baby's room.

The wedding was less than two weeks away. Dale had already packed up what he wanted to keep and transported it over to Lauren's, sold most of what he wouldn't need and didn't want. The only pieces of furniture left were his desk and bed and some chairs. And the bed had to go when he moved in with Lauren.

In an old fashioned, if rather silly, move, Dale had decided that he would sleep at home until the wedding. And he had decided, much to Lauren's dismay and displeasure, they would wait until after the wedding before having sex again. Lauren pouted any time she thought of it, but she was moved at the same time.

Everything was ready.

You have to tell him.

I will, today. As soon as he gets home.

* * * * *

He hadn't heard her right. That was all. He set the brown paper bag on the counter and asked, "Excuse me?"

Her gray eyes, stormy and turbulent, met his squarely. "I need to tell you about the night I got pregnant, Dale," she repeated. Behind her back, where he couldn't see, her hands knotted together nervously.

"Why?"

Her brows arched up and she repeated, "Why?"

He looked away from her solemn eyes, putting the carton of sherbet in the freezer. "It's not really important, is it, Lauren?" he said, his calm voice belying the thudding of his heart. The cold sweat of panic had settled over him and he had to concentrate to keep his hands from shaking.

Had the father changed his mind? Had she changed her mind? Did she still love the baby's father after all?

"I think it is," she said softly, hands locked behind her back. He knew she did this to hide her fidgeting.

"Are we still getting married?" he asked quietly. "Or have you changed your mind?"

"No," she replied, her voice urgent. "No. I haven't, and wouldn't ever change my mind about that."

He grabbed her arms, lifting her on her toes, lowering his face until he was nose-to- nose, eye-to-eye with her. "Do you love me?" he asked, his own voice mirroring the urgency in hers.

"With all my heart," she said. "Dale-"

The fist around his heart started to relax and he eased her back onto her feet, cuddling her against his chest. He wasn't giving her up.

"Is he going to try to take the baby from you? Do I have to worry about sharing this baby?" He sighed and shoved a hand through his hair. "It's his right, I guess. I can handle that, but I sure as hell don't have to like it."

"No. Dale, it's nothing like that," she said, reaching out for him. "I just think you should know-"

"Were you hurt? Did he…did he rape you?" The black rage welled up in him even from thinking it. By heaven, if somebody had hurt her, he would kill him, slowly.

"Absolutely not," she replied, her voice indignant. "I'd kill the man who tried it."

Dale smiled at the outrage in her voice, instantly reassured. "Thank God," he whispered, the tension draining out of him. He reached for her only to pull back when she held her hands out, warding him off.

She instantly regretted it as hurt filled his eyes. She wanted, desperately, to reach out for him. But she refused, her hands fell limply to her sides, and out of habit, she locked them behind her back. "Dale, you-"

He shook his head. Laying one finger across her mouth, cutting off whatever she had intended to say, he said softly, "Then, it's not important. He doesn't matter."

"Dale…"

Leaning back, staring down into her misty gray eyes, he admitted, "I don't want to know." Taking a deep breath, he schooled his features, calmed his voice. "I don't want to know, Lauren. I don't need to. I'm going to be this baby's father. I've been there with you on this practically from the beginning. I'm going to be there when you deliver. I'm going to be there when it's time for midnight and two a.m. feedings. That makes me the father. That's all that matters."

Coward. Lauren eyed her reflection owlishly, running a hand through her sleep tangled hair. She should have pushed it, should have just told him flat out. Why didn't she?

Because you're a coward, she told herself bitterly. She was afraid he would get so angry, angry enough to walk away from her. That was something people did rather easily, when it came to her.

Sleep eluded her all night. Guilt, she supposed. But, Lauren knew, if she had to make the choice all over again, not knowing how things would turn out, she would make the same choice. She had no way of knowing that Dale would fall in love with her, no way of knowing that he would be eager to raise a child. No way of knowing that she would fall even more in love with him than she had already.

If I lose him, it is going to destroy me, she thought helplessly.

"He's going to figure it out sooner or later, Lauren," she whispered to her reflection as she raised the brush to her hair. She stroked it through her heavy fall of hair as a tear spilled over and fell down her cheek. Stroke after stroke, tear after tear, she damned herself for being so pathetically scared.

She could only hope that he loved her enough to forgive her.

* * * * *

Her wedding day dawned cold and dreary. Lauren splashed cool water on her face, battling back a severe case of bridal jitters. She really could have used a drink or ten the previous night. Jennifer Langley, one of her few friends, spent the night, patting her back when the nerves got bad, letting her sniffle on her shoulder the one time tears arose.

But Lauren would have loved to be able to go out, party with friends, drink herself senseless so the guilt wouldn't keep her awake. Of course, even wishing to seek oblivion with alcohol had her cringing in even more guilt. *Bad mom, bad mom, bad mom,* she told herself silently.

Hours later, after a long bath and cool compresses to her red eyes, Lauren walked out of the house, clad in jeans and a sweatshirt, the last time as a single woman. Six and a half months pregnant, she was about to marry the father of her baby, only he didn't know he was the father.

Jennifer chattered on easily, used to Lauren's sometimes quiet moods. She was probably attributing this to bridal jitters and nothing more. Lauren hadn't confided in anyone, even though she desperately wanted to.

But if Dale didn't know, nobody would.

The small country church was tucked away in one of the valleys that hid in the hills of Floyd County. Simple and basic, much like the wedding itself. Lauren had considered just going to a Justice of the Peace, but had decided against it.

Dale had been relieved, even though she knew he tried to hide it. But she could almost hear him thinking, *A wedding is held in a church. Business meetings are held in the county courthouse.*

The ceremony was to be attended by close friends only, including her agent and his, his parents, his only brother, and a handful of others. Jennifer would stand as Lauren's single attendant, her simple suit of forest green matching the holiday decorations. Lauren stared at her reflection in the mirror as Jennifer swept her hair up in a Gibson girl style twist, leaving tendrils hanging at her neck and ears.

Her dress was old fashioned, with a high neck, long flowing sleeves ending in banded cuffs three inches wide at her wrists. The waist was low, around her hips. The dress fell straight down from her breasts, her rounded belly almost imperceptible. Simple ivory drops hung at her ears. She wore thigh high stockings more from necessity than out of a need to entice. She couldn't stand the way pantyhose felt against her sensitive belly. Low heeled lace up boots of ivory leather completed the look.

"You're nervous," Jennifer said quietly, smiling slightly as she looped a tendril of hair then secured it with a bobby pin. "I don't think I've ever seen you really nervous and I've known you for ten years now."

"I'm getting married. That's reason enough to be nervous, don't you think?" Lauren replied, keeping her voice low and level by sheer will power.

She only smiled, fussing a bit more with Lauren's hair. "I'm so happy for you," Jennifer said softly. "You love him."

"Yes." Lauren sighed, closing her eyes. "Yes, I love him. I can't remember not loving him."

"I can't remember you not loving him either."

Her eyes flew open and met the knowing green eyes in the mirror. "You knew?"

She shrugged. "I know you about as well as anybody could. I saw how you were around him. You were never indifferent to him, like you were with every guy I've seen you with since high school. He shook you up, he made you think. He made you mad." She laid the brush down, and came around to kneel by the chair. "You look beautiful."

"Thank you."

With a look at the clock, Jennifer sighed and said, "It's time." She hugged Lauren and rose to her feet. She handed Lauren her bouquet and headed for the door. They stood there, waiting until Jennifer's husband knocked to let them know. "One more thing."

She remained silent until Lauren met her eyes. "Don't you think you should tell him that he is the father?" Before Lauren could close her mouth, Jenny had opened the door and left her standing there.

Later, inside the elegant restaurant, Lauren met Jennifer in the bathroom while they waited for the dinner to be served. "How did you know?" she asked, her voice trembling.

Jennifer shook her head with a smile on her face. "You wouldn't have slept with anybody else, not loving him the way you do. Maybe it's just me, but I can't believe he never saw how you felt. He knows you; he should have seen it the way I did." Folding her hands around Lauren's, she asked, "But I'm kind of curious. Why doesn't Dale seem to know? Hell, I'm scared to say anything about it to Mike. He'd screw up and let it slip and that info needs to come from *you*, sweetie. "

Lauren remained silent, chewing nervously on her lip, wearing away her lipstick.

Jennifer sighed, glaring at Lauren as she repeated slowly, "Lauren, why doesn't he know? Most guys remember when they sleep with their best buddy."

"He was... he was drunk," Lauren replied, her voice soft, sad. "He doesn't remember. I don't think he even knew who I was." Her eyes misted over and tears welled up. Letting her head fall back, she stared up at the ceiling and said flatly, "He called me by her name, Jenny. That woman I told you about."

"Oh. Oh, honey," Jennifer murmured sympathetically, wrapping her arm around Lauren and hugging her tightly.

"He forgot all about it," she whispered. "It meant less than nothing to him. I had dreamed of being with him, of him making love to me and telling me how much he loves me. And instead, he fucks me up against a wall and calls me somebody else."

"I guess I understand," Jennifer said softly, her mouth twisting in a snarl. "I think I would have killed him, if I were you, but I understand."

"I know I should have told him. I still should," Lauren muttered, as the outraged feminine anger she had buried deep inside started to raise its ugly head.

"Why didn't you? I mean," Jennifer paused and spread her hands wide, staring hard at her best friend, "I mean, why didn't you tell him right up front? Smack him in the head with that damn whisky bottle and let him have it?"

Swallowing the lump in her throat, she blinked away the tears. "He passed out right after it happened. Right on top of me. I left. He didn't remember a damn thing. I didn't expect to get pregnant. Completely wrong time of month."

"How many babies started out that way?" Jenny asked, shaking her head. "I still don't understand why you keep avoiding telling him. He needs to know. Why don't you just come out and say it?"

"I tried." Lauren grimaced as she settled onto the stool in front of the lighted mirror. She stared at her pale, composed face and admitted, "Not very hard. But he said he didn't want to know, didn't need to know, so I let it go. I took the easy way out."

"Lauren…"

"Because," she whispered harshly, "I don't want to lose him." Tears glittered in her eyes but she refused to let them fall. She'd brought this on herself, and, damn it, she wouldn't cry about it.

Seeing those tears, hearing the fear that made her voice quiver, shook Jenny. This was a woman who had always been a rock, as steady and unflappable as they came. That vulnerability damn near broke Jennifer's heart. The smaller woman wrapped her arms around Lauren's shoulders and hugged her. "I'm behind you always, Lauren. I want you to know that. But this is going to backfire. He will find out. It will catch up with you."

Lauren raised haunted eyes to meet Jennifer's. "I know."

She was so beautiful it made his heart ache just to look at her. Dale watched as she walked with Jennifer back to the table, as graceful as a woman could possibly be, despite the fact that she was almost into the last trimester of pregnancy. As she walked, she brushed a lock of hair behind her ear, the diamond and pearl band on her finger sparkling.

His wife.

Cool to the point of being icy, serious, with eyes that could see clear to his soul. Lauren was not what he had envisioned in a wife. Life with her was not going to be easy. Loving her wasn't going to be easy.

His wife.

Hot damn, his wife.

The nerves were gone, almost as suddenly as they had come. Eagerness had settled in, eagerness to get home with his new bride and consummate the marriage he hadn't thought he wanted. Eagerness to start the family he had sworn he would never have.

With a contented smile, he placed his hand on her lower back, massaging the tension that so often lingered there. She slid him a slow, sweet smile, her eyes glowing with promises.

His wife.

* * * * *

Dr. Flynn beamed at the two of them as if she had paired them up herself. "Oh, I'm so happy for you, Lauren. And for you, Dale. You've got yourself a fine lady here."

"You're buttering me up so you can get me in an unflattering position," Lauren said dryly, with a slight smile as she lay back on the table. Gentle skilled hands probed her belly, judging the growth of the baby and the position. Lauren marveled at how the doctor was able to tell so much, simply by feel. "Time to check the heartbeat," Dr. Flynn said, squirting cold gel on Lauren's distended abdomen.

Moments later, the loud, steady, rapid beats filled the room. Dale's hand squeezed Lauren's as he placed a kiss on her brow. "Everything sounds fine. You've done well. You've only gained twelve pounds so far. These last few months are the tough ones, though. That's when cravings get stronger and when the baby gains the most weight. You just need to continue to watch yourself. Not too many sweets."

Lauren nodded, listening as the doctor warned her what to watch for, cautioned her against eating like there was no tomorrow, and advised regular exercise. "Now that we're getting close to the seventh month, I'd like to do ultrasounds every two weeks, just to monitor things more closely."

Dale frowned as she spoke. "You're certain everything is okay? Most women only get one or two ultrasounds. We've already had four."

Dr. Flynn wiped the gel from Lauren's belly before stepping back, allowing Dale to help Lauren into a sitting position. "Everything looks wonderful right now. I don't expect that to change, but I want to keep an eye on things." She smiled at Lauren. "Make sure he doesn't worry too much. These new fathers, sometimes, they are worse than the mothers."

* * * * *

Lauren burst into laughter when a huge Winnie the Pooh came through the front door. One hand resting on the swelling of her stomach, the other covered her mouth as she tried to quell the bubble of laughter. "Dale, that thing is huge."

His voice muffled, Dale said, "So, what? The baby will love it." He set the bear down on the couch before sweeping Lauren into his arms. "He can baby sit for us."

Lauren sighed as Dale set his strong fingers to work on the ache in her back while he nuzzled her neck. "Steve Young was over earlier," she murmured, arching her neck back as Dale trailed a line of kisses down it. "They're playing poker...tonight."

"Mmm." He slipped his hands under her shirt, over the high waist of her pregnancy jeans and over the sturdy bra comfort had demanded she buy. With a gentle tug, he pulled the shirt off her and flicked open her bra. "Have I told you today how much I love you?"

"Yes." She bit her lip as he gently bit her engorged nipple. "Tell me again," she demanded, her fingers diving into his gold streaked hair and holding his face to her breast.

"I love you." He slid his hands into the waist of her jeans and eased them down her hips, removing and tossing them aside as he dropped to his knees in front of her. He rubbed his cheek against her belly, smiling broadly when a tiny fist thumped against him. "Adore you." He grinned up at her. "No underwear?"

"I hate the pregnancy panties. They're hideous," she muttered, a flush rising to her cheeks.

Stroking his hands over her belly, hips, finally her buttocks, he pulled her down until she straddled his hips. The rough material of his jeans rubbed against her bare thighs. "Now where was I?" he asked absently, raising her hand to his mouth and nibbling on the fleshy part of her palm.

"Adoring me," she offered helpfully, guiding his mouth back to her nipple.

"Oh, yeah." It took a little bit of maneuvering, but he managed to get his jeans undone without moving Lauren from her perch. "Need you." He cupped her between her thighs, sliding his middle finger into her while his thumb pressed against her.

He nibbled at her neck and asked, "Is this where I was?"

Her breath catching on a sigh, Lauren answered, "Close."

"Mmmm," he murmured, trailing his mouth down her neck, her collarbone, dallying around her sensitive breasts. Taking her nipple in his mouth, he suckled gently until Lauren was shifting restlessly beneath him. "No. Not there either."

"Here," she urged, shamelessly guiding his head to where she wanted him to show his adoration. He chuckled as he shifted her weight, propping her on the chair behind her, settling between her thighs. "Now if I had been here," he murmured. "I'd have remembered." He closed his mouth over her clit, flicking his tongue lightly against her before pulling back and rocking his weight on his heels. "Now I remember." He ran a hand up the length of her leg and said, "Want you." Lowering his head, he lapped at her, slowly, lazily, while he rolled his eyes to stare up at her face.

"Dale, please," she panted, squirming beneath his mouth while he continued to play, carefully avoiding that sensitive bead of flesh she kept rocking against him.

"Please, what?" he asked with a grin. Her cream had his mouth and chin gleaming, and was now coating his fingers as he slid two of them inside her.

In answer, she only squirmed and tried to guide his talented mouth back down. With a frustrated groan, she said, "Your mouth."

His fingers left her body and he caught both of her wrists, pinned them down. "Just tell me," he coaxed. "What do you want me to do with my mouth?" Lowering his head, he blew a puff of air on her wet open folds.

"Suck on me, please. Oh, shit," she moaned when he lowered his head to comply. "Just keep, ah, oh, um, just keep doing that."

"I love your taste," he said roughly, sliding his hands under her ass and lifting her up. "I could just eat you up for the rest of my life." He swirled his tongue against her clit, and suckled against her, as ordered, groaning as she climaxed, so easily, against his mouth.

So primed, always so easily primed for him.

He rose to his feet and jerked his jeans down, freeing his erection, before reaching out and catching her abundant hair in his hands. She was still shuddering from her climax when he said, "My turn," in a thick voice, guiding her mouth to his cock.

Her lips wrapped around him and she nibbled delicately before lowering her head, slowly, steadily, until he was lodged in her throat. The woman could deep-throat his cock like nothing he'd ever seen. "Yeah, that's it," he muttered mindlessly, rocking his hips against her, holding her head still for his thrusts. "God, that's so damn good, baby."

His words, and his mindless pleasure fanned the fires in her groin again and she hummed low in her throat as she pulled back to nibble at the head of his shaft, savoring his warm salty taste before she started to take his length back inside her mouth again. The skin of his cock was satiny smooth, almost delicate, in contrast to the hardness and heat of it. Lauren doubted she'd ever tire of it.

She trailed one hand slowly up the inside of his thigh, loving how he jerked slightly when her fingers cupped his balls, massaging them gently and lowering her head to lick at the furry sac before placing a line of kisses back to his cock and down the length of it, laughing when he groaned in frustration and shoved his cock back inside her mouth, catching her head and holding her still.

He slid past her lips and she moved shallowly for a few minutes, until he started to move his hips and force her to take his cock further inside. Relaxing her throat muscles, she took him as far as she could while her hands slid up to cup his ass to squeeze and stroke. Lauren continued to take his large hard cock in her mouth, down her throat, over and over until he bucked and started pumping furiously, panting and swearing under his breath. His tight grip on her hair immobilized her mouth and his cock was half choking her.

She loved it. A current of excitement sizzled through her when he shot off inside her mouth, flooding her with the taste of his come. Above her, his whole body tensed, his skin gleaming with a fine sheen of sweat, his eyes, hooded and dark, locked on her face.

She was still swallowing him down when he slid to the floor and lay back, pulling her with him. He was still hard, still wild eyed. "Ride me, Lauren," he panted, positioning her until she sat astride him. "I need you."

With a pleased sigh, she lowered herself onto him, taking his cock into her body. The plum-shaped head of his penis stretched her tight sheath as he worked it in, her rocking motions taking him slowly, centimeters at a time. When he was fully seated inside her vagina, she planted her hands on his chest and rocked lazily back and forth, his large hands cupping her ass.

"You're so damn sexy," he murmured, using one thumb against the hardened bead of flesh at the top of her slit. The taste of her still lay on his tongue. Her wet, hot folds gloved him completely. Lids half closed, Dale stared up at her. Her head was thrown back, a small feline smile playing at her mouth. A delicate flush stained her face and neck, spreading down to tinge her nipples a rosy pink.

Lauren sat up straighter, taking him deeper into her body, laughing in delight when he bucked beneath her. A low hum of pleasure emanated from her as she stroked her hands up her torso, locking her fingers behind her neck, just barely moving atop him.

His eyes opened, focused on hers, locking their gazes for long moments before trailing down her body slowly, over her neck, lingering over her swollen breasts and rounding belly before settling his gaze where they joined, watching as she rocked slowly on his cock, rolling her hips and purring softly when he started to rotate the pad of his thumb against her clit. With a smile, she shifted and leaned forward over him, pumping her hips smoothly, feeling the hot length of him thicken and pulse inside her.

Lazy and sweet, easy lust slid through her as she stroked over him. His hands roamed over her body, down her thighs, up her sides, cupping her sensitive breasts before pulling her face to his. His brushed his mouth across hers, shifting until he had control of her body. Angling his hips, he pushed deeper, lifting her, sliding her back down over him in a hot wet caress.

The climax rolled through her as his hands cupped her face, his mouth nibbling at hers. Achingly slow and sweet, it lingered on until Lauren thought she'd cry from the beauty of it. With a low groan, Dale followed her, his fingers digging into her hips, clutching her tightly against him.

Nestled against his chest, Lauren drifted into sleep, listening to the beating of his heart. "I love you," she heard him whisper into her hair.

* * * * *

"You're sure you don't mind?" Dale asked for the fourth time five or six hours later. She had woken from her nap wanting to tackle the painting she had been ignoring for months. It was a turbulent scene of the Ohio valley, the sky an eerie gray green, the thunderheads full and ready to burst open. The colors weren't working.

She normally didn't try work like this but after a tornado had passed through the valley a few months earlier, leaving devastation and despair in its wake, she had started it, only to leave it unfinished after struggling over the right colors for weeks.

"Go on," she muttered, adding a bit of white to the thunderheads, then a touch of green. A little better. "Go have fun."

"Try to miss me a little," he told her, shaking his head with a smile when her only reply was a grunt. She was already too involved in her work to pay him much attention. Poker was as good a way as any to spend the night. He had finished his faerie tale only a few days earlier and sent it and the sketches to New York. There were no other ideas brewing at the moment and he had already tinkered on the Mustang in the garage.

So he got a six-pack out of the fridge and grabbed his jacket before heading outside.

Lauren didn't even look up when he said good-bye. Her face was folded into a scowl as she mixed a bit of this and that, narrowing her eyes when the color didn't work for her. It looked okay, but it wasn't right.

More than an hour later, after several more abortive starts and failures, she threw down her palette and brushes.

Why had she even started this? She didn't like to paint these sorts of scenes anyway. So why had she?

It sat there, almost mocking her. She snatched the palette back up, selecting another brush before attacking the canvas as though going to battle. This time, after judging the changes and finding them more lacking than most, she set her supplies down, taking more care this time.

And with a pleasant smile, she punched her fist through the canvas.

Stepping back, she surveyed the destroyed piece with satisfaction. The canvas was wrecked now, much like the Ohio valley had been for months following the terrible storms. "Much better," she decided before snatching up her sketchbook and pencils.

* * * * *

Dale sat at the table, frowning over his hand. An untouched beer sat at his elbow, his second of the night. A lousy pair, he thought with good-natured disgust. Tossing his cards down, he leaned back in the chair. The good doctor was a card shark. As he listened to the ribbing about folding so easily, he considered the changes in his old living room. Painting was underway. What little furniture they had was mostly covered with plastic or drop cloths.

The old wooden table they played at was the only thing unprotected. Steven Young, the pediatrician transplanted from upstate New York, said the table was the only thing his new wife wasn't worried about being messed up. Alexandra, his wife, was an interior designer and was as happy as she could be about having a place of her own to work her wonders on.

His eyes skimmed over the room, trying to picture some of the things Alex had mentioned, but failing. He pushed back from the table as another of the five folded to Steve. "I'm going to call home real quick," he said, heading for the kitchen.

Behind him, someone hooted. "Checking in?"

Dale looked back over his shoulder and flashed a grin at the speaker. He couldn't remember his name for anything. "You ever seen my wife?" Dale asked, propping a shoulder against the doorway.

"Nope. Can't even stand the word. Chained down to one woman. There's so many out there. Big ones, small ones. So many tasty little cunts my dick wants to try out. Chained to just one? It's unthinkable," he announced, shuddering before taking another swig of beer.

"You wouldn't think so if you saw his lady," Mike Langley, Jennifer's husband, said, raising his beer in toast to Dale. "A more perfect woman you're unlikely to ever meet. Me, I prefer my little red headed hellcat. But I got eyes."

"She's got these long legs, y'know," Benjamin Tallant said, blowing out a cloud of cigar smoke as he leaned back on the hind legs of the chair. He was more than a little drunk, otherwise he wouldn't have dared to say anything about Lauren. At least, not with Dale around. "Long black hair, big gray eyes, white skin. Doesn't do that tanning bed shit. And, man, is she built. Big tits, tight ass. Hips you can actually grab hold of. I'd like to-"

His fantasies were cut off as Mike kicked the leg of the chair, sending the drunken comic strip artist crashing to the ground. "Oops," he said mildly.

Dale turned his back and walked away as another voiced an opinion. They didn't know the half of it, he thought with a wicked grin. He was tempted to leave the poker game, go home and find his long legged wife. But when she answered the phone with a curt, "Yes?" he decided against it. Obviously Lauren was still irritated with that painting and she wasn't exactly a ray of sunshine. *Of course, what else was new?* he mused, hanging up after she told him, "I'm busy. Get back to your beer drinking and card games and lying about us little women." Lauren was rarely a ray of sunshine.

He strolled back into the living room, envisioning what he wanted to do when he got done with his beer, cards, and lies. At the doorway, he froze. Long legs, wrapped around his hips, face buried against smooth pale skin. Instantly he went rock hard. At the same time, his stomach clenched with guilt.

There were times when he could still feel her coming around him, times when he could still taste her sweet cream in his mouth while he drank her down. But the flashes were chaotic, and brief. And completely unenlightening.

Who was she? The dreams still came, but never saw her face. He backpedaled out of the living room and stumbled onto the porch as the flashback played itself through.

It wasn't a flashback, though, not really. Just little snatches, smooth soft skin, legs gripping his hips as he pumped into a body tight, soft and wet with welcome. A lush mouth eating at his while he palmed a firm round bottom. A tight little pussy that had writhed and spasmed around his cock while he fucked her slowly, his hands holding her legs wide and open. An elusive, hauntingly familiar scent. He no longer thought it was a dream. It had happened. He had been with a woman that night, but who was she?

She had been so tight, so hot, and so fucking good, climaxing around him, screaming in his ear.

Who was she? And where had she gone?

Scrubbing his hands over his face, he thought of Lauren. Made himself think of her, of her soft sweet scent, her strong confident hands and long lush body.

But her image paled as his body remembered.

Dale drank his second beer, a third, a fourth, and lost count after that. Sometime after midnight, pockets empty, he headed home. He had drunk the damn witch out of his head, he thought with satisfaction. And now…now he'd find Lauren. With a laughing snort, he thought finding her might be a waste of time, in his current condition.

Then he saw her, just a glimpse of her as she walked past a doorway, and he knew it wasn't a waste. He was instantly so hard he was aching from it. His cock was as stiff as a pike underneath his jeans, like it had been ten or twelve years since he'd last had sex, instead of ten or twelve hours. He stumbled across the living room threshold, grinning stupidly as his bride of three weeks looked up from a charcoal sketch she was working on. The unfinished canvas stood by the window, a fist sized hole in it.

Good and drunk from beer and the whiskey the young doctor next door had so graciously provided after fleecing him out of his money, he snatched the sketch pad from her, heaved it over his shoulder before lifting her and planting a hard kiss on her frowning mouth. Her scowl melted away as he nibbled and licked his way down her throat. "Are we celebrating your winnings?" she asked with a laugh as he jerked her shirt open and ran knowing hands over her rounding body.

"Nope," he said, grinning down at her like a fool. "You're consoling me."

"Am I?" she queried, her arch tone ruined as she hummed with pleasure as he aligned her body with his.

"Yup," he replied, removing her shirt and unfastening her bra and flinging it aside. It landed on the canvas by the back door, hung there for a second before sliding to the floor. "Damn doc stole my money."

"Did he now?"

"Umm," he muttered, nipping at her shoulder before working his way further south. "And now I wanna fuck your brains out. I want you to suck on my cock again, with that pretty little mouth. I want to slide into that wet little pussy of yours and eat it up."

"In that order?" she asked, slightly breathless. The way he talked, the pictures he put in her head…She went wet just at the thought. "May be physically impossible."

Her belly was a high hard little mound. He dropped to his knees and kissed it before jerking her loose sweatpants down so she could step out of them. Catching her hips in his hands, he planted another kiss, this one open mouthed on the patch of hair at her thighs. With a grunt, he said, "So I'll eat you first. Then, you can suck me off. Then we can fuck each other's brain out." Her knees buckled and Dale supported her as he eased her back down on the couch, nuzzling her. He ran his thumb from the hard little nub all the way down, opening her. Already wet and aching for him, she arched her hips up.

He thrust his tongue deep, laving at her inner passage while his thumb and forefinger caught her clit and pinched it roughly. She shrieked and twisted under his hands. "Be still," he muttered, releasing her so he could grab her hands, her left in his left, her right in his right so that her arms were crossed over her belly. He held hard, kept her pelvis still while he hardened his tongue and stabbed repeatedly at her swollen clit. "I've never seen a woman so easy to please, so ready for me to fuck."

Her face flushed and she twisted, trying to pull free from his restraining hands. He growled, his face still buried between her thighs, and tightened his hold. She fell back docilely at the look in those eyes, something ancient and female and instinctive rising inside her. Something willing to be dominated.

He closed his teeth around her clitoris and pulled, suckling and pulling until she whimpered deep in her throat. Then he released it and laved at the abused flesh with his tongue. Bite, pull, suckle, over and over until she was shrieking his name and coming in his mouth.

"Bed," she panted, when she could breathe again.

Dale lifted her and took two steps toward the stairs before he muttered, "The hell with it." He braced her back against the wall as he fumbled with his jeans. The alcoholic haze had lifted a bit, washed away by the sudden heat, the sudden urge to mate with his wife. His woman. "Here. Right here."

"Right here," she murmured in agreement.

She thought he would take her hungrily, like he had that first time, and she craved it, craved knowing he wanted her so desperately. But he entered her gently, carefully. The part of her that yearned for his rough strength, his domination cried out in anger.

Buried inside her, sucking much needed air into his lungs, he held still and asked, "You okay?"

"No," she choked, closing around him like a vice, legs wrapped around him. "You're not doing anything."

"Sorry, ma'am," he said, grinning like a loon as he pulled back and surged slowly back into her. He covered her mobile mouth with his as he pumped into her. She closed around him, wet, hot. Her skin dewed with sweat as she strained against him. Her legs, those long silky legs locked around his hips, holding him tightly against her. His mouth swooped down, covering hers, taking her mouth in a deep, drugging kiss. He fought down the need to take her hard and fast, fought down the urge to swallow her whole.

"Harder, damn it," she hissed, wanting, for some inexplicable reason, to be under his control. "Harder and deeper."

His head was spinning; it was unlikely that it was the alcohol that was responsible. It was Lauren, the taste of her, the feel of her, the scent of her. Shifting, he rode her a little higher, deeper, until she started to clench around him.

"Dale-"

The smell of her flooded his head, tickling some buried memory, and he clenched his eyes closed as he remembered another woman whose smell had driven him insane while he fucked her. He heard her cry out his name and he shook his head, shoving the thoughts away. Opening his eyes, he concentrated on Lauren, on her flushed face, on the feel of her tight little sheath as he pumped his cock inside her, on the hard firm mound of her belly. Blindly, he took her mouth, plunging his tongue deep, hungrily. The taste of her, the scent...smooth soft skin. Long legs, a body, tight, soft and wet with welcome.

Dimly, Dale realized in some part of his mind that something odd was going on. But the thought flitted away, lost in the fog of need and liquor. She climaxed around him only seconds before he emptied himself into her.

Dale awoke the next morning to only the third real hangover of his life. The sunlight that poured into the room had him cursing viciously under his breath as he was jerked without ceremony into complete, and horrible, wakefulness. A thousand little soldiers marched in his head, his mouth tasted like something at the bottom of a garbage can, and his stomach felt worse than that.

Rolling over, he moaned into the pillow, wishing hopelessly for oblivion.

Most of the previous night was a hazy. The last clear thing he remembered was stumbling onto the porch, feeling sick with guilt for fantasizing, hell, craving another woman. Then he decided to drown those memories, those needs out of his head with booze.

The quiet sound in the doorway didn't even reach his ears. His wife listened sympathetically to his not quite muffled curses and moans before turning and leaving him in silence. She already had coffee, real coffee brewing, when the shower started a few minutes later.

She waited a few more minutes and popped some bread into the toaster and hunted down a bottle of aspirin.

The shower stopped ten minutes later. Ten minutes after that, Dale still hadn't appeared in the kitchen so she put the toast, coffee and aspirin on a tray and headed into his office. It was another converted spare room, this one facing the front of the house. The curtains had been jerked closed and Dale sat in the murky light, half dressed, with a scowl on his face.

"What?" he demanded irritably when she started into the room. The aftereffects of the alcohol were making him feel mean. Son of a bitch, it was half her fault he was like this. He wouldn't have gotten so damn drunk if he hadn't felt guilty just because he had been dreaming of another woman, of a night that happened long before they had gotten together. He decided that a good honest fight would help and went about picking one with the only person available.

"I brought some coffee," she said, brushing aside his curt question with ease. She held it out to him, but when he didn't take it, she set it on the desk with a sigh. "Want some aspirin?"

He did, desperately, and he wanted that coffee, too. Even the toast looked good. But damn it, he wanted that fight more. Petulantly, his mouth drawing into a sulky snarl, he reminded himself why he had gotten so fucking wasted the night before. Her fault. He'd felt guilty about fantasizing about another woman and had a few drinks. Hell, that was why he hadn't wanted to marry anybody; get married and suddenly a guy had to start checking perfectly natural thoughts.

Narrowing his eyes at her, he growled, "No. I don't want any damn aspirin and I don't want any damn coffee. Lemme the hell alone."

He watched, in anticipation, as her eyes darkened and narrowed, watched as her mouth firmed in a flat, angry line. "Being ugly isn't going to make you feel better, Dale," she said, her voice mild.

His eyes narrowed on her retreating back and a growl started deep in his throat. Being ugly might not help, but a good hard fuck would. Especially since she wasn't going to oblige him with a fight. He went after her, caught her in the guest bathroom and pinned her against the sink. "I wanna fuck you," he muttered gutturally. "That'll make me feel better."

Her eyes widened with surprise, and darkened with instant lust, but she said coolly, "I don't think I want you touching me."

"Liar," he rasped, his hands streaking under the high cut night shirt she wore, one hand plunging inside her body, inside the folds that had gotten wet the second he whirled her around and pinned her against the wall. "Your little cunt's dripping, baby." Dropping his gaze, he stared at the hard nipples that pressed against her nightshirt. "And look here," he purred roughly, lowering his head and biting at one erect nipple until she arched up against him with a strangled gasp.

Without giving her a chance to breathe, he dragged her to the floor, spread her thighs and shoved them high, lowering his head until he could drink down the musky cream, until he could nip and suckle at the hard swollen bud of her clitoris.

She rolled her hips, trying to pull away but his hands gripped her hips tightly, his fingers biting into her flesh. A low, hot little ball of lust was expanding in her belly but Lauren fought against it, snapping, "Damn it, you get the fuck off me."

Of course, if he did, she just might die…

"Hmm," he hummed under his breath, spearing her with his tongue, lapping at her greedily. "Can't. If I don't get the fuck in you, I'll go crazy." He slid two fingers inside her, his breath catching as she closed tightly around him.

She gasped and struggled against him, worming her way free and turning her back to him before she stood. Big mistake.

Dale caught her hips in his hands and lowered his head to kiss her ass as he used his greater weight to take her back down to the ground. Shoving her shirt to her waist, he used one hand to free his turgid cock from his jeans before he thrust into her even as she tried, not very hard, to squirm away from him. The puckered hole of her anus beckoned. He had enough sense not to try it right then, not to try to fuck her ass for the first time while she was pregnant, but damn it, he wanted it.

Lauren's entire system went on red alert as he thrust deeply inside her. The urgency she felt coming from him was affecting her, either that, or she was losing her mind, because she wasn't sure she had ever wanted anything more than to give him what was he asking for.

Asking, hell. He was demanding, and Lauren was dying to give it, dying to know he wanted her like this, that he needed her enough to forget that he was used to handling her almost gently. She gasped and cried out when she felt him dig back inside her again, his fingers holding her hips tight and still for his cock.

"Oh, hell," she muttered, planting her hands on the ground, bracing her weight as he rode her hard, forcing her hips lower, her thighs wider so he could take her harder. The urgency in his hands, the heat in his eyes filled her, overwhelmed her.

Even if it wasn't completely overwhelming him.

He was already slowing his thrusts, not taking her so deep, and his hands had started to stroke and caress instead of take and take. Even now, when he used his body to completely dominate hers, he seemed...careful. She wanted him hungry and desperate, careless and greedy.

Dale lifted one hand to his mouth and licked his fingers, until they were wet and dripping. Then he slid his finger inside her tight little anus, lids drooping when she shrieked and writhed and climaxed around him while his finger invaded her.

Even as the orgasm ripped through her body, she moved hungrily against him, seeking more. Dale pulled out, his cock leaving her completely, his finger still seated in her ass.

"Don't stop," she whimpered, squirming and lifting her ass for him, her body silently begging.

"You want me?" he asked roughly, groaning when her tight little hole clenched around him. God, he wanted his cock in there, inside the tight hot little hole that was growing damp for him.

"Yes," she hissed, tossing her hair and staring at him, craning her head, glaring at him with hot, lust filled eyes.

"Then beg me," he told her, wrapping his other hand around his dick and stroking. Dale was being a bastard and he knew it, but he couldn't stop. He had her so deep inside his soul that it was driving him insane. "Beg me, or I'll come all over your ass and leave you there hungry." He seemed to be giving up little pieces of himself to her every fucking day, losing himself inside her until it felt anathema to even remember touching another woman.

Her eyes narrowed and she said, "I can give myself an orgasm just easily as you can do it."

"But you don't want that," he told her, while his hand continued to stroke, while he imagined the ring of her anus opening for him, closing around him, squeezing his cock.

He wondered. He wanted her until he was willing to beg, willing to lose himself, just to have her. Was *it* the same for her? Dale wasn't sure. He had to see. Could he make cool, proud Lauren Stoner beg? "You want me to fuck you. Harder and deeper, remember?"

"Damn it, Dale," she rasped, staring at his hand as it squeezed and rubbed his cock, while his other hand stayed where it was, with his lone finger penetrating her body.

"Beg me," he ordered, releasing his cock to slap lightly at her ass.

She jumped, startled. And the words tumbled from her lips before she could stop. "Please fuck me, Dale," she panted, lifting her ass again, spreading her thighs for him. "Pleasefuckme, fuckme, fuckme,pleasepleaseplease."

He withdrew his invading finger, planted his hand on her back and urged her chest low to the floor, until her ass was high and waiting and begging. Then he took her hands, braceleting them in his before he drove his entire length inside her body.

Her hands were pinned and she couldn't move. And Dale rode her hard, sending her skidding across the cool tile floor until she was at the bathtub. He pulled her torso up with his hold on her wrists, up until she was crouched over the rim of the bathtub. She whimpered and strained, unable to move, needing to, wildly excited at being imprisoned.

"Come for me," he ordered, releasing his hold on her hip so he could smack her butt again. "Now." He spied something from the corner of his eye, the belt to her robe. Snagging it, he wrapped it around her wrists, tying her hands behind her back. He went slowly, waiting for her to object, but she didn't. Dale wondered just how far he could take this, just how far Lauren was willing to let him dominate her. She started to shudder around him, her silken pussy gripping him even more tightly. Lowering himself until he could whisper in her ear, "This has you fucked up, too, doesn't it? You've got me so twisted up inside that it's making me crazy."

"I just figured it out, though. It's doing the same to you, isn't it, baby?" he asked as he started to rock inside her. "You'd give me anything I asked for, wouldn't you?"

She moaned and twisted underneath him before her heavy lidded eyes opened and met his. "So far, you haven't asked for anything," she drawled, her voice low and raspy.

He laughed shakily and rose up. "No, I guess not. And I think . . .oh, damn it, do that again," he rasped when she contracted her muscles slowly and deliberately, holding his cock deep inside her in a silken trap. "I think maybe that's what I've been missing. You, Lauren, aren't the kind to take orders. But..."

She was taking them, willingly and with pleasure.

Helplessly, she rocked back as far as she could and whimpered, "Will you please stop talking and just take me?"

He sank his fingers into the soft smooth skin of her hips, sank his cock into her wet swollen pussy and barked, "Come!" Then he rode her hard, pulling a climax from her bound body, and a second before she had even had time to catch her breath.

"Such a good little fuck," he muttered, his hips pumping against her ass as he came inside her in wet pulsing jets, his strokes slowing only slightly. Smoothing his hands down the orbs of her ass, he lowered his body until it cupped hers, until he could murmur in her ear while he continued to ride her. "Aww, Lauren," he whispered. "I love you, baby. I love being inside you, love the taste of you, the smell, the feel."

A whimper fell from her lips as he pushed back inside her slowly, his cock hard and hot, thick, filling her so unbelievably full.

His thrusts were lazy and slow, his hands gentle and soothing. Her hands were still bound. Her torso was pressed hard against the cool tile of the bathtub, biting into her flesh. Dale wrapped his arms around her lifting her upright, supported her body, one hand stroking caressingly over her belly while the other sought out her breasts, rolling and tweaking her nipples gently while he rocked slowly inside her.

She bore down on him for the final time, the climax flooding her body like a tidal wave. Dale cried out when he came, flooding her welcoming body again.

When he pulled out, he gathered her into his lap, undoing the knot in the belt so that her hands were free. And they came up to stroke and hug his neck. He closed his eyes and viciously kicked himself mentally, cursing his guilt and the need that drove him.

"I'm sorry," he whispered roughly. "I woke up feeling mean. I shouldn't be taking it out on you."

Still a little dazed, her head fell back against his arm so she could stare up at him. "Were you trying to pick a fight?"

"Yeah. Why wouldn't you cooperate?"

She chuckled, sighing as his mouth found her neck. "Sorry, Dale. I didn't realize that an argument was a cure for a hangover."

"Actually, I was looking forward to make up sex," he admitted.

"You should have said so sooner," she said, a smile curving her mouth upward. "So you decided to skip the fight and go straight to the sex, huh?"

He chuckled, feeling like the top of his head had come straight off.

She smiled sleepily against his chest. "Dale?"

"Hmm?"

"Why don't you take those aspirin?"

" 'Kay," he muttered, his eyes drooping.

"And then let's go back to bed."

His eyes flew open at that. "Are you suggesting we spend the day in bed?"

"Why not?" she asked, tipping her head back to meet his eyes. A smile came and went as she brushed her hand across his cheek. "You haven't started anything that needs work. And I can't paint a damn thing lately any way."

"Why not?" he repeated, the idea very appealing.

It was even more appealing a short time later when the clouds opened up and rain came in a steady down pour. Dale lay propped against the headboard, Lauren between his legs, curled against his chest. He stroked the tight smooth skin of her belly, marveling at the feel of it. A tiny fist bumped his hand and he grinned. "What's it feel like?"

"Hmm?" Lauren asked, drowsily. Her eyes opened half way, flying all the way open when steady pressure was applied in her pelvic area. "Good grief," she muttered, sitting up as the pressure increased.

"What's wrong?" he demanded.

She laughed, pressing a hand to her belly. "It feels like the baby is trying to push its way out," she answered.

"What?" he half shouted, jerking up from his relaxed slouch so suddenly, he dislodged Lauren.

After resettling her body, she patted his shoulder. "Don't worry. Dr. Flynn was saying I might start feeling something like this. It's just the baby getting ready."

"For what? You've got two months left." His eyes were wide and panicked in the dim light and he looked slightly gray.

She laughed and rolled to her knees, wrapping her arms around him before she said, "Think of it like the Olympics. They train for weeks and months and years ahead of time. The baby's got to train, too."

"I think we should go to the hospital," he muttered, ignoring her words as he swung his legs over the edge of the bed. He glanced down at himself and snagged his jeans, tugging them up over bare skin. Before he could button them, slimmer, paler hands covered his.

"Calm down, Dale," she told him, laughter lurking in her voice. "I'm fine. Forget I said anything." She wrapped her arms around him from behind, hugging herself to his naked back.

Queasy, Dale asked, "Is it too late to rethink this baby thing? Isn't there another way?"

Thinking of her swollen belly, Lauren laughed and said, "I think it's definitely too late to rethink anything." Then she sobered. "Dale, you're not rethinking, or regretting, this, are you?" she asked, her voice soft, uncertain.

He turned around and caught her up against him. "No. No," he repeated. Holding her tightly against him, he whispered, "This is the best thing that ever happened to me. You are the best thing that ever happened to me." Leaning back he studied her gray eyes, seeing the doubt there. Lowering his head, he brushed her mouth with his. "I love you, Lauren Stoner. And this has been the most amazing few months of my life."

With gentle, knowing hands, he caressed the bulge of her belly, delighting at the feel of the life within. No. He wasn't rethinking this.

And the only thing he regretted was not being the one who helped create the baby.

Chapter Six

Lauren awoke, achingly aroused, to the feel of Dale's hands on her body. His mouth was at her breast, feasting on her sensitive nipple while his greedy hands roamed the curves and contours of her body. He shaped the firm flesh beneath his hands, molding and stroking. His eyes were closed and his movements were hard, greedy, demanding. The way they had been that very first time.

They hadn't been like that since. Always so careful, so…gentle. Well, maybe gentle wasn't exactly the right word. But even the previous morning, when he had been so forceful, so demanding, he had taken care, care not to do anything he wasn't sure she was willing to do.

Right now, he didn't care.

Finally.

His big, hard hands buried in her hair and forced her head down, until she was on a level with his cock. Then he used his fingers to slip past her lips, until her mouth opened. Before she could pull away, he thrust his cock halfway down her throat before pulling back, urging her mouth into a steady rhythm, while he freed one hand from her hair and used it on the base of his cock. She quivered and jumped when he came inside her mouth, thick pulsing jets of come sliding down her throat.

And then she was flipped, rather carelessly, onto her back.

A throaty moan broke the silence when his free hand found her center, cupping her in his hand. His mouth cruised up her neck to hers and he took it at the same time he parted her flesh and plunged his fingers deep inside her body. Her short nails dug into his shoulders and she whimpered when he nipped at her lip before working his way back down her body.

"Oh, please," she whispered, as he dallied at the circle of her navel, pressed a kiss to the crease between thigh and groin. Hot hands cupped her bottom and lifted her up. Hot breath blew across her sensitized flesh and Lauren cried out when Dale pressed his face to her, drinking from her body as she climaxed quickly under the skill of his mouth.

Her breath was still caught in her chest when he moved, covered her quickly. His hands parted her legs, wrapped them around his waist and before she had time to come back down, he buried himself inside her body, buried his cock all the way down to his balls. Each hard, near brutal thrust shoved her closer and closer to orgasm. A second climax tore through her and she screamed, her flesh rippling and flexing around him.

Even as he put his hands on her, he knew he was dreaming. Like every other time, he would bury himself in her body and then, he would wake up, in bed beside his sleeping wife, sweaty and achy and needy. The need was a slippery, greasy thing that ate a hole in his gut every time he did this.

He didn't know her name, didn't even know her face. He only knew that this was the woman he wanted like no other, save for Lauren. And there were times when his obsession for her, whoever she was, paralleled his need for his wife. He knew when he woke, he would feel guilty, but for now…

Her throaty sigh caressed his ears as he learned her body by touch. Long slender legs, narrow feet with elegant high arches. Graceful wrists, fine boned hands and slender, tapered fingers. Was her waist thicker? Her breasts fuller? Her taste, her scent, was the same, innocence and musk.

He fought the urge to cover her and take her, knowing the moment he did, he'd wake up and the dream would end. Silky hair brushed against his skin and he caught it in his hands, pinning her thrashing head to the pillow, taking her mouth with his. He nipped and suckled at a full lower lip, dipped inside a sweetly moving mouth before pulling back.

He rolled onto his back, taking handfuls of the silky, thick hair and urging her down to suck on his cock. When her mouth closed around him, he shuddered and bucked, a climax ripping its way through his body in one quick, startling flash as she took him deep inside her mouth. He flooded the small tight caverns of her throat and mouth before pushing her away, and onto her back.

He moved to her mouth, pressing soft gentle kisses, then rough biting ones against her sweating flesh as he shifted and moved until he could lie between her thighs. He ate her wet pussy, licking and biting and thrusting his tongue as deep inside her as he could, lapping more and more of her tasty cream as he started to fuck her with his fingers, working her closer and closer to climax.

It burst from her with a gush, soaking his face and hands, while he suckled and probed inside her body.

Ravenous, needy, he moved, spreading her legs, piercing her. Her tight, wet vagina closed around him, like a hot silky fist. She convulsed around his flesh even as he buried himself to the hilt. A dream, he thought. How can a dream feel so real?

He wanted to see her face, wanted it so badly, he would have paid nearly any price.

A thin cry rent the air.

And Dale was jerked into complete and total awareness. He was atop a very familiar, very sexy woman, her legs wrapped around his waist, her hair wrapped around his hands. He could feel the swell of her belly against his and instinctively lifted his weight off her. At the same time, his demanding hands gentled. "Lauren?" he muttered even as he thrust deep inside her.

Beneath him, her eyes closed, face sheened with the sweat of good, hard sex. Lauren arched her hips up to meet his as she came. She was drifting back down to reality when his words echoed in her ears.

"…what?"

He shook his head, as if to clear it, then he groaned as the tiny silken muscles in her body caressed the length of him. Hot little tendrils were spreading out from the base of his spine and then before he realized it, his own climax was upon him. Regardless of the firm mound of her belly, he reared back and slammed into her, pumping his hips, working her against him with demanding hands. He came in an explosive rush, riding it with closed eyes, holding her hips tightly against his.

Moments later, Lauren shoved at his chest. Weakly, totally lost, he rolled from her body and lay staring at the ceiling. The bed shifted beside him and moments later, light filled the room. Lauren was standing by the door, tugging a discarded tee shirt over her head. Then she folded her arms over her chest and stared at him.

"Who were you dreaming about?" she asked, her voice quiet and calm. Her heart was breaking inside her.

"What?" Dale asked, his mind still foggy, the blood still pounding in his temples.

The sweet, heady delight of knowing how much he wanted her, needed her had disappeared and in its place was sickness and pain. He hadn't been making love to her, to Lauren. He'd been dreaming of, making love, to another woman. It hadn't been her he had urged down on him, hadn't been her who had torn a vicious glorious climax from him almost the moment her mouth closed over the head of his cock. Hadn't been her body he had filled with one hard thrust that had set her body to quaking.

"Who was she, Dale?" Lauren asked, unable to keep the quiver from her voice this time.

"I don't know what you're talking about," he muttered, but he averted his eyes as he swung his legs over the edge of the bed.

"No? Why were you surprised when you opened your eyes and saw me?"

"I was asleep, Lauren," he answered edgily. "I wake up, pounding myself into you like there was no tomorrow. And you're pregnant."

"Yes. I'm pregnant. Of course, that didn't stop you from tying me up and fucking my brains out yesterday, did it? Of course, you were in complete control then. I wake up with you touching me, like there was no tomorrow, and you were dreaming of another woman.

Totally out of control. Why can't you touch me like that? Who was she?" she demanded, her voice rising.

"I don't know."

"Oh, please." Lauren rolled her eyes. Then those cloudy gray eyes met his, turbulent and dark with pain. "I already know it wasn't me. Knowing who it was isn't going to hurt, now is it?"

"I said, I don't know, Lauren." And he didn't. And guiltily, he knew that he desperately needed to know who it had been. He was obsessed with knowing who she was. Again, feeling ill with the guilt, he turned his head away from his wife, away from the hurt he saw in her beautiful eyes. He stood and pulled his discarded jeans on, then turned to look out the window.

Lauren pressed the back of her hand to her mouth, fighting to hold back the tears that came so easily. "Your precious Nicole, I imagine," she finally said, her voice acid. "Looks like I became one of your little airheads, after all. How many times have you put her face on my body while you were inside me?"

Not Nicole's face. There was no face to go with these images of the woman. But he had closed his eyes before, imagining that his tender love making to Lauren was the hard, fast greedy sex he had with his obsession. Dale certainly couldn't tell her that. If she was this hurt over thinking it was Nicole, how hurt would she be to realize he had been dreaming, fantasizing, over a woman he had been with only once?

A woman, who if she came up to him now, he wasn't certain he could turn away.

So he remained silent, his gut churning with self-disgust.

Lauren read his guilt, in the slump of his shoulders, his refusal to meet her eyes. "So this isn't the first time," she said softly, a tear trickling down her cheek. "I'm such a fool. I actually thought you loved me."

At the despair he heard in her voice, he turned. "God, Lauren. Don't, please, don't." He crossed to her and wrapped his arms around her rigid body. "I love you more than life itself."

Her bitter laugh tore at his heart. "Sure you do. That's why you're dreaming of another woman."

"It has nothing to do with you," Dale insisted. Catching her face in his hands, he forced her to look at him. Her gray eyes were wet with tears and her wide mouth was trembling. "I'm sorry."

"Nothing to do with me," she repeated. Jerking her face from his hands, she stepped back. "Nothing to do with me. Well, you got one out of two right. You are a sorry ass bastard, but it has everything to do with me."

"I've loved you for years," she said passionately, backing away from him. "And you were too damn blind to see it, too damn blind to see I was the one you needed. You mooned over that stupid brainless fool who let her man run around on her and chose him, a faithless jerk, over you. He knocked up some stupid woman and married her, but when he came crawling, Nikki took him back, the spineless, foolish little bitch. What a woman, Dale. And now you're dreaming of her, and it doesn't concern me?"

He opened his mouth to tell her it wasn't Nicole, but he stopped himself. At least she knew about Nicole. She knew nothing of this other woman, when it had happened, where. Only weeks before he had realized he loved Lauren. Better the devil you know.

"What does she have that I don't? What makes her so damn special? She's a writer, but big deal. She probably couldn't draw a stick figure to save her life. I'd think she had a better body than I do, but I've seen pictures of her. She a scrawny little whey faced brat of a woman with the brains of a goat." She paced the width of the bedroom, tears streaming down her cheeks, hands clenched into fists at her sides. She whirled to face him, her hair whipping around, falling in a glorious tangle around her shoulders. "What does she have, Dale, that keeps you from wanting me like you want her?"

"I've never wanted Nikki the way I want you. I never loved her the way I love you," Dale said, jamming his hands in his pockets to keep from reaching for her. There was only one woman he had ever wanted the way he wanted Lauren. And he didn't know her damned name.

"Then why haven't you ever made love to me like that? Like you'd die if you couldn't have me?" she asked, her voice breaking, tears streaking down her cheeks. "Today was the first time..." her voice trailed off before she could say, since the night you got me pregnant. "Why don't you want me that way?"

"Lauren, you're pregnant. I don't want to hurt you-"

She cut him off with one icy glare. "Pregnant doesn't mean fragile, Dale. And you weren't exactly handling me with kid gloves when you fucked me senseless yesterday, huh? If that hasn't gotten it through your head that I can take it, then nothing will."

"Yesterday shouldn't have happened the way it did," Dale said stiffly, closing his eyes and remembering, with mingled self-disgust and a satisfaction that was mind-boggling. "I never should have done that."

She absently wiped a hot tear away as it streaked down her cheek, staring at him with hollow eyes. "Shouldn't have happened," she repeated. It had been exhilarating, mind shattering, and wonderful beyond words for her. And he didn't think it should have happened. "Well, it did. And you know I'm fine. The baby is fine. Get it through your head, pregnancy doesn't mean the same thing as fragility. But apparently it does mean stupid. Otherwise, I'd have realized I was your substitute."

Angrily, jealously, Dale snapped, "Well, if you've loved me for years, as you keep telling me, why in the hell are you pregnant with another man's kid? Why were you sleeping with another man while you were pining for me?"

"Because I wanted it. I've got needs, too, Dale. I got pregnant getting those needs met." *I got pregnant because I needed you too much to care that you just wanted a woman, any woman. I got pregnant because I had to be with you, even if it was only that one time.* But she'd be damned if she would tell him that now. Mournfully, she stared at him. He didn't love her after all. How could she have been so wrong?

"I'd have been happy to take care of those needs, Lauren. I would have been more than happy to give you a quick fuck. All you had to do was ask. Why in the hell didn't you ever tell me how you felt?" If she had, maybe he would have been the one to plant that child inside her. Maybe he wouldn't be dreaming of wild jungle sex with a woman he could never have.

"And have you feel sorry for me? Make love with me out of pity? I've got some pride, Dale. And you're walking all over it."

"Pride? You spent the night screwing some bastard who doesn't love you, because you're horny and ended up pregnant. Where was your pride then? Where was your pride when he didn't care enough to live up to his responsibility?"

"This baby isn't a responsibility, Dale. And you and I apparently have different ideas of what pride is. I had too much pride to go crawling to the man who seduced me, and cry, 'I'm pregnant. Help me.'" Lauren could have kicked herself, but the words had already left her mouth.

"Seduced you." Livid, Dale advanced on her, caught her arms in his hands, his grip gentle, but unbreakable. "Seduced you. One might see that as saying he took advantage of you, used you. Who was he, Lauren?" Who in the hell had seduced his woman, the other half of him?

Lauren saw the anger, the rage in his eyes, not knowing he was angry at himself, for not knowing, not seeing how much she meant to him in time to keep some Don Juan from using her and tossing her aside. "I tried to tell you once before. And you didn't want to know. That was your only chance," she said coldly.

"Who is he, Lauren?" Dale shouted. He had never been so angry, so furious. Who in the hell had touched her and turned his back on her? Who had hurt her that way? And it had hurt her, he knew it. Deep down inside, he sensed the pain she was holding in check.

"Go to hell," she whispered raggedly, trying to twist away from him.

Slowly, he let go of her arms. "You're not going to tell me?"

She shook her head, crossing her arms over her chest and giving him an icy look from cold, gray eyes.

He stepped back and without a word left the room.

Lauren sank to the floor slowly, listening as the shower down the hall started. "I'm sorry, Dale," she whispered, her own guilt rising, overshadowing the hurt.

* * * * *

Lauren woke hours later, after losing herself in sleep. Dale hadn't spoken a single word to her all night. It was early, before dawn, and the house was eerily silent. She knew, without even looking, he wasn't there.

She found the note on the kitchen table.

Gone to New York. I'll be back later in the week.

When I get back, you're telling me who he is. Or I'll find out myself.

You don't want me finding him on my own, Lauren.

He hadn't signed it, hadn't written I love you.

"Look in the mirror, Dale," she whispered, letting the note fall to the floor.

* * * * *

Later that day, Steve Young knocked on her door. "Dale called me earlier. He wants me to check in on you while he's gone," he said after following Lauren inside. "Feeling okay?"

"Yes." Arching a brow at him, she asked, "Isn't pediatrics your specialty?"

"That's what I told Dale. But when there's doctor next door, might as well take advantage of it," he said, eyeing her color. She was a little pale. He took her wrist, reassured at the strong steady pulse. "Just don't go into labor on me. I prefer taking care of them after they enter the world. Not while they're doing it."

Lauren smiled automatically, relieved when he let go of her hand.

"You're certain you feel okay? You look pale."

"Dale and I had a fight before he left." She shrugged, like it was no big deal, and played it down. "Nothing important, but it kind of wore me out."

Steve frowned. Nothing important. Dale hadn't mentioned this trip before; he hadn't known about it until Dale had called him from New York to ask if he'd check on Lauren while he was gone. "Is that why he left?"

"Of course not," Lauren replied, the lie rolling easily from her tongue. "He had something come up that he needed to take care of."

Steve left some time later, after watching her, making sure she was all right. She was as calm and as composed as she always was, distantly friendly, slightly aloof. He imagined that aloofness drove men crazy. If he didn't desperately love his wife . . .

He certainly wouldn't have left his pregnant wife alone, even with a doctor next door.

But then again, Alex didn't have the demeanor that Lauren had. She didn't have the calm look in her eyes that told the world, *I can handle anything you throw at me, and more.*

If any woman would be okay alone for a few days, pregnant or not, it was Lauren.

* * * * *

Lauren wasn't okay.

Her back was aching, her head hurt, and her heart felt as though it were bleeding. She was so confused. He said he loved her. It felt like he loved her. But he had been dreaming of another woman.

"That's just a man for you, sweetie," Jenny said over the phone later that night. "Their brains are controlled by their gonads. I know it hurt, but it doesn't mean he doesn't love you."

"It doesn't mean he does love me either," she said, pouting. She felt terrible, so completely unlike herself. But she didn't say anything to Jenny. She wanted to talk, not cry on her friend's shoulder.

She wanted to cry on Dale's shoulder. She wanted Dale.

"Lauren, I've seen how he looks at you. He does love you. He's crazy about you."

"You think so?" Lauren asked tearfully.

"I know so. Shoot, even Mike noticed. He said something the other night about how Dale's eyes got all glazed when he was talking about you, he was practically drooling just thinking about you. It was just a dream, Lauren. Dreams don't have to mean anything."

When she hung up a little later, she felt a little better.

After a warm bath and book, she settled into bed to sleep the night away. Dale was coming home day after next. The sooner the night passed, the sooner he'd be home.

She awoke in the gray hours before dawn, confused. The linens were wet.

Embarrassed, her first thought was that she had wet the bed. But when she flicked on the bedside light, she saw the sheet was streaked with blood. As though in a dream, she reached for the phone and called 911. She tried to get up, listening to the soothing voice of the dispatcher, but she could hardly move, for some odd reason, and getting out of bed was impossible.

The good doctor, who had checked on her shortly after nine, had been called to the hospital himself and missed the ambulance. His wife was out of town on business, so nobody saw as emergency workers were forced to break down the door to get in.

Distantly, as though she were watching it happen to somebody else, she felt her belly tighten, saw it happen, but it didn't hurt her, didn't disturb her.

Lauren had thought she would get through the whole thing without feeling any pain at all. But, half way to the hospital, pain ripped through her belly like fire, a startled cry bursting from her lips. Her labor had started and she was six weeks early and completely alone.

By the time she arrived at the hospital the pain wrenching through her was unbelievable. She had known it would hurt, had told herself she was prepared for it. It tore through her abdomen, ripped at her, and she cried out against it, arching her back, biting her dry lips. She had told herself that she could handle it.

Man, had she been wrong.

Another spasm gripped her, held her in its painful grasp. A nurse at her side spoke soothingly, telling her to keep breathing, yes, that's good. Good, keep breathing. Distantly, she heard the doctor tell her not to push, not yet.

Hell, she wasn't supposed to be pushing for over a month.

They had tried to stop the labor, but the baby wasn't listening. He or she was ready to come now.

But I'm not ready, Lauren thought hysterically.

Oh, God, she prayed. God, where is Dale? Why isn't he here?

But there was no answer, and Lauren hadn't really expected one.

God only helped those who helped themselves.

A familiar voice echoed outside the door and Lauren rolled her eyes in that direction.

"By God, her husband isn't here and she doesn't have any family. She shouldn't be alone!"

"Jenny..."

Just as she spoke, the slim redhead burst through the door and flew across the room. "Oh, honey," Jennifer murmured, hugging her tightly. "Lauren, honey, are you okay?"

"The baby, Jenny, it's too early-" her words were cut off with a gasp as another contraction seized her. "Dale!"

"Ma'am, you will have to wait outside."

"She's got a right to have someone with her," Jenny snapped, tossing an icy glare at the nurse.

"If this were a normal birth, yes. But-"

"But nothing," Jennifer interrupted. Vicious green eyes latched onto the nurse who had spoken. "I will not wait outside," she enunciated. "I am staying right here, damn it, until either she tells me to go or her husband gets here."

Dale…

Lauren grasped Jennifer's hand as the pain receded. "Stay, Jenny. Please, stay. Don't leave me alone." The nurse was reaching for the phone to call security when Lauren whispered pleadingly, "I don't want to be alone." Her hand hovered over the phone, then dropped. *What could it hurt?* she wondered. With that thought, she left the room.

"You won't be, Lauren. I'll be right here, honey. Right here," she promised, stroking her forehead. "I swear, I'll be right here."

"They tried to stop it," she whispered, exhausted, needing to talk. She was so scared. And she wanted Dale. "Dale's not here."

"Mike's at your house waiting for him."

"…Not there. New York," she murmured, slipping into sleep.

Finally, some of the medicine they were pouring into her veins was taking effect. The painkiller dulled the pain enough that she could rest a bit, but even in her exhaustion, she ached for Dale. "He's gone, Jenn. He left me. Left me. Why does everybody always leave me?"

* * * * *

Dale answered the phone wearily. It wasn't even dawn. The digital clock read three thirty two. A clerk murmured an apology before saying, "There's a Dr. Young on the phone. He says it's an emergency." The bone deep weariness that had plagued him all day was gone, replaced by pure panic as he waited for the connection.

An agitated Steve came on the phone. "You've got to get home, Dale. She's here at the hospital. I was called in to check on a patient in the ICU when she got here. She's in labor."

His hand closed convulsively over the handset. Quietly, shaken, Dale said, "That can't be, Steve. She's not due for six more weeks. She can't be in labor. It's too early."

"I'm sorry, Dale. But that baby is coming now. I've called the airlines. You have a seat on the red eye. Gate 82. It leaves in less than an hour. Mike will meet you-"

The rest of Steve's words went unheard. Dale had already thrown down the phone. Labor. She was in labor. And she was alone.

The next few hours took days. The short flight stretched on endlessly. Dale was out of his seat even before the flight attendant could speak. "Sir, you need to return to your seat-"

"My wife's in labor, damn it," he snapped, pushing past her to wait for the door to open.

He was in the terminal only seconds after the walkway was opened. He took the moving sidewalk in a loping run, ignoring the security officer that called after him and started chasing him.

He saw Mike pacing just beyond the security barrier and caught him by the lapels of his coat. "How is she?" he demanded roughly. "What's going on?"

The sun was just barely touching the horizon, and the security officer saw panic in the eyes of the man he had been chasing. "Is there a problem here?"

Turning wide panicked eyes to the security guard, he said, "It's too early."

Confused, the officer looked at Mike. "His wife's gone into premature labor, officer. She's not due for almost two months."

"I'll get you a police escort," he said, turning away. He had a wife and a daughter of his own. And a son who had died because he had come too soon.

"It's too early," he whispered numbly as Mike followed the wailing sirens. Red and blue lights flashed across his face, but he didn't even notice. His terror stricken mind was imagining Lauren, the pain she was in, the fear she felt. She was alone.

He had left her alone.

"What in the hell were you thinking, running off to New York with your wife pregnant?" Mike burst out, unable to stop himself. His friendly, affable face was cold and ruddy with anger.

"She's not due until February," he said numbly. He frowned when Mike took the exit for the downtown hospitals. "What are we doing here? She's having the baby at Floyd."

"Sorry, pal. She's having it in Louisville. They have to be close to the NICU at Kosair," Mike replied. "They flew her over right after the doctor finished examining her at Floyd. Steve tried to tell you that but you had already hung up."

"NICU?" Dale repeated, numb, confused.

"Neonatal intensive care unit."

"Something's wrong with the baby?" His hands fisted uselessly on his jean clad thighs. His eyes, blind with panic, turned to Mike.

"Easy, Dale. They don't know. The baby's early, not due yet. Its lungs may not be fully matured," Mike explained. "They just want to be closer to the children's hospital if the baby needs treatment."

"Why would the baby need treatment? Why would they think it might?" He reached across the seat, clutching at Mike's coat as he slowed, then stopped, in front of the hospital.

Taking a deep breath, Mike calmly said, "Listen to me, Dale. We need to get inside. Lauren needs you. She should be okay, both she and the baby. But the baby is premature. It may not be able to breathe on its own. The lungs are one of the final things to develop. They need to have access to people who can help if they need it. They won't take any chances."

"And...and the baby is breech. It hasn't turned fully, yet. Lauren needs better than what Floyd has. The doctors wanted her at Nortons, with better access to specialists, and they need the baby near Kosair."

"Breech," he repeated, his voice almost soundless.

Breech.

He knew what that word meant.

If they couldn't turn the baby, both she and the baby could die.

I shouldn't have left her, Dale thought bitterly as they took the stairs to the labor and delivery floor. I never should have left her. "They're certain she's in labor?" he finally asked as they burst through the stairwell door.

"Yeah. She may have already had it by now. Jenny hasn't called in nearly an hour." His hand went reflexively to the cell phone at his belt, as if touching it would bring a call to let them know everything was fine, it hadn't been labor after all.

"Why don't they stop it? They can stop labor, right?" he asked, hopefully, desperately. It was too early.

"No. They can't stop it, Dale. I know one of the nurses who works the floor. She broke several federal regulations, but Grace told me that Lauren's water broke and her blood pressure's skyrocketing. If it was just the blood pressure, they could deal with it. But once the water breaks, the baby has to be delivered. They have to get the baby to turn, and then deliver it. If Lauren doesn't have the baby soon, they'll have to do a cesarean."

"Cesarean? Like cut the baby out?" he asked faintly. Lauren, under a knife, on a surgical table? Fuck, he could lose them both. Why did it sound so much safer *outside* the hospital?

Dale was starting to feel queasy.

"That's generally how it's done," Mike drawled, rolling his eyes. Then he caught a good look at Dale's white, panicked face and he sighed. "They have to take the baby, Dale. They've got no choice."

Her water had broken. Breech. High blood pressure. Cesarean.

Dale pressed his fisted hands against his eyes. "Do they know why she's gone into labor?" he asked, voice rusty. Had he done it? The bathroom. His eyes closed and he remembered how he had fucked her on the floor, with her hands bound. And then again that night, dreaming of some woman who didn't really matter, not compared to how much he loved Lauren. And then, after fucking her like a wild animal, he up and left, leaving her alone and pregnant and, oh, shit, this was all his fault.

"Nobody knows why women go into labor early. There probably isn't a reason," Mike replied as they took the long hallway in ground eating strides.

Dale's response to this was a self-directed curse. Mike had to murmur agreement.

He slowed then, stopping before a closed door. Behind it, they heard Lauren cry out. Dale was ready to lunge into the room but before he could, Mike barred the doorway. "I know you two had a fight, Dale. I'm not saying this is your fault, but, man, you shouldn't have left her."

"Get out of my way," Dale ordered, shoving against the body barring his way.

"Not until you calm down," Mike told him, shoving back. "Damn it, I know what I'm talking about. She can't see you upset like this. Whether or not you two fighting had anything to do with this doesn't matter now. She matters. Now calm down. Seeing you like this will do her more harm than good."

"Back off!"

"Calm down," Mike said, his sturdy boxer's frame going tense and ready. "I know what I'm talking about. You have got to calm down."

Dale reared back, ready to toss the shorter man aside when the Mike grabbed his jacket, pivoted and slammed him into the wall. Dale's head cracked against the wall and his vision swam dizzily for a brief second. "Now listen to me, you stupid son of a bitch. Your wife is in there, scared to death and hurting. Are you going to be there for her? Or act even more stupidly than you already have and scare her even more?"

Dale stared into the calm hazel eyes of his friend, seeing his own panicked reflection there. Up until he started dating Lauren, he'd spoken to the quirky, stocky nurse on a rare basis. Since then, he had become a good, close friend, one he trusted. One he could count on.

Staring into those glaring, angry eyes, he shuddered and fell back against the wall, the anger draining out of his body. No place for it, not here. Not now. Forcing a calming breath deep into his lungs, he held it briefly, letting it out in a shuddering sigh. He scrubbed his hands across his gritty eyes and nodded. "I'm okay, Mike. I need to see my wife."

* * * * *

I should have told him, Lauren thought as another contraction tightened her stomach. She could feel it more this time and knew the medicine was wearing off. The nurse had told her it wouldn't be long now. They had finally gotten the baby turned, and now they were waiting for her to finish the delivery.

Jenny brushed her hair back from her face. "I should have told him," Lauren said aloud.

"Yes, you should have. But this isn't your fault," Jenny said quietly.

Yes, it is, Lauren thought sadly. *It is. All my fault.*

But that didn't mean Dale and the baby should have to pay for it.

Four minutes went by and another contraction had her arching her back against it. "Felt that one," she muttered, panting to catch her breath. "Dale..." she whispered mournfully, closing her eyes against the emotion and pain that arced through her. When the contraction ended, she sagged back against the pillow, whispered for ice and zoned out.

Exhausted, she barely flinched when the door flew open, crashing into the wall. Nurses rose, issuing orders that weren't heeded, requests to be quiet and careful, demands on the intruder's identity.

Dimly, she heard Jenny snap, "It's about damn time. Where in the…"

Time lost all meaning again as another contraction seized her. A hand closed around hers, but she didn't marvel at how Jennifer could hold both hands at the same time from one side of the bed. She rose into a half seated position, panting, grasping at the hands that held hers as though it was all that kept her from being ripped in two. When it finally eased, she closed her eyes and escaped temporarily into oblivion.

Impersonal efficient hands were pressing, poking and prodding, taking measurements and making notes. Her eyes opened blearily and she looked around, confused. First, she saw the nurse who was between her upraised legs. "Nine inches, Lauren. Full effacement. It's just about time." Then her head rolled to the side as Dr. Flynn entered the room. Something like disapproval flashed in her normally placid eyes before she became all beaming smiles. "Everything will be fine, Lauren. You're young and healthy…" the platitudes rolled off the doctor's tongue without Lauren hearing them.

Jennifer sat at her left hand, smiling shakily and gripping her hand tightly. Her mouth moved but what she said, Lauren didn't know.

Finally, she rolled her head the other way. Cheek resting on the pillow, her eyes met deep pools of blue, full of sorrow and panic. The last time she had seen them, they had held only anger. "Dale," she whispered, reaching out. "You're here…"

Dale entered the room, afraid of what he might find, schooling his features as best he could.

What he saw was something from a man's worst nightmare. Lauren was on a table with her legs propped up, feet in stirrups. She was naked from the waist down, a hospital gown rucked up around her waist. Her eyes were closed and her face was pale, deathly pale. Her mouth was open as she breathed rapidly, shallowly. Her belly, that tight hard little mound that was nowhere near the size it should be, was much lower than it had been when he had left only two days earlier.

There was blood. He jerked his eyes from below her waist, away from that red fluid that smeared her thighs as he rushed to her side, taking her hand. He met Jennifer's stony glare without flinching, knowing damn well he deserved every hideous thing she was thinking. He'd much rather face that than look at the blood that streaked Lauren's flesh.

Birthing was a messy business, a painful one. He'd known that technically, but it hadn't really hit home. And he thought he'd have some time to prepare for it.

She was so pale, Dale thought, jaw clenched. All around him, everybody scurried about, doing this, checking that. After examining Lauren, Dr. Flynn donned gloves, and spoke tersely to Dale. "Dr. Norland, a very fine neonatal specialist, is in the facility and will examine the baby as soon as we deliver it. He comes highly recommended by your chosen pediatrician, Dr. Young. I'm most concerned about the lungs. But I am thinking things will be fine. Lauren's young and healthy. We got the baby to turn and now we just have to deliver the little tyke. She's taken good care of herself and this baby."

She didn't look so fine now.

Her cheeks had a spot of high color on each cheekbone, but the rest of her face was parchment white. Her lips were dry and cracked and as he watched, as her hand closed painfully around his, she sank her teeth into her lip, arching her back. In horrified fascination, he watched as her stomach tightened. "Don't push yet, Lauren," Dr. Flynn ordered briskly. "Not yet. Keep breathing."

Tendrils of hair had escaped the messy braid to cling to her cheeks. She panted shallowly at the doctor's request, but her eyes were wild with pain. Finally, the muscles in her abdomen eased and her grip on his hand loosened.

He watched, astonished moments later, as Dr. Flynn once again left the room. "Not time yet," she said. Not time yet? Dale thought as he watched Lauren slip into sleep swiftly.

How could she sleep? Dale wondered frantically. He'd never sleep again. He raised his eyes and met Jennifer's accusing glare over the bed. In a flat calm voice, she said, "You really are a bastard, you know that?"

He said nothing, just turned his eyes back to Lauren's pale face, raising her limp hand to his lips. After a minute, her eyes fluttered open and she looked up, meeting his worried gaze. As he watched, the distress, the fear, the exhaustion in her eyes disappeared and she said in a calm, if hoarse, voice, "Stop worrying, Dale. I'm fine."

"Sure you are," he murmured, clinging tightly to her hand when she would have pulled it away. "But I'm not."

Her mouth quirked into a slight smile as she turned her head to Jennifer. "Ice?" she asked. Dale watched as his wife's friend held a cup of ice to her mouth, watched as she sighed in relief. "How much time?"

"A minute or so," Jennifer replied, glancing at her watch. "Are you ready?"

Bitterly, he closed his eyes and lowered his head. It should have been him she turned to; he should have been there for her. His mouth spasmed once and his throat ached with grief.

Time and again, it happened, the four minutes between contractions dwindling to three, to two. Finally, there were only seconds between contractions and the serenity had faded from her eyes, even the echo of it gone. "Shit," she cursed weakly as the final spasm faded. "How do women survive this?" she gasped, trying desperately to catch her breath.

"No choice." Jennifer quipped, "You don't really think men could do it, do you?"

Before she could answer, a moan slid past her lips and she arched up again. Dale sat there, helplessly, while she panted and breathed. No words of comfort or encouragement could he find as he sat, frozen, watching as she bit back a cry. Harsh, shallow breaths came from her mouth and her face paled even more, a grimace twisting her features.

When it finally ended, she again tried to tug her hand from Dale's. Quietly, he said, "No, Lauren." Meeting his eyes, she sighed, weakly, unable to fight with him. She had barely caught her breath before another contraction was on her.

The pain twisted through her again, obscene in its intensity. Her chest felt tight, as though an iron band was clamped around her. "Don't push," she heard a nurse shout out. Another said, "I'll get Dr. Flynn."

Before she could even blink, another pain shot through her and she screamed, unable to hold it back any longer. No more, she thought wildly. No more. Then Dr. Flynn was there, again, between her upraised legs. "Don't push, Lauren, not yet," she said, her voice soothing, calming, and irritating as hell. She had a brief moment to reflect on how undignified this was before another contraction started.

As it eased, she waited, hopelessly, for the doctor to order, yet again, not to push. But this time, when the pain came, the doctor said, "Okay, Lauren. Bear down...Now!"

The pain built until she thought it would rip her in two, then, with a suddenness that left her floundering, it eased.

Dale's hand was holding hers and his other arm was under her shoulders, supporting her. In her ear, he whispered, "I love you, Lauren. I'm sorry..."

"Breathe again, Lauren. Don't push any more until I tell you to," Dr. Flynn said from between her legs.

Dale raised his head, to ask something, but the words died in his throat as he saw what the doctor held in her hands. A tiny little head. She worked quickly, suctioning out the tiny mouth. she ordered Lauren not to push as another contraction gripped her, but with the next one, she ordered, "Now, Lauren. One more time."

As his wife arose to her elbows, pushing down, Dale held his breath and prayed. And then it was over. Dr. Flynn held a tiny little girl in her capable hands. He started to ask if the baby was well but then, to his amazement, she opened her mouth and squeaked out, indignantly, hoarsely, voicing her protests of the treatment she had just received. "My God," he whispered reverently.

"Is it okay?" Lauren asked weakly, trying to raise her head.

"I think she's going to be just fine," Dr. Flynn said, smiling broadly as the baby gave another squeaky little cry. "Just fine."

Several hours later, Dale finally held his daughter. Lauren was sleeping soundly in the bed next to him. After Dr. Flynn had reassured her, she had dropped into sleep as though she had just been waiting for permission. The neonatologist had examined the baby and pronounced her fit as a fiddle, if somewhat tiny. At each vigorous cry, he had laughed, assuring Dale that her little lungs were functioning exactly as they should.

His daughter. He'd watched as this tiny infant pushed her way into the world, and screamed her protest at being taken from her snug little nest.

He was scared to death of this tiny thing. She didn't even weigh five pounds and one of his hands was almost as big as her whole body. A knitted pink and blue stocking cap was on her head and she was swaddled in blankets as she slept soundly on his chest. "How in God's name did you do that Lauren?" he asked in wonder. Tiny little lashes fluttered but the baby slept on, oblivious to her father's fascination. For the first time, he didn't even feel bitter toward the unknown biological father. He would raise this child, he and Lauren together.

More than a half an hour passed with him just staring at the little bundle in his arms. He was startled to hear his name, more startled to look up and see Lauren watching him with gray eyes that revealed nothing. Her eyes dropped to the baby and a slow smile bloomed on her face. Dale rose and gingerly held the baby out.

"Oh," Lauren whispered. Tiny lashes fluttered at the sound of her voice. "Oh, my." The little eyes flew open and locked on her mother's face. Watching the face above hers intently, the baby didn't even squeak as Lauren gently unwrapped the snug blankets. "She's so little, so tiny." She traced a finger over the perfect cupid's bow of the tiny little mouth.

"Dr. Norland, the specialist, said she's fine. Just a little small," Dale said softly, tucking his hands in his pockets. "Her lungs…the specialist said they're working just fine."

"I know," Lauren said softly, examining tiny fingers, palms no bigger than a nickel, wrinkled red skin and a wizened face. "I heard her cry and I knew she was fine."

He had heard the cry, too, but it hadn't sounded too fine to him. Dr. Norland had assured him that a newborn cry didn't sound like much.

Nothing else was said until nearly an hour later when a nursery nurse entered the room to assist Lauren with the first feeding.

"What's to assist?" Dale asked curiously, watching as the nurse, Brigit, showed her how to hold the baby, "Isn't it instinct, or something?"

"Of course, it is. But, sometimes, we all need a little help. Even with instinct."

It humbled and awed him to watch that tiny little mouth fasten and feed avidly at her mother's breast. Krista Dawn Stoner. Lauren had whispered it over the baby's head as little Krista latched on the first time and Dale had agreed. They hadn't discussed any names, but it seemed to fit.

Not that she'd care much for his opinion right now any way. He realized, much too late, of course, how badly he had bungled the situation. And he was deathly afraid he knew what had caused the premature labor.

Just then, Dr. Flynn entered the room and that was the first question out of his mouth after she cooed over the baby and examined Lauren. "There isn't always a reason," Dr. Flynn replied, briskly watching her hands. "There was no sign-"

"I think there might have been," Lauren said softly. "I wasn't paying too much attention. I thought it was too early and that it was just symptoms of late pregnancy."

"What symptoms?" Dale asked, frowning, eyes narrowed. And why in the hell hadn't she said anything?

Lauren shrugged, stroking Krista's stocking covered head. "Backaches. The backaches were pretty bad for a couple of weeks. And I was more tired than before. It's been like that for almost a week. And more irritable, more emotional than usual. Sleeping a lot more. I had the hardest time getting out of bed yesterday morning. I didn't even think of calling about it. Too tired to care. Nothing specific, just a few little things. I didn't think anything of it, but maybe I should have."

Dr. Flynn listened, nodding, frowning a bit. "Before you went to bed, was there anything odd?"

"Just the backache. The past few days it's been almost nonstop. But I figured it was because I was lying around so much all of the sudden."

"I should have been there," Dale said, quietly, looking intently at his wife and daughter, ignoring the doctor.

"Damn it, Lauren. I'm sorry." He turned his back to stare out the window. "I should have been there."

"It's unlikely anything you did caused this, Dale," Dr. Flynn said, sighing. It was hard to be mad at the guy when he was so clearly kicking his own butt over it. No fun in kicking a guy who was already down. "Sometimes, there is no reason, no why, no answer. It just happens."

His neck flushed red but he forced himself to ask anyway. "Sex?"

The doctor laughed. "Not likely."

"Rough sex?"

Her laughter faded and she felt a stir of sympathy. "Not very likely, Dale. The majority of women can have as much sex as they like, in just about any form, as long as it isn't painful," Dr. Flynn said, sliding Lauren a questioning look.

"It's never hurt," Lauren said softly. "If it had hurt, I wouldn't have kept it up."

"Could we have stopped it if we'd known earlier?"

"Honestly," Dr. Flynn said, "I doubt it. This little girl was in a hurry to meet her parents. I doubt I could have changed her mind, no matter what I did." She patted Lauren's shoulder and said, "I've got to be heading out, but call if you need me. I'll be by tomorrow."

Dale said nothing else for a long time. And when he did, it was in a rough, hoarse voice that he asked, "Will you forgive me?"

Her eyes teared up at the humility she heard in his voice. And the guilt, once again, reared its ugly head. "Do you love me?" she asked quietly. "Tell me the truth. Do you love me?"

He turned and met her eyes across the space that separated them. Intently, he whispered, "I didn't know it was possible to love anybody the way I love you. I need you more than I need air. You're my life."

Krista had fallen asleep, cuddled against her, tiny mouth damp and slack from exhaustion. Gently, her hands still awkward, Lauren shifted her, covering her naked breast, before she raised her head. "I know you think I'm a strong woman, Dale. But I'm not, not as strong as people think I am. It hurt to realize that you were dreaming of somebody else, that you could want somebody else that much."

"I'm sorry," he said roughly, moving to her side slowly. When her eyes didn't ice over, he sank down and shifted her until he was behind her, supporting her tired body. Resting his chin on her hair, he said it again. "I'm sorry. I don't know why I was dreaming of her." He didn't correct her assumption that he had been dreaming of Nikki, knowing she was too fragile just yet. "I'd undo it if I could, because I don't love her."

"Don't you?" she asked, her voice quivering.

How had he thought her so calm and in control? Dale wondered. Had it been an act all these years? Had she hidden her vulnerable heart away, like she'd hidden how she felt about him? Gently, he turned her head, angling her face until he could press a soothing kiss to her mouth. "I think about you day and night. I feel your body against mine even when you're not there. The way you laugh, the way your skin smells, the way you sigh in your sleep and gasp when I touch you, all of it, it's there inside me all the time."

"You're in my blood, in my heart. Anything I felt for her pales in comparison to what I feel for you."

Sometime during the endless flight home, he had acknowledged how foolish it was to dream of a woman whose face he didn't know, whose name he never knew. And he had sworn it would end, even if he had to end up on a shrink's chair to do it.

He had a beautiful wife who loved him with everything she had in her, and now they had a daughter together. They were what mattered, nothing and nobody else.

He would never put that pain in her eyes again.

* * * * *

Krista was able to go home with them after five days in the hospital. Lauren, on the doctor's orders, stayed the five days for observation. The bleeding had been difficult to stop and she required a blood transfusion the day after Krista was born. It wasn't until the third day that bleeding slowed enough to suit Dr. Flynn.

Dale carried the tiny baby as Lauren came inside, moving slowly, tiredly. It's no wonder they called it 'labor,' she thought as she carefully lowered herself onto the couch. She said nothing to Dale as he handed Krista to her. He said nothing to her. The awkwardness between them saddened her.

Dale stood there helplessly while she cuddled the baby to her chest, her sexy mouth a sad straight solemn line in a somber face. He was turning to go to his study and sulk when Krista opened her eyes, gazing up at her mother before opening her mouth and yawning hugely.

"How can you be tired, huh?" he asked, squatting in front of Lauren and stroking his daughter's cheek. She turned her head, looking at him with the unfocused gaze of the newborn, watching him while he spoke. "You've done nothing but sleep the past five days."

"Being born is tough business, I guess,"Lauren said, smiling as Krista closed her tiny hand around Dale's index finger.

"I'd say you had the hardest part. It wore me out just watching." And completely humbled him. Terrified him. "For a minute there, I decided I wasn't ever going to lay a hand on you again. I hated seeing you hurt like that."

"Well, you can do it next time," she offered, reaching up for the buttons of her shirt as Krista started rooting around with her mouth. Tears burned her eyes when Dale took over the task for her, flicking open her bra and helping her shift the baby. Her throat ached when he jogged into the bedroom and returned with a pillow to prop under the baby.

"I love you, Lauren. I really do. But," he said a few minutes later, "I wouldn't do this if my life depended on it, even if I could. Thank God, I can't."

Moments later, Dale lifted her chin with his index finger. Crouched in front her, the awe he felt still showing in his eyes, he told her, "God gave me the greatest gift I've ever known the day you told me you were pregnant. It made me see you as something other than my best friend. It made me see you."

* * * * *

Krista was one month old today, Lauren thought. Depressing. It was going by so quickly. She had gained a good two pounds and her little face was filling out. Lauren sulked as she tried to fasten a pair of pre-pregnancy jeans. Still too tight through the hips and waist. Eyeing the little pouch of flesh with acute dislike, she threw the jeans down and reached for a pair of stretch pants to wear with her sweater.

She was tired of stretch pants.

Dale strolled into the room, a pair of unfastened jeans tugged around his lean hips, rubbing his gold streaked hair with a towel. Licking her lips, she watched as a drop of water slid down his neck, his chest, to disappear into the vee of his open jeans. She was thinking about heading over to him and helping him back out of those jeans when he shot her a vague smile before tossing down the towel and heading out of the room.

She was also tired of celibacy.

Krista was in the bassinet in the living room, down for her afternoon nap. She'd sleep a good two hours, Lauren knew, and wake up starving. She picked up the towel Dale had thrown across the bed and carried it into the bathroom to hang up. The air was hot and steamy from the shower, the scent of his soap hanging in the air.

It was pretty pathetic when the scent of a man's soap turned a woman on, Lauren decided. It would be another two weeks before the doctor released her and Lauren was still too uncomfortable to even be entertaining the thought of going and seducing her seemingly uninterested husband.

She had been expecting, even anticipating, his suggestive bantering and teasing. It hadn't come. He hadn't teased with her or joked with her in more than a month. They were polite to each other, friendly even. But Dale treated her like she was made of spun glass.

Worse, he treated her like his best friend again.

Her hand reached out and she tugged the towel off the bar, pressing her face to it, willing herself not to cry.

Chapter Seven

"He doesn't even act like he wants me any more," Lauren said morosely, picking at the salad she had ordered for lunch. Dale was watching Krista so Lauren could get out of the house. She and Jennifer were having lunch at a little cafe in Louisville and then heading out for some shopping. She firmly pushed the little twinges of guilt away, knowing she wasn't the type of woman who stayed by her baby's side twenty four-seven. She didn't want to be; it wasn't good for her or for Krista.

Krista had taken to the supplemental bottle-feeding well enough, as long as Lauren wasn't the one feeding her. If Lauren held her, Krista absolutely refused to have anything to do with the bottle. Any time Lauren tried, Krista set up a wail to wake the dead.

"Sugar, you've got almost two weeks before you could even do anything, even if you wanted," Jennifer replied.

Narrowing her eyes at her friend, Lauren scowled. "There are other ways," she loftily informed Jennifer. "And he's damned good at them. But it's not that, it's the way he acts. Like I'm his...sister, or just good ole Lauren again. I can't go back to being his buddy, Jennifer."

"Then maybe you should show him that you're not his buddy. Start teasing him a little. By the time Dr. Flynn gives you the okay, he'll be absolutely mad for you."

"Not with this body," Lauren muttered. She had yet to lose ten of the sixteen pounds she'd gained and her belly would never be what it had been. Faint purple stretch marks marred her ivory skin and her rarely exercised vanity was coming into play. Worse, nursing hadn't just made her breasts a little larger, it had also taken away the firmness. She looked plain and dumpy, and she hated it.

Jennifer eyed Lauren over the rim of her glass and rolled her eyes. The woman was an idiot, she decided. She knew exactly what Lauren was thinking and was hard pressed not to laugh over it. Her figure, always gorgeous, was more lush than before and she had this glow about her. Being a mommy suited her well. With a sigh of disgust over her rather scrawny body, she hoped she'd come out of pregnancy as well as Lauren had.

"Lauren, you are an idiot," Jennifer said, deciding not to be subtle. Lauren was feeling way too much self-pity. "Most of the weight is because you're nursing. The rest will come off in time. You're too self-disciplined for it not to come off."

"Great. So until I'm done nursing my child, which is the best way to feed a baby, my husband isn't going to want me."

"That's not what I said," Jennifer snapped. "Stop feeling sorry for yourself and do something about it."

Lauren opened her mouth to tell Jennifer to go to hell. But she closed it with a snap as she realized she was feeling sorry for herself. She was pouting, for crying out loud. "Honestly, do I look okay?"

She was seated, but Jennifer could visualize well enough. Long legs showcased in leggings that fit like a second skin, a sweater that would make any man who saw her want to cuddle her against him. Her hair was twisted into a French braid, a perfect look for her, allowing one to see the heavy lidded gray eyes, perfectly arched brows and wide mouth. "Lauren, I'd kill to look like you do right now. I can't look that good on my best day," Jennifer said with disgust, because it was the honest truth. Lauren had given birth four and a half weeks ago and had drawn more looks of male appreciation in the past few hours than Jennifer drew in a week.

A slightly pleased, slightly embarrassed grin on her face, Lauren set her glass down and reached for the check. "Let's go shopping."

* * * * *

Dale glanced up as Lauren said from the doorway, "She's asleep. I think I'll take a shower." He replied with an absent hum as he tapped away at his keyboard. It wasn't until he heard the water running that he scrubbed his hands over his face.

He knew, technically, a man couldn't die from unrequited lust. But it sure as hell felt like he could.

The last month had been rough, but the past week had been pure hell. As the images of delivery faded, his hunger for Lauren grew steadily. Certain that the last thing she wanted from him right now was any sign of that, he had hidden it as best as he could, rising early in the morning, exercising like a weight trainer gone mad, and taking enough cold showers for a battleship of sailors.

One more week. He could handle one more week. But, hell, what would he do if she weren't ready after another week? Physically or emotionally?

She was so damn cool to him any more.

After that fight, the one that had made him take off for New York, things hadn't been right between them. Dale was starting to worry that things weren't going to ever be right.

They could have lost Krista.

He could have lost her.

And it would have been all his fault.

A cold sweat broke out over his body as he listened to the running water. He could see her, standing under the pounding shower, hair slicked back from that lovely face, her body wet and warm, flushed from the heat.

Shit, he thought with disgust. If he kept this up, he wouldn't survive the night, much less the week.

Closing his eyes, he concentrated on anything that would settle his body. His blood had started to cool and his head had started to clear when he heard a sound at the door. Lauren was standing there, wet and fragrant from her shower. Thick ropes of ebony hair hung around her strong shoulders. Beads of water clung to her face, neck and shoulders, ran down her legs. The thick white towel she had wrapped around her was far too brief for Dale's comfort.

"You need something?" he asked, voice a little hoarse. In a move he hoped was casual, he spun the chair around so that he was once more facing the keyboard.

"Yes."

That single word was all she said and after a minute, he cautiously turned his head. When he was looking at her, she moved out of the doorway, a smile playing at her mouth. She laid her hands on his shoulders, turning him back to her. His throat was too tight for him to speak as she smiled down at him.

A ragged groan left his throat as she dropped to her knees in front of him. Busy fingers unzipped his jeans and pulled them down over his hips. Before he even had a chance to hope he knew what she was up to, she was already doing it, her mouth closing around him, wet and warm, while her fingers played delicately on his skin.

A witch, he thought. Or a dream. But the reality of her mouth moving on him, as she took the initiative as never before, was no dream. She deep throated him, a sexy little hum leaving her throat when he shuddered underneath her mouth. Closing his hands in her wet hair, he gasped out, "Lauren, what are you doing?"

She paused, lifting her head to smile at him, her mouth red and swollen. "If you have to ask, I can't be doing it right."

"Sweetheart, you get it any more right, I'll be dead," he rasped as she lowered her head once more. Her teeth nipped delicately at the sac of his balls before she nibbled her way up his shaft, taking him deep in her mouth again.

His skin was hot and smooth under her fingers, and the taste of him, salt and musk, had an ache throbbing between her thighs. Uninterested, my butt, she thought smugly.

She had missed this, missed feeling his smooth, steely cock in her mouth, missed feeling his hands in her hair as he pumped his shaft in and out of her mouth until he came, shooting come down her throat that felt like and tasted like molten fire.

The look she glimpsed in his eyes when he first looked at her had her wondering and what she had come into the room for was forgotten.

Until she was on her knees in front of him, she had no idea what she was going to do. It certainly hadn't been this. She had never gone down on him with the sole intent of giving him a blowjob. The few times he'd urged her to go down on him, she had enjoyed it, but she generally avoided doing it. Dale let her get by with it and she was always repaid in kind, which made it even more worthwhile.

But, the surge of power she was riding on had her wondering why in the hell she had ever avoided it. So what if she wasn't getting an orgasm of her very own? Feeling him quiver and surge against her, feeling his powerful body shaking was almost as good as an orgasm. The ache between her thighs spread to her belly and breasts but she didn't mind.

He wanted her. Still wanted her. She could sense it, feel it, and after a few moments more, she could taste it as he climaxed with a groan. Hot semen flooded her throat and she swallowed it, swallowed more of him, stroking up and down until the last of the quivers faded from his body, until his cock stopped bobbing and jerking in her mouth.

She settled back on her heels, wiped her hand over her mouth and smiled serenely at him. Then she rose, adjusting her towel and calmly said, "I'm going to bed. Good night."

It was one hell of an exit line, she decided, as his eyes burned into her naked back.

Dale watched through dazed eyes as she sauntered out of the office, his chest heaving as he sucked in much needed oxygen. Damnation, but what had brought that on? Not that he was complaining, mind, but he wanted to know so he could be sure to do whatever it was again.

Shortly after Lauren bid him good night so sweetly, Dale shut down the computer and got ready to join her. He went to check on Krista, lingering over her crib while he studied her sleeping face. Her little mouth was puckered in a slight pout and she shifted in her sleep.

She was so perfect, so tiny. Dale's hands felt huge and clumsy when he held her, and he thought his heart would break from the emotion that swelled inside him every time he looked at her.

He left the nursery after checking the monitor. The moonlight was spilling across the bed, their bed. Lauren was lying on her side, turned towards him. As he shucked his jeans, she opened her eyes and smiled a sleepy smile before sighing and snuggling deeper into the pillow. He slid under the covers and wrapped his arms around her, pressing a kiss to the top of her head.

"You're the best thing that has ever happened to me," he murmured, hoping she wasn't asleep.

She curled her hand around his shoulder, smiled against his bare skin and said softly, "I know." Then she pressed a kiss to his chest, yawned, and fell asleep almost instantly.

Sometime near dawn, Dale rose and gently lifted Krista from her mother's arms. Having eaten her fill, she was ready for her own bed again. Lauren refastened the button down shift she wore, already falling back to sleep. Dale slid in bed behind her, wrapped his arms around her middle, and pressed a kiss to her shoulder. She murmured as he pressed another kiss to her skin, this one on her neck.

"…Dale?"

His only answer was to glide his hand up and down her side, stroking her skin with a feather light touch.

Lauren's eyes blinked open and she rolled her head forward, baring her neck. One hand slid around her, cupping her breast, shaping it while he nibbled along the cord in the side of her neck. A bead of milk gathered at her nipple, wetting the front of her shift as she rolled back against him. Heat spiraled in her body, spreading from the inside outward until even the tips of her fingers tingled.

Hands slid down her hips, pulling her into contact with a hard, aroused body. "Dale, I can't…"

"Sure you can," he murmured, slipping one finger into the nest of hair between her thighs, sliding back and forth through her slick, wet center. "I just can't."

A low hum of pleasure sounded in the back of her throat as he slid the one wicked finger inside her, slowly, gently. She whimpered and he stilled abruptly. "Am I hurting you?"

"No," she whispered, pressing her hips forward, against his hand. "Dale, please."

He chuckled, burying his face in her hair. "If you insist." Then he secured her against him with one arm and shifted until he was sitting with her cradled in his lap, facing away from him. He caught her legs with his, spreading them, opening her wide to his touch. Then his hands resumed their play on her heated skin. One hand fondled her breasts while the other found her center, pressing against her, circling around her clit, dipping inside to stroke.

Against her neck, he whispered, "God, Lauren. You can't know how it feels to hold you, to touch you and hear the sweet sounds you make." He slid one finger in and out, slowly, carefully, aware of her tight, still healing body.

"I felt like half of me was missing, and now you're back. Come for me, baby. Let me feel it again."

Lauren arched backward, half sobs rising in her throat as the pressure built inside her body, inside her groin, until she thought she would surely burst from it. Dale was muttering in her ear, praising her, adoring her, while she shot swiftly to the peak. With a flick of his thumb, the dip of his finger inside her body, she fell over, the cream from her body flooding his hand as she arched back against him. Her breath caught in her chest as she plummeted back to earth.

She was still gasping for air when Dale straightened her shift and slid back down in the bed, cradling her against him. She had barely registered the whispered, "I love you," before she dropped into sleep.

* * * * *

The day of her six-week check up, Lauren woke with her mood sky high. Krista seemed to sense her mother's happy state of mind, for she was cooing and gurgling with pleasure almost from the minute her eyes opened.

A portrait stood by the back door, kitchen lights casting a glow into the far corners. Outside, the sky was overcast and gloomy, but Lauren hummed gaily as she added a bit of color to the cheeks. It was a portrait of Dale and Krista, him seated in the rocker, bare chested, while he cuddled his newborn daughter against him. She was reaching upward with one little hand, and Dale had a bemused, awed smile on his gorgeous face.

She surveyed it nearly an hour later with critical eyes. It wasn't the best work she had ever done, but portraits had never been her strong suit. It was damn good, though. Dale's birthday was two days away. She'd hide it until then. She cast her napping child a look before heading for the little spare room tucked behind the stairs. She stored her off-season and evening clothes there. If she was lucky, the portrait would fit in the closet.

Several hours later, the doctor was giving her the okay. Dale, cheeks a dull red, couldn't hide the broad grin on his face. Dr. Flynn turned away while Lauren donned her jeans, dropping the paper drape into the trash while the doctor cooed over the baby sleeping in Dale's arms.

"You know, she has your mouth, Lauren," Dr. Flynn said, tracing the tiny cupid bow that was a diminutive replica of Lauren's. "But the rest of her, that's her daddy all over. Call me if you have any problems."

Lauren froze in the process of straightening her hair, the color draining from her face as Dr. Flynn left the room, unaware of the storm that was about to break. Dale smiled, about to make a remark when he noticed the odd look in her eyes. He started to speak, but his throat closed. Looking down at Krista, her face, so similar to his. Her nose and chin, the shape of her ears.

She was him all over.

And he remembered.

Drunk as a wino, opening the door to see Lauren wearing a gauzy purple shirt, the amethyst he had given her around her long pale neck. Lauren sighing, closing her hands over his, telling him, "Doesn't matter much who, or what. I know how you feel, though." Offering to fix him some supper, then him grabbing her, pulling her up against him.

He remembered, clear as day, stripping her naked, going down on her while she tried to push him away. Taking her against the wall like a sailor with a hooker after months of celibacy. Remembered the hot wet embrace of her body, her long legs wrapped around his waist.

And he wondered how he could have possibly forgotten.

His baby. Really his.

Cold fury settled in his belly as he rose, Krista still sleeping peacefully against his chest, unaware of the tension in the air. In silence, he walked out of the room, Lauren standing behind, staring at him.

His baby.

He slowed his steps in the waiting room when he saw Jennifer's grinning face. She scooped Krista out of his arms, taking the diaper bag from Lauren who trailed after him. "I'll have her back to you in a few hours. I'll call first," she said cheerfully.

"Jenny, this isn't a good time after all," Lauren said slowly, closing her eyes briefly. "I-"

"Nonsense. Dale, this was Lauren's little surprise for you. An early birthday present, some time alone. Have fun," she called out, already sailing out the door.

"Jenny, wait-"

"No," Dale said, speaking for the first time. "Go on, Jenny." Then he grasped Lauren's arm above her elbow, guiding her outside.

"Dale-"

He cast her a frigid glance that froze the words on her tongue. She fell silent. After all, what could she say?

'I'm sorry,' sure as hell wouldn't cut it.

The rest of the drive home passed in the quiet confines of the Explorer. Lauren wrapped her arms around her body, cursing herself endlessly. Why didn't you tell him sooner? He was so angry. Lauren doubted she had ever seen him this furious before. She thought she had the knack of being cold down to a science, but Dale could teach her a thing or two.

Dale was cursing them both. Lauren, for hiding this from him. Himself for not remembering. For his rough assault on her. Seduction was too polite a word to describe what he had done. It had been the most glorious minutes of his life and though she had climaxed, though he hadn't been brutal, she hadn't given consent. Had tried to push him away.

Was that why he had blocked out the memory of it being Lauren?

When they were in the house, Lauren took a deep breath and braced herself.

"Were you ever planning to tell me?" he asked quietly, throwing his keys on the table. He slung his jacket across the back of the chair and advanced on her. Hands buried inside the pockets of her long black leather trench coat, she eyed him warily, as though fearing he would pounce on her.

He was tempted. By God, he thought praying for patience. He was tempted. He wanted to turn her over his knee for not telling him. Wanted to shake her for standing there so calmly, as though she hadn't just shattered the foundation of his world. He had accepted it, that Krista wasn't his. Even had the sense to be grateful for whatever circumstances put her in his life.

And all along, it had been his baby.

"Answer me," he rasped after she remained silent too long. "Were you going to tell me, if I hadn't figured it out?"

"I don't know," she answered quietly. Damned if she'd lie about it, she had her reasons, good ones.

"Were you just out slumming?" he asked casually, turning away to grab a beer from the fridge. He opened it with one vicious twist of his wrist and drained half the contents before glaring at her.

She opened her mouth to speak but closed it, realizing there was nothing she could say. She lowered her head, her eyes on the floor.

"Why did you lie to me?"

Her chin went up several notches and she met his frigid eyes squarely. Now she did speak. "I never once lied to you, except by omission. You were the first I told. And you told me more often than I could count that if you couldn't have a family with Nicole, you didn't want one at all. I wasn't about to force one on you."

"I had a right to know," he said, his voice vibrating with fury.

"Yes, you did," she agreed quietly. "But I know you, Dale. I wasn't going to force you into something you didn't want. I didn't want an obligated father for my child."

"And what you want is what counts," he replied, silkily. "Screw anybody else. If we hadn't ended up together, would you have robbed your kid of a father?"

"It takes more than sperm to make a father, Dale. You have to love the baby, want it. I would no more raise my child in a home where she was an obligation than I would sell myself on the streets." She spoke levelly, keeping her voice calm even as her stomach churned sickly. In concession to her weak knees, she did walk over to the table and sit, folding her hands in front of her.

"So you waited around, hung around, until all I could think about was you," he accused, realizing as he spoke how stupid he sounded. "Until all I could think of was you, until I fell in love with you and you had your damned husband."

"That," she announced, "is the most foolish thing I have ever heard. I never expected you to love me."

"You sure as hell didn't fight it, did you?"

"Why would I? Damn it, Dale, I've loved you for years. Why would I fight what I wanted most in life?" she demanded, shoving herself to her feet, her voice passionate, eyes hot.

That slowed him a little, that emotion, the flare of temper. But the anger was too great and won over again. "You have no idea how much I hated him. How jealous I was. And it was me all along," he said, his voice rough with the rage he was trying to hold in check.

He turned and met her eyes. "That night that we fought, before I left for New York. It wasn't Nicole. It was you I was dreaming of. I'd been dreaming of you for months and could never see your face. You haunted me, turned me inside out. I felt guilty all these months for dreaming about it, for fantasizing about fucking my own wife!"

Hr eyes widened, her mouth formed a soundless, "Oh," but Dale was too furious to care about how his admission affected her. "And all the damn time, it was you that night!" he shouted, hurling the half full bottle of beer against the wall. It shattered, beer splattering the wall, small shards of glass flying. "You!"

"Why in the hell didn't you tell me?"

"I tried," she said, hating how shaky her voice sounded. "You said you didn't want to know."

He remembered. "You should have told me before that. And no matter what I said that night, you should have told me any way. Why the hell didn't you?"

"I didn't want to lose you," she whispered, closing her eyes. She wanted desperately to go to him, but the rage in his eyes, the anger, the very stiffness in his shoulders, kept her where she was.

"I love you. I would have understood. I'd have been angry, but damn it, if I'd heard it from you...Damn it, Lauren. I don't even know if I can trust you. This is the most important thing that has ever happened to me and you kept it from me."

He turned away, staring out the window while Lauren forced herself to take deep calming breaths. "I'm sorry. I can't do or say anything that will change it. But I did it because I thought it was best. You told me you didn't want to get married and didn't want a family if you couldn't have Nikki. You didn't love me. This child deserved better than that. So did I."

"You deserve the best, Lauren. I would have done my damnedest to give it to you."

"You couldn't have. Not as long as you loved, or thought you loved, Nikki. Do you remember the whole of it, Dale? You called me her name," she hissed, closing her eyes against the remembered pain, the humiliation of that. "I've loved you for years and when you finally touched me, you called me by her name."

She dashed away the tears that had seeped through her closed eyes before bitterly saying, "You were having sex with me and making love to her and you called me

Nikki. You ripped my heart out and didn't even know it. I couldn't be your substitute for her. So I didn't tell you."

"I could have been a father without being a husband." He said it without turning around, aching inside.

"Yes. You could have. But that isn't what you would have done. And I couldn't have told you no. You're my weakness, Dale. And there's nothing I wouldn't do to make you happy."

"Except tell me the truth."

"I'm sorry," Lauren repeated, her voice dull.

"Sorry," he said, laughing bitterly. Then he took a deep breath and opened the door. "I'm going outside."

Lauren closed her eyes as the door shut and gave in to the urge to weep.

Dale entered the bedroom, listening to the shower running in the master bathroom. He didn't know what the hell to do, how to feel. The only thing he did know was that he wanted his wife.

It had been far too long.

He reached behind him, grabbed the material of his tee shirt and pulled it off, kicked off his shoes, shucked his jeans. Lauren stood under the shower, soaping her body while he stood there watching her with hot needy eyes.

He opened the door to the shower stall and stepped under the spray and pulled her up against him, ignoring her startled cry. "It doesn't matter right now," he muttered thickly as she stiffened. "Dale-" she said, trying to move away. She'd tried to pull back that first time, as well, he remembered. At first. Running his hands over her wet body, he lowered his head to nuzzle at her shoulder. I'm not waiting any longer to touch you," he said gruffly, cupping her full breasts in his hands.

He dipped his finger inside her, shuddering as she closed tightly over him. She had been tight that night too, clinging to him like he was all that mattered in the world, like he was the only man to have ever touched her, had gloved him as though she had been created just to fit him. "Lauren," he groaned against her skin.

He turned the shower off abruptly, picking her up and carrying her out of the steamy bathroom. But he didn't put her on the bed. He braced her back against the wall. "Like this," he muttered, his voice thick.

"Dale, no. You're still angry-"

He covered her mouth with his, cutting her protest off. When she turned her head away from his mouth, he caught her face in his hands, covering her mouth with his and taking it roughly. He cursed when she bit his tongue, but when she tried to dart away, he snagged her wrist, turned, pressed her up against the door. He caught her narrow wrists in one hand, the other hand closing over a milk heavy breast. He tipped his head back, watching with satisfaction as her eyes darkened to the color of storm clouds.

"Dale, wait," she insisted once more.

He plunged his fingers deep as she gasped. "I've already waited long enough," he told her. "So have you. Can you tell me you don't want me?" Mutely, she stared at him, and slowly, shook her head. "I didn't think so. Give me your mouth." Then he covered her mouth with his, his tongue mimicking the motions of his hand.

Her hips rose helplessly against him, a dazed whimper coming from her parted lips. She stared at him, bewildered, as he lowered her hands, but before she could even acknowledge that she was free, he cupped her bottom and lifted her. "Dale…" she gasped, sucking in air, before trying again. "Dale, wait." Her voice ended in a breathy gasp when he settled between her legs.

"Are you sure you want me to wait? Really sure?" he drawled as he traced a fingertip along the entrance of her body. She was wet and so hot, it was a wonder she didn't singe his hand. Her wet folds were almost dripping with need. She wanted, all right. She might not be happy with it, but she wanted. Her eyes were full of emotion now, hot with need, clouded with confusion and uncertainty.

"Not like this," she whispered raggedly. *Not with all this anger left between us.*

"This particular position has always worked well for us, don't you think?" he asked conversationally, ignoring her plea as he braced her back against the wall, ignoring her halfhearted attempts to push him away.

She was strong enough, skilled enough, to stop him, if she had really wanted to. Later, he would wonder why, only to realize she'd already given him her answer. *You're my weakness, Dale. And there's nothing I wouldn't do to make you happy.*

Her mouth opened, but Dale covered it with his before she could speak. As he plunged his tongue inside her mouth, his hips thrust forward, burying himself in her body. He filled her roughly, completely burying his cock inside her tight, wet little pussy to the hilt. She flinched, pulling away from him, recoiling in pain.

A little trickle of awareness rolled through him and he wondered at it. The pain in her eyes looked familiar, distressingly so. Those eyes looked huge and dark in her pale face and her hands were bunched into fists against his shoulders. What had he ever done to make her look like that? When had he seen that distressed, confused, and needy look in her eyes before? When?

Dale stilled, guilt flooding him as he rested inside her tight body. She was wet, yes, needy, yes, but her body, only just now recovering from childbirth, was far from ready for him. The distress in her eyes ripped at his heart. Soothingly, he pressed a kiss to her eyes, her trembling mouth before locking an arm under her bottom. He moved away from the wall, carrying her to the bed. Her legs locked around his hips and as he moved, she shuddered.

He started to pull out of her, but she tightened around him, her damp flesh growing more welcoming by the second. Cupping her face in his hands, he kissed her gently, grieving inside. He hooked his arms under hers, holding her tightly to him as her arms wound around his neck.

Gently, he moved against her, closing his eyes at the hot pleasure of it. She surrounded him tightly, smoothly, her body hot, wet, fitting him to perfection. A rippling sigh escaped her, followed by an eager little moan. Heaven and hell, he loved her. His heart felt as though it were breaking inside him.

She hadn't trusted him to take care of her, to want a child he had helped make. What kind of man did she think he was?

He propped himself on his elbows, cupping her face once more in his hands as everything inside him died a slow withering death. Her eyes were bright with tears he knew instinctively she would never shed. He pressed a kiss to each eyelid before covering her mouth with his.

With slow, deep strokes, he took her, using his hands to help drive her to the brink of madness while he nuzzled and sipped at her milk heavy breasts. Thirstily, he suckled as tiny beads of milk escaped her nipples to trickle down her breasts. Moaning, he lapped it up, hungry for more.

It was slow and bittersweet, not the way Lauren had wanted this first time to be.

She cried out as he sipped from her nipples, when he pulled away to mutter, "God, that's sweet," before returning to lap at her again.

Dale swallowed the tiny droplets of milk that tasted like honey before he took her mouth again, diving his tongue deep to seek out hers, tangling with her tongue and tasting her while he trailed one hand down, shifted his position until he could stroke her clit.

Lauren gasped out his name, everything inside going tight. She lifted her hips, taking his cock deeper as he continued to flick her clit lazily, tweaking and tugging on it until she was whimpering and straining.

"Dale, please," she pleaded, seeking his mouth, seeking his body with hers as she climbed toward release. He rolled his hips, until he was brushing her now throbbing clit with his body every time he rocked against her. His hand palmed her ass, and he slid one finger between her cheeks to press against her anus.

It shot her straight over the edge and her milking contractions pulled him along with her.

As she climaxed around him, tears slid silently down her cheeks. He followed her with an anguished moan that he stifled against her neck. He shifted to prop his weight on his arms, unwillingly to pull away from her just yet; how had it come to this? Her silken sheath still shuddered around him and her long slim body was trembling in the aftermath. They had lain together, just like this, so often.

But this was the first time he had wished he had never laid hands on her, that she was just like she had always been, his best friend. That first night was what had led to this, and the love that had always seemed so natural felt like it was withering away to ashes.

For long minutes afterward, he remained ranged atop her body. Then he rolled to the side and closed his eyes. The guilt and the anger were there, swirling inside him. This was her fault, damn it. He tried to thrust the blame on her, knowing it would do no good. He couldn't fool himself.

He had hurt her, physically and emotionally. The one thing he'd sworn never to do to a woman, hadn't thought he was capable of. She hadn't wanted it, had said no, and he hadn't listened. Hadn't cared.

He only cared about burying himself inside her body, getting as close to her as he could, in the only way she would let him.

The fact that he hadn't brutalized her, or even done more than cause her a little discomfort, made no difference. He had taken her choice away.

Maybe that was why he had done it, to even the score. She hadn't given him a choice, so he hadn't given her one.

"Are you okay?' he finally asked into the silence.

"Of course," came her distant reply. She turned to her side, away from him and he wanted to yell with frustration.

Even after what had just happened, she could close him out and shut down on herself. She couldn't even get angry like a normal person, or cry and make him feel like a jackass. How could he go crawling to her when she so obviously didn't care?

"I'm sorry," he said, knowing how useless, how pointless those words were.

He stared at her, willing her to turn around, to look at him. Open up to him. But she said nothing, merely lay there in silence. He wanted to reach out to her, but how could he? Finally, unable to bear the silence that echoed in the room, he rose and dressed. Shoving his hands deep into his pockets, he stood at the edge of the bed, watching his wife as she lay with her eyes closed, shutting him out.

"I'm sorry," he repeated softly and then he turned on his heel and left the room.

Moments later, she heard the muffled roar of the engine as his truck sped away from the house. She opened her eyes and stared at the ceiling. "Sorry for what?" she asked quietly.

* * * * *

When Jenny arrived less than twenty minutes later, she took one look at Lauren's face and asked, "What happened?"

Lauren took Krista in her arms, nuzzled her satin skinned cheek. "He knows, Jenny."

Those simple words, combined with the heartbreak in her eyes had Jenny groaning. "Oh, no. How bad?"

"Pretty bad." She settled on the couch, cuddling her sleeping daughter against her chest like a little girl with a favored teddy bear. "He left just a little while ago."

"Are you okay?" Jenny asked worriedly. Lauren always hid everything so deep inside. Even now, when any other woman would have been wailing, Lauren sat there, calmly, her face placid.

But she held Krista to her like a life preserver tossed to a drowning man. And her eyes were stormy, swirling pools of emotions that Jenny couldn't identify. "Is there someplace he would go?"

"The river," she responded, her voice almost dreamy. "Always to the river. Across from the Belvedere."

Jenny frowned as Lauren started to rock back and forth. "I lost him, Jenn. He's too angry and he left. Why do I always have to figure things out too late?"

"It's not too late," Jenny whispered, closing her hands over Lauren's shoulders, shaking her gently, mindful of the resting child. "It's never too late."

"He left me, too, Jenn. Just like everybody else. But this time, it really was my fault." Eyes glassy, she looked up at her worried friend and asked, "Is there something about me that just keeps other people from wanting to stay with me? Something that chases them away?"

"Don't say that, Lauren. Damn it, I'm still here."

When Lauren didn't respond, she rose and headed out the door.

Moments later, the door swung open again and Alexandra Young entered, her face concerned. Lauren didn't even look up as Alex promised to stay with her. Jenny cast her one last worried glance and headed out the door.

Nobody could hide their emotions indefinitely. And nobody could withstand countless rejections and not suffer for it. Lauren's parents hadn't wanted her. None of the foster families had wanted her and too many had tried to abuse her. Dale had loved another woman for years before he married Lauren. And though Jenny knew Dale loved his wife, she knew there were some details that Lauren hadn't shared. Hell, a lot of details.

Speeding down the twisting roads of the Knobs, Jenny got to the interstate leading to Jeffersonville and punched it. She wouldn't lose this time, Jenny swore. Lauren had stood by her too often, had helped her through too many rough times.

She found Dale standing on the stone at the river's edge by the dam. Arms crossed over his chest, eyes staring sightlessly across the river, he stood there, looking as lost as Lauren had looked only minutes earlier.

"You're not going to let something like this end things, are you, Dale?" she asked, coming up behind him in silence. He turned his head, glancing at her briefly, eyes shielded by mirrored aviator sunglasses. "It's not like she tried to pass another man's child off as yours."

"Is she okay?" he asked, ignoring her question as he turned his eyes back to the slowly moving river.

"No. She's not, Dale. She's hurting. She's afraid you're going to leave her."

"Shit. She's probably praying that I will leave," he muttered, shaking his head. He'd practically raped his wife. The guilt inside him was threatening to choke him. He was certain if there had been anything in his tight stomach, he would have vomited it back up. "She wasn't...was she hurt?"

"Hurt how?" Jenny asked, her eyes narrowing. The slump of Dale's shoulders, his silence told her everything she needed know. Rage bloomed inside her. "You son of a bitch!" she hissed, hands curling into small fists. She started to leap forward, but halted. "What happened?" she asked haltingly, fury making her voice shake.

"I raped my wife," he responded flatly. "And she let me."

"That's a damn contradiction in terms, Dale. Thanks so much for clearing this up," Jenny snapped, nails biting into her skin. "What happened?"

"Not a contradiction, not when it comes to Lauren. She didn't want it, she said no. But she let me, because she wouldn't deny me anything." *You're my weakness,* her voice whispered in his mind, taunting him, sickening him. "Was she okay?" he repeated roughly.

Lauren hadn't been hurt, not physically. She was hurt inside, and afraid. But not for the reason Dale was thinking. The initial surge of anger faded quickly. No. She wasn't hurt the way he was thinking she was. Whatever had happened hadn't been against Lauren's will. Otherwise, Jenny figured, Dale would have left the house in a body bag.

"No. She's not hurting like that, Dale. If she were, you'd be in the river right now and I'd be throwing rocks at your worthless carcass." She took a deep breath and said, "Whatever happened wasn't against her will, Dale. She wouldn't have looked like she did when I left if it was otherwise. That kind of assault would have infuriated Lauren, and you damn well know it. She would have been cleaning your blood from her hands. She wouldn't be sitting there looking like her heart had been ripped out of her body.

And you don't have it in you to hurt her that way."

"You weren't there." He could still hear her voice as she said, *Dale, wait. Not like this.* He hadn't cared, hadn't listened.

"No. But I know her. Probably better than you. And I've seen women…" her voice trailed off. Seen the kind of hurt he was thinking, seen the lost vacant eyes, the terror that bloomed if a man so much as entered the room, the way a woman would cringe in fear like an animal. "I've seen the kind of hurt you're talking about. Lauren is heartbroken because she thinks she chased you away. She's not hurting because of something you did, but because of something she did. She's hurting inside. I think you are, too."

Raggedly, he asked, "Why didn't she tell me?" His jaw clenched and his eyes closed. "Damn it, Jenny. Why didn't she tell me?"

"I don't think she knew how," Jenny said, sitting down on the concrete ledge. The cold wind whipped her hair around her face and she tugged her hood up.

"The same way she told you, I imagine. That would have worked."

Jenny smiled sadly. Shaking her head, she said softly, "No. It wouldn't have. I knew, Dale, the minute she told me she was pregnant. I knew who the father was. She never said a word."

He dropped down, crouching on the ledge and shoving his sunglasses back on his head. "How did you know?"

"I've always known how she felt about you. I've known her for ten years, since we were in high school together. And I've never seen her even remotely interested in a guy. And then she told me one day about this guy who had moved in next door. 'He makes my heart flip over,' was what she said. And I knew it was the real thing."

"Am I the only one who didn't know how she felt?" he asked, shaking his head.

"I doubt that. Only people who know Lauren well would know. And very few know her at all. But I saw how she looked at you. It was written all over her face. I can't believe you didn't see it."

"Maybe I didn't want to," he admitted, sighing heavily.

Jenny shrugged, not knowing the answer to that. "I have a hard time believing you didn't figure it out before now. Lauren doesn't do anything casually. She couldn't have slept with another man while loving you."

"So now I'm supposed to believe she's been celibate for five years," he muttered.

Jenny looked up, meeting his eyes levelly. "If I know Lauren, I'd say twenty five years is a closer guess." She smiled as he paled, as what she was saying sank in.

"No." He said it roughly, his eyes dark. That was it. That was when he had seen her eyes staring into his, wide with distress and pain, but swirling with the same need that burned inside him. The night he had gotten her pregnant, Lauren Spencer had been a virgin. "Absolutely, no."

But he already knew otherwise. He had been the first. The only. "Hell."

"Are you going to let this slip away?" Jenny asked quietly. "She loves you so much. And I know you love her."

"No. I'm not going to let her go. She can be as cold as she damn well wants. But I'm not letting her go." He spun around, striding to his car.

"Wait," Jenny said, jumping up and going after him. "Wait, damn it. Lauren isn't cold," Jenny said, blocking Dale's way when he would have headed for his car. "She hides behind that. But she isn't cold. She's got the biggest heart of anybody I've ever known. It's been stepped on too many times, by the people who were supposed to love her. She doesn't trust herself any more. Hasn't trusted herself for years. She's gotten the worst from people for so long she's learned to expect it, to think that's all she deserves."

He paused, frowning. "I know my wife, Jenny. She's got a little more belief in herself in than that."

"No, she doesn't. Dale, Lauren's scared to death right now that you're going to leave her. She hurting inside and she doesn't know how to show it, or how to tell you." Her hands rose and fell helplessly as she struggled to describe the Lauren she knew existed. "She doesn't fight like you and me. She doesn't know how. Damn it, every time she ever cared about something, she lost it. She stopped letting it show when something mattered. Stopped pretending anything mattered. All she knows to do is shut down. And the more she hurts, the colder she gets. You'll feel like you're fighting a glacier."

Dale shook his head, not linking the woman Jenny was describing to the one he knew. "I know she loves me. But she doesn't trust me."

"Yes, she does. She didn't tell you because she didn't trust you. She didn't tell you because she does trust you, too much. She knew you'd do the right thing and she didn't want to lock you into something you didn't want." Jenny stomped her foot and raised her clenched hands to her temples, shaking with sheer frustration. "She didn't want a man who was there only because he felt obligated. And she deserves better than that, she and Krista both."

Was it really that simple?

"She doesn't love easily, Dale. She doesn't trust easily. But she loves and trusts you; she was afraid of tying you in a place you didn't want to be. And later, she was afraid of losing you. Be careful with her, Dale." Jenny's mossy green eyes filled with tears and she pressed her fingers to her mouth, forcing herself to take a deep calming breath. "She's on the edge right now, she can't keep getting rejected by the people she loves. She needs you so much."

No, she doesn't. He even opened his mouth to say that, but then he closed it, frowning. How well did he really know her? He didn't know her any better now than he had less than a year ago, not really. He never would have known how she felt about him if it wasn't for Krista.

Lauren never would have told him if he hadn't gone to her first. If he hadn't fallen in love with her.

Dale reached out, drawing Jenny close in a quick hug. Brushing a kiss across her cheek, he said, "Thank you."

Chapter Eight

The house seemed oddly quiet when he entered it. Alex had been sitting on the couch, flipping through a magazine, but rose when he came in, took one look at his face, and left.

He stood in the living room, wondering what he should do, how he should do it. If he should even bother.

A noise in the doorway had him raising his head. Lauren stood there, her face pale but otherwise composed. She wore a neatly buttoned black shirt tucked into a pair of slim fitting khakis. Her hair, dry now, was secured in its usual French braid.

She met his eyes squarely, levelly. He couldn't see any clue that she was hurting, or scared, or even the slightest bit nervous. From a distance of ten feet, she stood with her hands tucked causally into her back pockets, head cocked slightly to the side.

"Where's Krista?" he finally asked, unsure what to say, what to do.

"Sleeping. I just fed her," Lauren said, her voice polite, distant. Cold.

He closed his eyes, turned away. "I'm sorry about what happened earlier. I can't say that I didn't mean to hurt you. I didn't think about it, didn't even care. And there's nothing I can do or say that will change it, but I wanted you to know I'm sorry."

Lauren took a deep, quiet breath and forced her shoulders into a casual shrug. "You didn't hurt me, Dale. I'm fine. And there's nothing for you to apologize about."

"You said no. I didn't listen." He turned to look at her, knowing that avoiding her eyes was cowardly.

She flicked away a speck of lint from her black oxford cloth shirt before looking back at him. "I've said a lot of things in my life, Dale. I haven't meant every single word I've ever uttered." Then she headed into the kitchen. "I've got a yen for lasagna tonight. I'd better get it started if we want to eat any time soon."

Dale followed her, watching with a dark frown on his face as she set a pot of water to boil. He gave it a minute, thinking maybe she just wanted to keep her hands occupied while she talked, but she said nothing, merely humming quietly under her breath as though nothing was wrong, as if her husband wasn't standing there, waiting.

"We need to talk about this," Dale said, his frustration level starting to rise as she continued to pull out ingredients for supper. Bell peppers, tomatoes, garlic, sausage. Her hands were rock steady and her face placid.

"Not much to talk about. You remembered what happened, after all, and we said everything that needed to be said already."

Dumbfounded, he watched as she set about browning Italian sausage. She had just started slicing tomatoes and bell peppers when he walked up behind her. "I think this is a little more important than food, Lauren."

She turned her head to him and asked, "What's more important than food?"

"We had a fight. We need to settle it."

"Oh, that." She shrugged and turned her attention back to the food. Slicing an onion quickly, she added it to the pot that was starting to simmer on the stove. After washing her hands, she said, "I thought it was settled. I kept that night from you, did my best to make you think nobody had been there. I didn't tell you I had gotten pregnant. You found out, were understandably angry. As for what happened this afternoon, I'm not hurt. What's left to settle?"

Grabbing her elbow, he spun her around to face him. "How about the fact that you hid this from me all along? How about the fact that I damn near raped you earlier? How about the fact that I took your virginity with you standing up against a wall?"

A slight flush stained her cheeks and she looked away. "You didn't rape me, Dale. It was uncomfortable for a second, but that's all. And why on earth do you think I was a virgin?" she asked, her voice flat. God, please don't let him know that. It was humiliating. It had been the most miraculous night of her life, up to that point, and he hadn't even remembered it five minutes after it was over.

He moved his hands to her shoulders, giving her a gentle shake. "Damn it, Lauren. Stop it. I remember the whole damn thing. I hurt you. I remember how tight you were, and I remember seeing you flinch. You'd never been with a man before, and I fucked you like some whore in a cheap motel room."

She rolled her eyes and said, "It had been a while, Dale. What's the point of this? What does this have to do with me not telling you? That's why you're mad, right?"

Even as she spoke, the emotion faded from her eyes and her voice dropped several degrees. The ice was forming so quickly, Dale was ready to scream himself hoarse with frustration. "*All she knows how to do is shut down. And the more she hurts, the colder she gets. You'll feel like you're fighting a glacier*".

A glacier. The frost was in her eyes, in her voice. *So help me God,* Dale thought, his hands tightening on her shoulders. *I'll break through that ice if it's the last thing I do.* Drawing her stiff body closer, he took her face in his hands, forcing her eyes to meet his.

"It has everything to do with it," Dale whispered. "You loved me for years. I took what I wanted from you and called you another woman's name. Do you expect me to believe that didn't hurt? That it had nothing to do with why you didn't tell me about Krista?"

Her only answer was a careless shrug of her shoulders.

"So it didn't bother you at all? Won't bother you if it happens again?"

Her eyes darkened, only for a moment, but it was enough. "It tore you apart," he said quietly, caressing the satiny underside of her chin with his thumbs. "If I hadn't done that, if I had just slept with you and forgotten it, you would have reminded me, you would have told me about the baby."

She clasped her hands around his wrists and tugged them away. "I dealt with it, didn't I?" she asked, tossing her head arrogantly. Her gray eyes were as cold as the winter sky outside. With every word she spoke, the distance between them grew.

No. Dale thought viciously. She wouldn't do this, not again. Not now. He stared at her for a moment, his mind racing. How did he get through to her, how did he touch her?

The same way he had the first time he had ever gotten through the remote wall she kept around herself.

And then, he moved around her, turned off the stove, then the lights. "Dale-"

Before she could finish her question, he scooped her up in his arms and headed out of the kitchen. He'd tried earlier to break through to her with words. He had already tried anger. It hadn't worked.

This time, he swore, carrying her up the stairs, this time, he'd get through. He'd do things the way they should have been done from the beginning. "Dale, put me do..." Her words ended in a muffled groan as Dale covered her mouth his, pressing a chaste kiss to her mouth before pushing the bedroom door open with his shoulder. The lights were off, the only light being the pale, watery twilight outside.

He gently laid her on the bed, following her down and gathering her tense body up against his. He pressed gentle kisses to her eyes, his hand unweaving the intricate braid of her hair, then smoothing the wavy locks. "You said one time that you'd been seduced. Calling what happened a seduction is being kind, Lauren." He straddled her hips and reached for the buttons on her shirt.

"Dale-"

"A seduction," he told her softly, nuzzling her neck, "isn't flash and fire. At least not right away." He laid one hand against her collarbone, smoothed it down her torso, spreading her shirt as he stroked his way down to her navel. "It's about soft words, promises."

"I don't need-"

Interrupting her, he said, "Of course, I realize you don't have much in the way of comparisons. But I think I can remedy that." When she reached for his hands, he caught her wrists gently in one hand, pinning them to the mattress.

"You have no idea how you haunted me," he whispered, stretching his length out beside hers. "I'd wake up at night, aching for you, and you were there beside me all along."

Her thick lashes fluttered over her eyes, a faint flush rising from her breasts upward. Still, she shifted and twisted against his hands. "Dale, stop it. This isn't solving anything," she ordered, her voice just the slightest bit ragged.

"You said it was solved," he murmured, nuzzling his way down her neck.

"I've changed my mind," she hissed, arching up against him.

"Are you saying you don't want me to make love to you?" he asked, conversationally, propping himself up on his elbow and staring down at her. His blue eyes looked into hers with pure innocence while his free hand found the catch on her bra. As her breasts fell free, he caught one in his hand, plumping it, dragging his thumb lightly across her distended nipple. A tiny droplet of milk glistened there and he caught it on his finger, lifting it to his mouth, all the while staring into her eyes, waiting for her answer.

Lauren's eyes were locked on his hand as he slid one long finger between his lips, licking it clean before tracing the damp finger down the center of her chest. Circling her navel, back up to tease at her sensitized breasts, then up to her chin, forcing her gaze to his. He caught her hand and raised it to his mouth, nibbling on her knuckles before telling her, "I'll stop if you want me to. I swear it. What happened earlier won't ever happen again."

Guilt darkened his eyes briefly and he closed them, willing it away.

When Lauren's hazy eyes cleared enough to see his face, his eyes were the way she had seen them the first time he had kissed her, sleepy, sexy, and just slightly wicked.

"Should I stop?" he asked roughly.

Words were frozen in her throat. Yes. Yes, she wanted him to stop. She opened her mouth to speak, but all that left her was, "No. Please, don't."

He smiled at her, tenderly. Lowering his head, he bussed her mouth with his before resuming his tactile exploration of her body. "I'd wake up after dreaming of that night, hard and aching. Sometimes, I thought I'd die if I couldn't touch you again. And I felt so guilty, because you were lying there beside me, my wife. My life. I'd move all of heaven and earth to make you happy. But I couldn't stop thinking of the woman I'd been with that night."

Her eyes closed against the backwash of her own guilt, and the shameful pride of knowing it had been her, all along. The tiny smile playing at her mouth caught his eyes and he nipped her shoulder with sharp teeth. "Like knowing that I'd been going out of my mind?" he asked gruffly. That sly female smile, the desire that darkened her eyes to smoke tightened his skin, heated blood already hot. "Hell, you drove me damn near insane. Both of you."

He buried his face in the curve of her neck and whispered, "Damn it, I love you, Lauren. So much it hurts. So much I ache with it. When I'm not with you, it feels like part of me is missing."

"And I'm not..." he nipped gently at the cord in her neck "going to let this come between us. Nothing will do that."

He slid his hands inside the waistband of her khakis, dragging them slowly down the length of her smooth pale legs. He knelt at her feet, his eyes lingering on her body. How could he not have known it had been Lauren? he wondered. Those spectacular breasts rose and fell with each ragged breath. The scent that had haunted him rose from her heated skin. Her mouth parted and her teeth sank into her lower lip, her eyes fluttering closed. He grasped one ankle, raising it, massaging it with the pads of his thumbs. An involuntary groan of pleasure escaped her lips as he rotated her ankle, moved his way up her calf. "I'm not going to let you close me out, Lauren," he murmured. "You're too much a part of me."

"Dale..."

He released her ankle, moving upward until he was kneeling between her thighs. With a feathery light touch, he stroked one finger down through the patch of hair, hot moisture dampening the tight curls. "I hurt you earlier. And before. As God is my witness, it'll never happen again." Tiny little droplets of her cream had collected there and were gleaming like pearls.

She opened her mouth to say something but the words locked in her throat when he lowered his head, parted her flesh and licked her. A startled climax tore through her only seconds after he touched her, leaving her gasping and panting for air as he began again. He paused only long enough to ask, "All better, Lauren?"

Her only answer was the low ragged moan that left her body when he lowered his head and caught the bud of nerves gently between his teeth. He shifted until he had one leg draped over his shoulder then he tilted her bottom higher, braced his weight and slid one finger inside her body. Back and forth he stroked, suckling at her clit with his mouth, biting down gently, caressing the quivering folds of her body with a knowing hand.

Her hands fisted on his shoulders, closed around his head, tightened on his hair. Her body twisted restlessly against the smooth linen sheet. "Dale," she choked. "Dale, please." Her pleas faded away into a soft moan as another climax rolled through, slower, sweeter.

He drew away from her after the last wracking moan escaped her lips. "Why did it take me so long to find you?" he asked quietly. "What did I do to deserve somebody like you in my life?"

"...what?" she asked, her voice husky and thick, her eyes befuddled.

A grin tugged at Dale's mouth. Nothing stroked a man's ego like making a smart mouthed sassy woman speechless. Leaning over her, he cupped one hand over the wet heat between her thighs, dipping inside her swollen quivering entrance, he eased one finger inside her body, shuddering himself at the feel of her. Just as slowly he withdrew, then entered her again. And again. Repeatedly, until with each entry she was rising up against his hand, meeting him with her hips.

He felt her tensing again and he pulled away. "I'm going with you this time," he told her, tearing open his jeans, spreading her thighs wider and lowering himself atop her. Her tightly beaded nipples pushed into his chest, her hands clutched convulsively at his shoulders. Her satin soft skin met his and Dale stifled a groan. Her thighs opened and her knees came up, one on each side of his hips, so that from groin to mouth, their bodies touched.

"Don't lock me out, Lauren," he pleaded as she tried to turn her head away. Catching her face in his hands, he held her gaze as he entered her slowly, bit by bit, until he was buried inside her quivering sheath to the balls. "Don't lock me out."

Her heavy lidded eyes fluttered but she kept her gaze on his. "It's always been you," she whispered, as the pressure within her loins spread through her body. Her heart beat wildly against his, his hips recoiled and plunged into her arching body. "Always you."

Unbelievably moved, he lowered his head and took her mouth in a long deep kiss, hooking his arms under her shoulders and holding her tightly against him. She convulsed around his rigid cock as he pounded hard into her. "I can't wait," he rasped against her ear, reaching down with one hand to draw her knee higher.

"Then don't," she replied only seconds before another climax exploded in her, a keening cry rising from her lips as she went into spasms around him, milking his flesh as he emptied himself into her, filling her with his seed while he roared out in agonized pleasure.

* * * * *

Hours later, he rose, pulling the blanket over the sleeping body of his wife, his dream lover, his best friend. She slept curled up on her side, one arm tucked under her head, lashes fanning over her ivory cheeks. As he watched, she turned onto her back, flinging one arm over her head, frowning in her sleep. Restless. As calm as she was, or seemed to be, on the outside, at night, the restlessness came through.

Why hadn't he known it was Lauren?

In the stillness, the answer came to him.

He had known. He had always known. Why else would he have asked her to marry him? Why else would he have wanted that baby so badly? Somewhere inside, he had remembered.

Just as somewhere inside, he had already loved her. There was no other reason why he would have touched her that night. As much as he loved women, loved touching them, lying with them, tasting them, he didn't bed his friends. He never had. Sex changes things, he had always known that.

Dale opened the door to Krista's nursery, flipping on the light just as weak little snuffles started echoing from the crib. He scooped the baby out just as her eyes fluttered open. Warmed bottle in hand, he carried her over to the rocker, easing down into it as Krista latched onto the bottle with an avid mouth. He started to lean his head back.

And froze.

There was a canvas standing next to the window, one he hadn't seen before.

It was a portrait of him, holding Krista.

Lauren had captured them in the rocker of the nursery, shafts of sunlight falling across part of his face and Krista. Her tiny little hand was reaching up for his face and he was smiling down at her. Looking for the signs now, he could see how closely Krista resembled him, the shape of her face and eyes, her hairline and the dimples in her cheeks.

His daughter.

Nobody looking at the picture, even without knowing the two, could deny that the two were linked by blood.

She had been planning to tell him.

How long had she been working on this?

A soft noise in the doorway pulled his attention from the portrait and he looked up, meeting Lauren's eyes. She met his eyes somberly, before closing her eyes briefly. Then she looked at the baby and said, "She's gone back to sleep."

"She didn't wake you, did she?" he asked gruffly as Lauren gently took Krista from him, kissing her brow before settling her back in the crib.

"No. I woke up out of habit, I suppose." She turned then, crossing her arms tightly under her breasts. Studying the painting, she said nothing.

"It's...it's beautiful," he finally said.

"I'm glad you like it," she replied politely. "It's your birthday present."

"Thank you. I know you don't think you do very good portraits, but it's unbelievable," he said. Reaching out, he traced his finger down the painted edge of Krista's cheek. "How long did you have to work on it?"

"A month or so, I guess. I was only able to work on it a little at a time." She still didn't look at him.

"She looks like me."

She turned her head at that, meeting his eyes with hers shuttered. "Of course she does. We've already established that's she's your daughter."

"I meant that anybody who has eyes is gonna see the resemblance," he said, shoving splayed fingers through his hair. His blue eyes were dark with frustration and confusion. "I thought you weren't planning on ever telling me."

"I wasn't planning on it. But if you ever asked, I wouldn't have denied it." With that, she turned her eyes back to the painting, studying it as if she had never seen it before.

"This was your way of telling me," he murmured out loud, realizing. She had been planning on telling him. "Why didn't you just come right out and say it?"

"Haven't we already been over this?"

He moved closer, until he was standing behind her, and rested his hands on her shoulders. Together they stared at the picture in the dim light. "You're not going to lose me, Lauren," he whispered in her ear. He moved his arms down to her waist, dragging her stiff body against his. "I'm not going to get tired of you. I'm not going to abandon you. Nothing short of death will ever take me from you. God willing, we'll grow old together, die together." Hugging her tightly against him, he told her, "You don't have to be afraid to open up to me."

A slight tremor wracked her body and she covered his hands with hers, but said nothing.

"Will you trust me, Lauren?"

She stood with her head lowered, chin tucked against her chest. He gently turned her to face him, lifted her chin to his. A single tear fell to trickle down her face as she stared up at him, her eyes dark and miserable. Dale felt his heart twist inside his chest. "I'm not going anywhere, Lauren," he promised, lifting his hands to frame her face.

Lauren stared up at him, those ice blue eyes seeing clear down into her empty heart. "Dale, I don't know how to handle this," she whispered, her lower lip quivering slightly before she firmed it. "Nobody's ever loved me. I've never loved anybody. I was so sure I'd mess it up, and I did."

"We both did. And it's nothing we can't fix. But, baby, I can't do it alone. And I can't do it if you keep thinking I'm going to leave sooner or later. Isn't that what's been going on inside that head of yours?"

A dull flush turned her cheeks pink and she averted her eyes. "Yes," she whispered. "I mean, why would you stay? Nobody else ever has."

"I'm not them, Lauren," he told her, wanting to shake her. "I'm me. Just me. The man who loves you, who loves our daughter." He brushed her tumbled hair back from her face. "I've got a wife who loves me, a beautiful sexy wife. A sweet, beautiful little girl. Why would I leave?"

Lingering panic kept the tension in his shoulders, hardened his face. The doubt in her eyes would tear them apart. He knew it. He could fight most anything that threatened their marriage. But he couldn't fight her fears. They went too deep. "Lauren, if you don't believe in me, in us, we won't last. You know that."

Her hands came up to grip his. "Dale..." Tears gleamed in her eyes, making his image blurry. She blinked and the tears fell, his image cleared. And the love she saw in his eyes, the determination was like nothing she had ever seen.

"I will never willingly leave you, Lauren," he swore again, his hands moving down to grip her shoulders. Her hands crept up, linked behind his neck. "Never."

She shuddered as a sob burst from her lips, tears she had kept hidden for fifteen years. Swiftly, Dale scooped her up and carried her to their bedroom. Hot tears fell on his neck as he cradled her on his lap on the edge of the tumbled bed. "Believe in us, Lauren," he whispered in her ear, stroking her hair with a soothing hand. "Believe in me."

Harsh sobs tore from her, wracked her body. The torrent of grief, of hopelessness, of loss filled the room. Her fingers kneaded at his shoulders, clutched desperately at his hair as she cried helplessly. The sobs eased into sighs and her tears dried. Unbelievably weary, and unbelievably embarrassed, she raised her head, forced herself to meet his eyes. "I don't think I ever cried over her leaving me," she told him, rubbing the back of her hand against her cheek. "My father...I really don't remember him being around much. Just my mother. And then she was gone. I didn't even matter."

Stroking her hair back from her face, Dale said, "You've always mattered to me. Always." Sliding his fingers through her hair, he drew her closer, until his brow touched hers. "Believe in us, Lauren."

She closed her eyes and rested her aching head on his shoulders. His strong arms came around her and held her close against him. "I believe in us, Dale. I think I always have. I just have to work on believing in me."

With a relieved smile, Dale kissed her hair. "I believe in you enough for both of us."

Epilogue

Two Years Later

The door flew open, revealing Dale standing in the doorway glaring at Lauren with irritated eyes. "You forgot me at the damn airport again."

She raised her head from the couch where she and Krista had been napping. Face flushed, eyes heavy with sleep, her eyes wandered from Dale to the clock and back before they widened. "Dale, I am so sorry," she whispered, moving carefully, trying not to wake Krista. It was exhausting, trying to get a rambunctious toddler to nap. "I fell asleep..."

Dale's eyes narrowed and he glared at her, a sulky snarl on his gorgeous face. "You plan on making it up to me? You had me worried."

"Did not," she replied. "You didn't even try to call." Turning around, she threw a light throw over Krista and headed out of the room, beckoning for Dale to follow. "Besides, I had a very good reason."

"Yeah. I saw. Taking a nap. Good reason to stick me in a damn cab."

"Dale, don't sulk. You look just like Krista when you do. And I had a good reason, too, for taking that nap."

He had been reaching out to swat on her butt when he started thinking. "A good reason?" he asked, his gaze thoughtful and curious as it trailed a path down her slender body. "How good a reason?"

With a coy smile, she tossed over her shoulder, "I'm pregnant." And with a laugh, darted out of the room.

"Pregnant…" Dale whispered. Stunned, he dropped down on the nearest step. "Pregnant." Studying his hands, he replayed what she had said in his head.

And then, with a whoop, he was on his feet, dashing up the stairs after his long legged woman.

The End

Enjoy this excerpt from

Whipped Cream and Handcuffs

© Copyright Shiloh Walker 2003

Chapter One

There was another letter, sitting there on her desk. She felt her heart skip a beat as heat pooled low in her belly. Glancing around, she made sure nobody else had seen it. More instinctive than anything, since she was usually one of the first ones in the office.

Slowly, her hands shaking, she reached out. A poem this time? Another short story that would have her quivering and ready to beg for climax?

Nope.

Not this time.

This time it just read, *Soon.*

Holy shit, he had meant it.

Whoever it was that called her late at night — whoever it was that left these dirty little stories, or romantic poems — was going to finally come out and meet her. Face to face.

The first letter had come nearly four months earlier, on Valentine's Day, with a basket that held some interesting little items. A pair of cloth restraints — like handcuffs — but made of soft material that wouldn't cause pain. A feather. A bottle of massage oil.

A can of whipped cream.

And a magnet.

The magnet had read

You.

Me.

Handcuffs.

Whipped Cream.

Any questions?

Since then, only the stiff ivory envelopes made of a heavy bond paper that had linen in it. The writing was all handwritten and looked familiar, but she couldn't place it. Sweeping, rather elegant looking, especially for a man.

A month after the letters had started, the phone calls had begun.

She rubbed her left hand nervously against her pants, the ring on her finger flashing at her mockingly.

The letters had started less than a week after Tyson had proposed. And when she told, rather reluctantly, the mystery man — who refused to give his name when he called her — he had only responded, "The man isn't right for you."

She suspected the letters had started because of the proposal. And she also suspected her mystery man was right. Just reading his letter left her more turned on than foreplay with Tyson. Very tepid foreplay, at that.

If just his letters, his voice were enough to make her cleft wet and aching, what would touching him, him touching her, be like?

She was going to find out.

But maybe she should tell Tyson.

* * * * *

The cool eyed blonde sitting across from her started to tap his fingers steadily on the white tablecloth. He lifted his water glass and sipped from it before setting it back down and staring her like she was a lab specimen under a microscope.

He was angry.

She had rarely seen Tyson James angry, but the tic throbbing in his chin was a pretty good give away. "Why haven't you called the police?" he finally asked.

The police? Why on earth would she call the police? The thought must have been written all over her face because Tyson leaned forward and said, "You have somebody stalking you, leaving you threatening presents and notes, calling you at home, and you haven't called the police, you little idiot. This isn't like you, Tessa."

Her eyes narrowed as she said slowly, carefully, "I am not idiot. He doesn't want to hurt me, Ty."

"Handcuffs? You don't think that's threatening?" Tyson drawled, shaking his head.

No. She thought it was exciting.

Handcuffed to a bed, maybe even blindfolded, while a man ran knowing hands over her body? While he fucked her from behind, slapping at her ass...Tessa felt her nipples tighten, and through the silk of her shirt, she knew Tyson could see it as well. Her cleft was aching again, and dripping. She could feel the cream soaking through her panties and had an image of the mystery man sitting beside her, sliding his hand high up her thigh, dragging his fingers through her wet folds, caressing her clit while carrying on a conversation.

"Tessa."

She shook her head and opened smoky eyes to stare into Tyson's face. His face was tight and grim. Slowly, he stood, tossing some bills down on the table. "I need to get back to the office," he said quietly, the rage throbbing in his voice. "And I think you need to figure out what you want in life. If it's me, then you're going to go home like a good little girl, gather up all those letters and take them to the police."

He came closer and lowered his head to whisper in her ear, "And for God's sake, have some dignity. You look like you're ready to get fucked right here."

Her face flamed as he walked away. She was certain everybody was staring at her, but when she glanced around, no one seemed to be watching her. She waited until her breathing slowed and then she stood up, leaving a few extra ones on the table.

Tyson was one of the area's most respected physicians, a gifted cardiologist who repaired the damage done to the human heart with his own surgical skills and the help of modern medicine.

But when it came to understanding the human heart, the man was clueless.

About the author:

They always say to tell a little about yourself! I was born in Kentucky and have been reading avidly since I was six. At twelve, I discovered how much fun it was to write when I took a book that didn't end the way it should have ended, and I rewrote it. I've been writing since then.

About me now... hmm... I've been married since I was 19 to my high school sweetheart and we live in the midwest. Recently I made the plunge and turned to writing full-time and am looking for a part-time job so I can devote more time to my family—two adorable children who are growing way too fast, and my husband who doesn't see enough of me...

Shiloh welcomes mail from readers. You can write to her c/o Ellora's Cave Publishing at 1337 Commerce Drive, Suite 13, Stow OH 44224.

Why an electronic book?

We live in the Information Age—an exciting time in the history of human civilization in which technology rules supreme and continues to progress in leaps and bounds every minute of every hour of every day. For a multitude of reasons, more and more avid literary fans are opting to purchase e-books instead of paperbacks. The question to those not yet initiated to the world of electronic reading is simply: *why?*

1. *Price.* An electronic title at Ellora's Cave Publishing runs anywhere from 40-75% less than the cover price of the <u>exact same title</u> in paperback format. Why? Cold mathematics. It is less expensive to publish an e-book than it is to publish a paperback, so the savings are passed along to the consumer.

2. *Space.* Running out of room to house your paperback books? That is one worry you will never have with electronic novels. For a low one-time cost, you can purchase a handheld computer designed specifically for e-reading purposes. Many e-readers are larger than the average handheld, giving you plenty of screen room. Better yet, hundreds of titles can be stored within your new library—a single microchip. (Please note that Ellora's Cave does not endorse any specific brands. You can check our website at www.ellorascave.com for customer recommendations we make available to new consumers.)

3. *Mobility.* Because your new library now consists of only a microchip, your entire cache of books can be taken with you wherever you go.

4. *Personal preferences are accounted for.* Are the words you are currently reading too small? Too large? Too...**ANNOYING**? Paperback books cannot be modified according to personal preferences, but e-books can.

5. *Innovation.* The way you read a book is not the only advancement the Information Age has gifted the literary community with. There is also the factor of what you can read. Ellora's Cave Publishing will be introducing a new line of interactive titles that are available in e-book format only.

6. *Instant gratification.* Is it the middle of the night and all the bookstores are closed? Are you tired of waiting days—sometimes weeks—for online and offline bookstores to ship the novels you bought? Ellora's Cave Publishing sells instantaneous downloads 24 hours a day, 7 days a week, 365 days a year. Our e-book delivery system is 100% automated, meaning your order is filled as soon as you pay for it.

Those are a few of the top reasons why electronic novels are displacing paperbacks for many an avid reader. As always, Ellora's Cave Publishing welcomes your questions and comments. We invite you to email us at service@ellorascave.com or write to us directly at: 1337 Commerce Drive, Suite 13, Stow OH 44224.

Discover for yourself why readers can't get enough of the multiple award-winning publisher Ellora's Cave. Whether you prefer e-books or paperbacks, be sure to visit EC on the web at www.ellorascave.com for an erotic reading experience that will leave you breathless.

WWW.ELLORASCAVE.COM

Printed in the United States
52597LVS00001B/109-129

9 781419 950414